SALT AIR
SECRETS

ALSO BY JOANNE DEMAIO

The Seaside Saga
Blue Jeans and Coffee Beans
The Denim Blue Sea
Beach Blues
Beach Breeze
The Beach Inn
Beach Bliss
Castaway Cottage
Night Beach
Little Beach Bungalow
Every Summer
Salt Air Secrets
Stony Point Summer
—And More Seaside Saga Books—

Summer Standalone Novels
True Blend
Whole Latte Life

Winter Novels
Eighteen Winters
First Flurries
Cardinal Cabin
Snow Deer and Cocoa Cheer
Snowflakes and Coffee Cakes

salt air
secrets

A NOVEL

JOANNE DEMAIO

ISBN: 9798625162401

Joannedemaio.com

To my loyal Seaside Saga fans

For embracing the beach friends' ongoing story,
and taking this coastal New England town into your hearts.

I tip my beach hat to you.

one

Late Sunday Morning

IF IT'S TRUE THAT SALT air cures what ails you, Shane Bradford hopes everyone he knows is taking a good long breath of it. He sure is. As a matter of fact, he's taking several. The first comes after heaving his duffel aboard the lobster boat and hearing the thud of the bag hitting the deck. That first breath of sea air clears his head. Because any seasoned lobsterman knows the Atlantic Ocean shows no mercy for distractions. One wrong move on a boat pitching on the sea can be deadly. Can land you tripped up in an uncoiling rope delivering a lobster trap to the bottom of that sea. And delivering you to those depths right along with the trap.

So Shane boards the boat, pauses, and breathes the salty tonic.

The second deep breath comes after shooting the breeze with the boys onboard. It doesn't take long to catch

1

up on any news he missed—being away at Stony Point for the past two weeks. Then he resettles his cap on his head, faces the distant blue sea, and inhales. All the while, amidst the laughter and seafaring tales of the crew, there's the rocking motion of the lobster boat moving through the harbor. A bell buoy clangs; gulls swoop overhead. Seawater sloshes against the boat's hull.

Shane's third calming breath of salt air, the sweetest, comes when he turns to take one more look at his harbor house beyond the docks. It's routine for him; a good-luck tic, if you will. Taking one last glance at his little shingled house is almost a way of blessing himself. Of praying for a safe journey out at sea—one returning him to shore, and home, intact.

But today? Today, that third breath of salt air is cut suddenly short. It happens when he seeks out his seaworn, dockside home—and sees something else.

Sees *someone* else. Someone hurrying along the docks.

Sees Celia Gray.

Which right away throws him. Celia's *here*? In Maine? Five hours from Stony Point? Trying to keep her in his sights, Shane grabs up his duffel and crosses the moving boat's deck.

Yes, it's Celia.

No amount of squinting into the sunlight, of rushing around the stacked lobster pots to get to the boat's stern, of his hand skimming those pots to keep steady as he maneuvers through the tight space, proves otherwise.

The problem is, he's helpless to do anything about it.

2

Helpless to talk to her. Not anytime soon, anyway. Especially with the number of towering lobster pots he just passed—each one ready to be thrown overboard and eventually hauled back up, full and dripping, from the bottom of Penobscot Bay. He'll be gone for days.

Squeezing into an open space near the stern, Shane tips up his newsboy cap and takes a better look across the harbor water to the docks. Celia is just turning away. She's got on cropped white pants and a sleeveless denim blouse. Little Aria is strapped to her in a baby sling. Shane can't miss that, especially with the way Celia's face is tipped down to the baby. She's whispering some sweet nothing, some secret words meant only for her daughter.

Well, now. Only days ago, Shane had told Celia to come to Maine. Anytime.

I'll be damned, Shane thinks. *She did it*. She drove hours on the highways throughout New England to be right here. To come to the docks in Rockport, Maine—looking for him.

And there's not a blessed thing he can do. Not as the harbor grows smaller. Not as the captain—Shane glances at him up in the wheelhouse—navigates the boat past a stretch of rocky coast. Deeper water slaps at the hull now.

Still, Shane drops his heavy duffel and leans against a secured stack of lobster traps. On the docks, Celia keeps walking away. She passes boats moored there; she talks to Aria. Worst of all, she doesn't look back. That's all Shane wants now—one glimpse at her face to be sure she's okay. Just a reassuring glimpse, a hint of a smile, or some ease in her expression. He stands there, looking across the lengthening span of water between Celia and himself. He considers calling out her name, but his voice would be lost in the sound of the engine.

So as the boat chugs past idle sailboats and local lobster boats anchored in the harbor, Shane only watches Celia. Just her, and nothing else, lest he miss her giving one look back—even a brief glance over her shoulder.

Minutes pass as the boat heads out, leaving Celia further behind. But she's still within view, Celia and her daughter. And Shane's still worried that something might very well be wrong for Celia to have made the trip. If she'd been only *minutes* sooner, he would've given her his house key. Would have pressed it into her hand and insisted she and Aria rest after their long drive. Insisted they stay at his home for a day, at least.

Instead, the boat chugs along, leaving a white froth of water in its wake. Still, Shane watches Celia cross the docks.

Watches until a hand suddenly claps his shoulder.

"What? What's this?" one of his shipmates asks. He looks beyond Shane to Celia walking away. A seagull perched on a roped dock piling ruffles its wings as she passes by. "Two weeks gone, and you're in love?"

"Shut up," Shane tells him. He picks up his duffel and jokingly shoves the guy. "You don't know shit."

"Listen, Shane."

Shane moves past him, but he can't miss the warning being issued from behind.

"You bring a woman on the boat—in your head—and

you know what happens? She'll sink the ship. You'll be thinking of your lonely sweetheart and … cut your hand. Or go overboard. Or mess up."

When Shane feels a hand firmly grab his arm, he turns around.

"Let her go, man," his shipmate evenly says. "Set her sailing and clear your mind."

Shane waves him off. But before turning to bring his duffel below deck, he manages one last look off the stern of the boat.

One last look at Celia.

two

That Same Morning

ELSA'S WORRIED. FROM THE DOCKSIDE Diner's restroom, she'd secretly called Maris. But, no answer. Back outside now, Elsa reads the chalked words on the A-frame sign at the patio entrance: *Reserved for Private Event.* Then she looks past it to the tables beneath open umbrellas. She'd assumed that Maris would be here by now. Certainly her niece wouldn't skip out on Neil's memorial brunch. Maybe Elsa missed her. Yes, that could be it. Enough people are gathered that someone *might've* pulled Maris aside to chat. Or maybe Maris is sitting at a table surrounded by folks milling around. Maybe she's taking a look at the distant harbor across the street; finding a seat; talking.

Unfortunately, it's the talking that does it. That clues Elsa in that her hunch is right. Maris *isn't* here. Because everyone's debating some take on her absence. Their urgent words blend, making it hard to tell one voice from the other: Paige, Lauren, Eva. Or Vinny, Matt, Cliff. Even Nick.

Maybe she went to buy flowers.
Or else Jason picked her up, and she's coming with him.
Could she be sick?
I'll bet she forgot something. And had to stop home.
But I heard Jason left her.
Yep, it's true. Something's going on with them.
Jason did look shot at church.
Seriously, are we gossiping?

When the voices suddenly go quiet—pin-drop quiet—Elsa lifts her cat-eye sunglasses and turns to see Jason and Kyle walking through the parking lot. Jason's presence is enough to put a stop to any marriage musing. But one voice starts prattling again, regardless. It's Eva. She wears a fitted striped sheath and is pulling her phone from a straw clutch, just as Elsa heads her way.

"Well, I'm texting Maris," Eva is saying while her thumbs fly over the phone. She pauses, keeps her eyes glued to the phone screen and says to anyone listening, "No reply."

"Don't worry!" Lauren hushes her words now that Jason's nearing.

"Don't *worry*?" Eva glares at Lauren. "I come back from Martha's Vineyard and my sister's marriage is falling apart?"

Enough, Elsa thinks. She rushes up behind Eva before her niece has a chance to disrupt the brunch. "Put your

7

phone away. *Now*," Elsa says under her breath, then motions toward Jason talking to Vinny and Cliff. Beside them, the diner staff is setting up a buffet table. "Maris is an adult and can take care of herself," Elsa goes on. "And this brunch is for Jason, anyway. And Paige. Remember that. It's also for Neil, who *can't* be with us."

Eva brushes aside her blonde-highlighted bangs and looks back at Elsa. And takes a breath. And nods. "*Okay*," she whispers, returning her phone to her clutch.

"But what about Celia?" Lauren asks. She's sitting in the shade of an umbrella at one of the round patio tables set for brunch. "Celia *said* she'd be here." Lauren pulls out a chair beside her for Elsa. "Did she say anything to you?"

"To me?" Elsa cautiously sits as Paige comes up beside Eva and *they* both look to her now, too. "No. I haven't talked to Celia."

"But didn't you see her this morning? When you left, maybe?" Lauren gives Elsa's hand a squeeze. "Or out the inn window? Celia *had* to get Aria into her car to come here."

"The thing is," Elsa quietly admits, so quietly that the other women move closer. Elsa glances at Cliff, now talking to Kyle and his cook Jerry at the outdoor grill station. "I wasn't home, actually."

"What? Really?" Eva pulls out another chair and sits across from Elsa.

"Okay." Elsa gives the ladies a small smile and turns up her hands. "I spent the night with Cliff. I didn't plan to, but, it's just that … well, his futon is really something."

"Oh, I'll bet." Lauren raises a suggestive eyebrow.

"No!" Elsa insists. "That's not what I meant. His futon is *so* comfortable, it knocks me right out and I sleep incredibly deeply."

"The futon knocks you out?" Eva leans very close and drops her voice. "Or what happens *on* the futon knocks you out?"

"Eva! Seriously?" Elsa lowers her sunglasses to her face now. "I simply fell sound asleep and never woke up until I heard some strange noise this morning. Some ... *scratching* ... at Cliff's door."

"Scratching. Like what? An animal?" Eva asks.

Paige steps closer. "Maybe a raccoon? I hear they're all over the place this summer."

Elsa looks up just as someone clasps her shoulder.

"I'll get you a plate, Elsa," Cliff says from behind her.

Elsa reaches up, pats Cliff's hand and silently nods.

But Lauren wastes no time worrying about Celia. "So let me get this straight. You never saw Celia, *and* no one's heard from her?"

"Apparently not," Elsa says. "I mean, after Cliff brought me home, I quickly showered and got dressed. Then we went directly to the church—thinking Celia would be *there*."

When a phone dings, they all reach into their purses and clutches. "Oh, wait!" Elsa squints at her dinging phone. "Aha! That's Celia now. Texting me. She must be on her way," Elsa says while lowering the phone, whipping off her sunglasses and digging her leopard-print reading glasses from her tote.

"Oh, good." Lauren slides her chair closer. "What's she saying?"

"Hm." Elsa adjusts her reading glasses on her nose. "She's actually in Addison."

"Addison?" Paige asks. "Isn't that where her father lives?"

"It is." Elsa looks at her phone as another text message dings. "She says there was a mini-minor emergency and her father's car is in the shop. The ... the engine wouldn't start. So she's with her father all day doing errands and helping out." With a sigh of relief, Elsa rests her phone-laden hand in her lap. "She sends apologies for not being here." Another glance at her cell phone has Elsa skim the rest. "Back tonight," she reads before beginning to type a return message.

"*Ahem,*" Eva loudly says.

Elsa looks up at her niece. And oh, Eva's pointed finger can't be missed.

"*Put away the phone, Aunt Elsa,*" Eva gently admonishes, returning the same words Elsa gave her moments ago. "And remember who this brunch is truly for." Eva stands, gives Elsa a wink and crouches to hug her. "Anyway, Matt's at the buffet table. I'm going to check out the spread."

Elsa watches her go, then quickly texts Celia back before dropping her phone in her tote.

⌒

One hour, Jason thinks. He stands on the outdoor patio of the Dockside Diner. Kyle cordoned off the space with rope

10

swim-line secured to wooden dock posts. Fishing buoys of red, green and yellow dangle from the rope. Umbrellas are opened at the round tables. Fishnet is draped from white stockade panels behind the patio area. And clear zip bags dangle from the low branches of a tree beside the parking lot. The bags are oddly filled with water and copper pennies. There's got to be some classic Kyle rationale there.

But the buffet table? It's loaded with food: fruit salads and muffins; scrambled eggs and bacon; stacks of blueberry pancakes and trays of cinnamon rolls; egg-and-hash-brown lasagna; ham-and-cheese casserole; pitchers of breakfast sangria and flutes of lemonade spritzers.

And the people ... Jason sees it, how everyone's here.

Everyone except Maris.

One hour, he thinks again. *If I can just get through one hour, it'll be done. Everyone will be on their way.* He checks his watch to begin the countdown, then heads to where Mitch Fenwick stands at a table. Framed photographs of Neil are displayed there, beside vases of fresh-cut hydrangea blossoms.

Of course, Jason's waylaid right before he gets to Mitch. Stopped in his tracks by someone grabbing his arm from behind. No surprise, it's Eva.

"I have to talk to you later," she practically growls. "Before you go."

"I'm sure you do," Jason calmly tells his sister-in-law as she releases his arm and heads to the food table.

Mitch must've heard them and looks over his shoulder. His fading blond hair is in a tiny ponytail. He wears a loose

11

button-down with cuffed linen pants and leather two-strap sandals. And he holds one of the framed photographs.

"Mitch," Jason says, approaching him at the table. "Nice of you to come today."

Mitch nods. "I remember your brother. This picture seems like it's from around the time Neil and I talked. Can't believe it's been ten years since he toured my cottage."

Jason looks over at the photo. It's of Neil and himself, both in their late twenties. The picture was taken on the stone bench on the bluff. Neil's dark hair is wavy in the sea damp. He wears cuffed jeans and a tee, and holds a journal. Jason sits, leaning forward—elbows on his knees—beside Neil.

"May I?" Carol asks, coming up beside them. She takes the picture from Mitch. "You and your brother were close, Jason?"

"Definitely." Jason glances at the photo again. "My father snapped that, out on the bluff behind my place."

"It's a nice shot," Carol says, setting the picture back on the table.

"And how about Maris?" Mitch draws a hand along his goatee and turns to Jason. "Your wife still working on Neil's book?"

"She is."

Mitch glances at the small crowd gathered. He throws a look to the food table, too. "She around?"

"I saw her at Mass, didn't I?" Carol asks, lifting her round sunglasses to scan the crowd.

"Because we thought, well," Mitch adds, "we thought

maybe *she'd* like to tour our cottage before any demo begins. You know, like Neil did. For the book. Get some details of the original structure for the story."

"That's really generous of you," Jason tells him. "She'll appreciate the offer."

"Where *is* your wife, anyway?" Mitch asks then.

"Unfortunately," Jason begins, then hesitates. "Well, Maris couldn't make it to brunch today." He doesn't miss it, either. Doesn't miss the beat of silence that follows.

"Oh, too bad," Carol says. "Tell her we were asking for her." She gives a sympathetic smile before turning to the food table. "I'm going to grab something to eat, Dad."

But Mitch doesn't. While eyeing Jason, he tips his head. "Maris on deadline?"

"Something like that," Jason says, with no explanation. But he does have a thought. Just one. *Fifty more minutes.*

~

And so it goes. Jason's marriage comes undone under the microscope of everyone. The microscope of one brunch. One where his sister, Paige, wanders over and chats with Mitch while looking at the framed pictures. And Nick passes by to tell Jason he has to bounce for his guard-duty shift, then leaves with a bagged plate of food.

Jason waves Nick off before turning back to Mitch— still standing close by. "Listen, Mitch." Jason looks over to Lauren and Kyle's table, and sees Elsa sitting there. Can't miss her, actually, with her plum sheath, long chain

13

necklaces and honey-highlighted thick brown hair held back by big sunglasses propped on her head.

More than Elsa, Jason sees something else—his out. "I'd like you to meet someone," he says while motioning for Mitch to follow him. "Elsa. Elsa DeLuca." On their way to her table, they pass Cliff headed to the food station. He gives Jason a brief nod.

Moments later, when Jason's making introductions, Elsa tries to stand and shake Mitch's hand. "No, sit. *Sit*," Mitch tells her, all while taking her hand in both of his. "So nice to meet you, Mrs. DeLuca," he says while warmly clasping that hand of hers as she sits again.

"Elsa! Please, call me Elsa." Her eyes take in Mitch's small ponytail and a short braided-leather necklace. "I've heard a lot about you, Mitch. Or, well, about your *cottage*. The one ... right on the beach?"

Mitch nods and moves to the empty chair beside hers. But he doesn't sit, Jason notices. Instead he stands *behind* the chair and casually leans his forearms on the chairback— so that he's actually pretty darn close to Elsa.

Which is when something happens. Kyle and Lauren quiet. Not only that, but they give each other a look and a discreet nudge. So Jason turns to see what prompted *that* exchange. It surprises him that Elsa, who is normally cool and collected, is flustered talking to Mitch. Throughout some trivial small talk, she trips on her words. Smiles a lot. Fiddles with her chain necklaces. And wait, is her face flushed from the summer heat? Or from this laid-back dude rambling on with a slight Southern bent?

"So, we're still on for tomorrow evening?" Mitch is asking her. "Meet at my place? I'd like to show you the cottage before the reno gets started."

"That way," Jason adds, "you can tell Mitch and his daughter what to expect once the cameras are really rolling."

Elsa glances from Mitch, to Jason, then back to Mitch. "Yes, of course," she agrees.

Mitch tips his head and slightly squints at Elsa. "Plenty of space on that deck of ours, so bring along your husband, why don't you?"

"Oh, no." Elsa reaches out and briefly clasps his arm. "It'll just be me. My husband passed away several years ago."

"Now I'm sorry to hear that," Mitch tells her while patting her hand on his arm.

"Well, thank you." Elsa pauses, gives him a small smile, then tugs her hand from beneath his and folds both her hands on the table.

The whole time, Kyle and Lauren lean close and share some words. They sip lemonade spritzers from flutes. And keep a wary eye on these two new acquaintances.

So does Jason, while crossing his arms over his chest and listening.

"Anyway," Elsa continues. "I'll see your cottage *before*, and it might help if *you* see one after—mine."

"Give them a feel for the outcome," Jason says. "Not a bad idea, Elsa."

"I think so, too." She turns completely in her chair,

15

toward Mitch. "You and your daughter should come to the inn's grand opening. The ribbon-cutting ceremony is Friday night."

"This coming Friday?" Mitch asks.

"Yes!" Elsa answers. "Can you make it?"

"Sure to be a big turnout at the Ocean Star Inn that night." Jason, still standing beside the patio table, drags a hand along his jaw. "Everybody'll be there," he says.

"Friends, dignitaries, you name it," Kyle adds from his seat at the table.

Carol, balancing two loaded plates, walks up beside Mitch. "Dad, I got you some food."

Mitch stands straight and pushes in the chair he'd been leaning on. "Friday night okay with you, Carol?" he asks, then turns to Elsa. "Elsa, this is my daughter."

"Wonderful to meet you." From her seat, Elsa gives an easy wave.

"Elsa's invited us to her inn's grand opening," Mitch tells Carol.

Jason turns to Carol, too. "She wants you both to see firsthand the work my crew did there."

"Friday?" Carol asks, then hesitates. But only for a second, when she gives a quick nod. "Okay. Friday's good."

"Excellent," Mitch says.

Carol leans close to her father. "Dad, come on. We can't stay long. You promised to help me today, cutting flowers."

Mitch takes a plate from her before nodding to Elsa. "Nice talking, Elsa," he says. "We'll see you tomorrow night, then. At my cottage."

What Jason notices when Mitch walks away is this: Elsa doesn't take her intrigued, brown eyes off of him. Not for one second. Not when Cliff returns with their plates. Not when Cliff sits beside her in the seat Mitch had leaned on. Not when Kyle clears his throat and asks Cliff about the food. Only when Cliff nudges her plate closer does she look at him, then at her food, before standing and picking up her plate.

"Oh, Cliff. I wanted to eat over there, with Paige and Vinny."

"But, Elsa. We're settled—"

"I know. But the brunch, it *is* for Paige. *And* Jason," she adds, nodding to Jason still watching the way Elsa's world is spinning this morning. So Cliff stands. Together they move two tables over, sitting with Paige and Vinny now.

Jason just shakes his head and walks to the food table alone, thinking only one thought the whole way there. *Forty-five minutes to go.*

⁓

Problem is, as Jason walks past the tables—past Eva, Matt and their teenage daughter, Taylor—he *hears* only one question in his mind. It's the question Mitch had asked him. Because walking alone, without Maris beside him, without her leaning into him, waving to the others, straightening his collar or touching his arm, Jason can figure that everyone here is thinking the very same question as Mitch Fenwick: *Where's your wife?*

Good question.

As Jason fills his plate with eggs and bacon and a muffin, he hasn't one lousy clue where Maris is. Oh, but he knows damn well *what* she's doing. Maris is giving him a hefty spoonful of his own medicine, disappearing like this. And honestly? It doesn't taste too good.

When he sits beside Paige at her table, the talk is quiet. Right now, everyone's more interested in the meal.

"Oh, *Marone*," Vinny says, chewing with his eyes closed. "Whoever heard of a *breakfast* lasagna? Amazing."

"I'll have to get the recipe from Jerry," Paige says, raising her own fork dripping with the egg-and-hash-brown concoction, pausing only to swipe it through a swath of ketchup. "Mm-hmm."

Jason scoops up a forkful of scrambled egg, right when someone comes up behind him and gets him in a pseudo headlock.

"You'll be at the diner tomorrow morning for your regular cruller, right?" Kyle asks, bending low. "I'm expecting *you* at your reserved counter stool, bro."

"No can do," Jason tells him.

Which gets Kyle to release his grip around his neck. "What? That's two weeks in a row you'll be MIA."

Jason straightens his shirt collar. "Got a commitment tomorrow."

"For what?" Kyle asks.

"Live interview happening for Boston's public TV station," Jason replies. "The host of *Today's New Englander* is driving down for a morning chat, on-camera."

"I've seen that show," Vinny says. "Nice coup."

"Thanks. I guess they reserved dining space for the talk. At that historic inn over in Essex."

"Sweet, Barlow." Kyle grabs his coffee cup and swings a chair around. He sits backward on it, hanging his hands over the chairback. "That place is top-shelf."

Jason nods. "Good New England vibes to shoot there, with all its dark paneling, maritime artifacts, seafaring paintings."

"What a beautiful backdrop!" Elsa leans close on the table. "How'd this all come about?"

"The Boston station picked up *Castaway Cottage* for their programming," Jason says around a mouthful of scrambled eggs. "So my producer—"

"Trent?" Kyle asks.

"That's right. He put this Q-and-A thing together," Jason tells him.

"Kudos. Big-time stuff." Kyle sips his coffee. "When's it airing?"

Jason adds salt to his eggs. "Tomorrow morning. It's a live segment for their show."

"Wow, live TV," Kyle says. "I'd be sweating, for sure. You nervous?"

"Nah. Some of it will be off the cuff, some I'll prep for tonight."

"Good luck, dude." Kyle gives Jason a slight shove. "I'll put the TV on in the diner. Watch for it."

"That's wonderful, Jason," Cliff adds. "Good publicity, too."

19

Elsa wastes no time. She hooks two fingers in her mouth and attempts a whistle that fails.

"Allow me, Elsa." Kyle stands and taps a knife on a glass. "Listen up, everyone!" he calls out, tapping that glass until all the guests quiet. "A brief announcement for you. Tune in to *Today's New Englander* tomorrow morning, guys. Our pal Jason here? They're doing a big profile on him and his show."

When a few more whistles ring out, and random applause sounds, Kyle sits again.

"Jason," Elsa says. "On *this* day, remembering Neil together, I can't help but think how proud he'd be of you. *And* your show."

"Oh, let me tell you," Paige interrupts. "Neil was proud of *everything* his big brother did. Jason was his idol. I remember how he'd tag along with Jason everywhere he went."

"He was something," Jason agrees. He takes a sip of iced sangria then. "Definitely my shadow, growing up. Always there. When we were kids, Neil's favorite thing was playing soldier in the woods. Or the marsh. He'd wear Dad's old boonie hat, and load his camping vest with rock grenades and rations. Man, we'd make forts in the woods to Little Beach and hunker down there, patrolling for the VC. Secretly following poor unsuspecting folks walking the trail."

"I never met Neil," Elsa says, raising her flute of lemonade spritzer. "But I *feel* like I have from all the stories I've heard about him."

"Yo, Barlow," Matt calls out from his nearby table. "Remember how he'd start up with his drumsticks? In Foley's back room?"

"Then Shane would come in with the harmonica," Eva adds.

Lauren raises her own glass. "They'd both get the place stomping."

"I remember the time I told Neil about the driftline," Kyle says from his seat beside Jason. "I read about it in a little beach handbook in the cottage my old man rented every summer. Told Neil how all the things you find in the high tide line—sea glass, shells, hermit crabs, stones— they're all connected. And you know something? Your brother was fascinated with that concept. Thought people were connected like that, too." Raising his coffee cup, Kyle says, "To Neil."

Jason raises his own glass. Raises it, nods, and thinks one thought as he feels suddenly fatigued by it all. By Neil and his own fading memories of him. By Maris not being here. By the silent scrutiny placed on his marriage at the diner today.

One thought fills his mind. *Thirty-five more minutes.*

Those minutes tick slowly past. Jason feels each one, sitting in the shade of the patio umbrella. A waitress breezes through and refills coffee cups. Laughs rise. Slow stretches happen. At one point, a bee buzzes around, getting Lauren to jump in her belted maxi dress.

21

"Don't swat at it," Cliff calls out. "It'll chase you."

Elsa turns to Lauren's table. "Stay calm, hon. Zig to one side. It'll zag to the other."

"I might add some netting out here," Kyle says. "Especially late summer, to keep away those pesky yellow jackets. But the bags help."

"Bags?" Jason asks.

Kyle hitches his head to those clear plastic bags hanging from a tree's low branches. The bags are filled with water and shiny pennies. "Bugs don't like the light reflecting off the pennies. It bothers them, so they buzz off in another direction."

"Seriously?" Vinny asks as he lifts a forkful of coffee cake.

"Yeah, man. I read something about it in the paper. Gave it a try and it's been working all right."

As Kyle talks, someone taps Jason's shoulder, getting him to turn in his seat.

"Good luck with your interview tomorrow," Mitch tells him. "And we'll see you later this week."

"Will do, Mitch. Carol. Thanks for coming."

Mitch pats his back. "Sure thing. Peace and love, all," he says before heading off to his vehicle with Carol.

And the minutes, they keep ticking. Slowly but surely the clock hands move as the crowd thins. *Twenty-seven more minutes*, Jason thinks. *Under a half hour.*

22

But the hangers-on, well, they do just that—hang on.

"I have to get inside the diner," Kyle says as he stands and swings his chair back around. "It's mobbed already in there."

"And I should get home," Lauren announces. "My mom's babysitting Evan and Hailey. Paige's kids, too."

"Jason." Paige reaches over and gives his hand a squeeze. "Hey, what happened here?" she asks, pointing to his forearm.

"Where?" Jason twists his arm around and glances at the nasty bruise showing beneath his cuffed and pushed-back shirtsleeve. The bruise is purple now, and mottled. "Hit my arm on a door," he lies, instead of admitting his shocking fall from bed last week. "At Ted's cottage."

"You're still there?"

"Yeah. And I'm not too familiar with the place."

"Oh. That bruise looks painful," Paige tells him. "And all the more reason you *should* come on the beach with us this afternoon. Get some sun and kick back. You look tired." She brushes a finger beneath his eyes. "And the kids need to see their Uncle Jason," she reminds him.

"Okay, fine." He gives in, because he knows. With his sister, sometimes giving in is easier than resisting. "For a little while. I'll catch up with you guys there."

Paige leans closer. "I don't suppose Maris will come, too."

He shakes his head. "Not today," he tells her. And thinks, *Fifteen minutes left.*

23

Which gives Jason enough time to hit the buffet table for dessert. A slice of strawberry cake with cream-cheese icing suits him fine, so he takes a large piece. Before he can even turn back to his table, though, he's trapped. Trapped by the angry hiss of one sentence whispered in his ear.

"I knew things were bad with you and my sister just by the sorry state of my deck pots."

Jason, with his back to Eva behind him, closes his eyes for a long moment before turning around. "What?"

"My deck pots! I came back from Martha's Vineyard and my flowers were all withered and ... and *dead*. And Maris *promised* she'd water them, so I knew something was up."

"I can't answer for Maris, Eva."

"Oh, yes you can. Because you're the cause of her distress."

Jason looks long at his sister-in-law, then turns to the buffet table and picks up a clean fork.

"How can you even eat?" Eva demands under her breath, all while squirming around him to face him head-on. "What's the matter with you?"

"Eva." Jason steps back and slices off a piece of cake with his fork. "I'm asking you not to make a scene," he says around a mouthful of the dessert.

"But my sister's not *here* today. On this *very* important day." She looks from his plate of strawberry cake to his face—but not without dropping her gaze to his too-casual chambray button-down and dark khakis. "And you don't even know where she is, do you?"

24

While taking a second bite of cake, Jason notices Matt approaching.

"Jason!" Eva says, jabbing his shoulder. "I'm *talking* to you."

"Evangeline." Matt tugs her away from Jason. "Just go sit down."

"What?" Eva asks.

Matt simply hitches his head.

Eva, well she does it. She says what she wants to Jason with a look alone. With her winced eyes and pursed lips and a certain tip of her head that gets her to glare out from under her long, sideswept bangs. And Jason doesn't miss that look, even as she turns and walks off in a huff.

"Matt, thanks," he says with some relief.

"No problem. You know how protective she gets. Maris being her sister and all."

"Yeah. Hey, listen." Jason holds up his plate. "The strawberry cake's good."

"That's right where I'm headed."

Jason moves aside, eats another forkful of cake and walks back to his seat with Paige, Vinny, Cliff and Elsa. On the way to his table, he glances at his watch and thinks, *Eight more minutes.*

three

Sunday Noontime

IF HE'S QUICK, SHANE FIGURES he can get this done. Even if it's only a few lines, he needs to write a letter. Just a note will suffice. A few words will do. Below deck, he first grabs the orange waders from his duffel and steps into those bib pants before adjusting the overall straps on his shoulders. His deck boots go on, too, so he won't be slipping on the wet floor above. This way, he's ready to get to work on a moment's notice—should one of the crew come looking for him.

Next up? A pen. So he digs a ballpoint from his duffel. An envelope, too. A few are stamped and folded into the side zip compartment. That's his way—keep close a little bit of everything and he'll want for nothing.

Except paper, damn it. He brushes through his duffel, unzipping here, zipping there.

"Paper, paper," he quietly says then, turning and scanning

26

the small space below deck. There, on the side table. A pad of paper used for keeping score when a card game gets going. He grabs the pad, leans against the doorjamb, puts his pen to paper … and stops.

Because, shit. There's no time to think. No time to answer one nagging question. Does he really want to do this? To send Celia a note? Hell, he *could* act like he never saw her on the docks and ignore the whole scene. She'd never know the difference. He could just go out to sea and get on with his life. His lobstering life, in Maine.

"*Right*," he says under his breath, with a glance up the stairs to the boat's deck. A life spent alone with no family around. No close connections. Oh, there's some friendly company here and there. A few good times, a few casual relationships.

But no strings. No ties. No history.

Which gets him remembering his old captain and mentor, Noah, and how happy they *both* were to see each other again last week. There was something about their time together at Noah's seafood shack, and during an afternoon fishing on the Sound, that Shane's missed— some deep-rooted connection reaching far back through the years.

Years that ticked by unnoticed, until Shane landed in Stony Point for two weeks. Some evenings there, sitting on the open back porch of his rented cottage, he felt *every* single one of those years gone by. And sometimes in a sad way. A way that had him feel very much alone in his life.

So that does it. He starts writing. Just the date and

salutation. Which is where he stops and looks at his words. The formality of them has him rip off the paper, crumple it and shove it in his duffel.

"*Aargh*," he says. Because he felt it, writing those few words. Sending a letter? It *means* something. Something more than a chance greeting. It means Stony Point actually has a hold on him.

From below deck, Shane hears the boys. Hears their voices carry down, hears their shuffling around getting things ready—the traps, the bait bags. And he feels the motion of the boat as it moves through deeper water now. There's the call of seagulls, too, swooping over the vessel while trying to steal any scrap of lobster bait.

And there's no time now. He *has* to join the crew, fast.

Again, he starts writing. Whatever comes to mind, he puts it on paper. Quick, quick. In under a minute, his pen scrawls out the words. A few more seconds to sign his name, rip off the paper, fold it into the stamped envelope. He grabs Celia's address from his phone, seals the envelope and is done.

Just like that.

His shipmate was right. For the next couple of hours, doesn't Shane know it. Getting a woman stuck in your head is the worst distraction on the water. Already, his worry about Celia is messing with him. To start, he nearly skewered his hand while prepping bait bags. And once the first string of pots started going overboard, only a quick hop and a twist kept his foot out of the uncoiling rope—a narrow escape that barely kept Shane out of the sea.

Thankfully, fate smiles down and gives him just what he's been waiting for. Another lobster boat is headed their way. A boat *returning* to harbor after a long excursion. It's a familiar boat, too, with a crew Shane knows well. He's worked with them many times. Even better, his own lobster boat is idle right now, so Shane's able to flag down the approaching vessel.

"Hey, hey!" he calls over to one of the men on that returning boat. It slows to a crawl as it nears. "You guys headed back to port?" Though Shane figures they must be. This fellow looks tired; his clothes, hanging; his hair, a mess.

"Sure are," the deckhand aboard the other vessel calls back. "What's up, Bradford?"

"Could you drop this in the post office there?" Shane pulls Celia's letter from his shirt pocket beneath the suspender straps of his waders.

The other boat stops beside Shane's. "You don't want to just email? It'll get there faster."

"No. Signal's crap. Don't know the email address, either."

The fatigued deckhand shrugs. "Send 'er over," he says, reaching out for the envelope.

So Shane does, leaning far over the port side of the boat.

"Got it!" The guy snatches the envelope from Shane's hand and signals a *good-to-go* thumbs-up to the captain in the wheelhouse.

That's all it takes to clear Shane's head. To eliminate the distraction of Celia Gray. He's done all he can—letter written and hopefully soon mailed. So he salutes the other captain, who gets his vessel moving again. But *this* time, the captain has the boat going full speed *astern*, backing far away.

Shane watches, slowly grinning as he realizes just what the captain's doing. It doesn't take long. When enough distance falls between the two boats, the other captain reverses direction to full speed ahead. He flies past Shane's lobster boat in a friendly old roustin', sending a splash of the sea right over Shane on deck. The droplets arch high above him—glistening in a silver spray against the summer-blue sky.

four

Sunday Midafternoon

EVERY SUMMER SINCE NEIL DIED, Paige and Vinny have spent time on the beach on this day—the afternoon of Neil's Memorial Mass.

After brunch, Jason joins them in Stony Point. He sits beneath their umbrella. Ocean stars sparkle on Long Island Sound. The sun beats down hot on the sand. He relents when Paige's kids call out *Uncle Jason!* and get him into the water. Earlier, he'd stopped at Ted's cottage to square away his prosthesis with a waterproof cover. So now he splashes around with the kids. And swims with Vinny. Gets some sun.

But the whole time on the beach, Jason's really doing something else. With every breaking wave, every cry of a soaring seagull, he's hoping Maris might walk down the beach. Might head down the footpath, to the boardwalk, to the sand. Might wear her straw cowboy hat. Might have a

31

tote slung over her shoulder, an easy smile on her face.

Apparently his sister hopes so, too. Paige says she's worried about Maris.

"I never imagined she'd walk out of Mass *and* miss brunch," Paige tells him. Her sand chair is set beside Jason's. "Do you know where she is?"

Jason glances over to the footpath, then out at the water. A few teens are climbing onto the floating raft anchored in front of the big rock. "At this point, I wouldn't even know where to look."

"Will you stop at home to see if she's there?"

"Not sure." Because even though *he* decided to leave their house last week, it feels like Maris has since evicted him. But this Jason keeps to himself, sitting beside his sister.

That's how the afternoon goes, those couple of hours on the beach. From laughing fun with the kids and Vinny, from splashing and swimming beneath the August sun, to silent worry about Maris. Eventually the worry overtakes all else, so Jason's glad when his brother-in-law announces they have to leave.

"Convocation at the high school tomorrow. Then a meeting with the history department. Full day starting the new school year," Vinny says while toweling off after one last swim.

Jason helps carry the gear to their car in the Stony Point parking lot. There, he says his goodbyes, tells the kids to get straight A's at school, and gets into his SUV. When the door thuds closed, it's like the whole outside world is shut out. Gone are those splashing waves, the gulls, the vacationers' voices on the beach.

Now, there's nothing. Nothing but him and his thoughts as he drives the cottage-lined streets. Folks carrying sand chairs and swim tubes, and pulling wagons of beach toys, amble back to their cottages. Flip-flops flip on the sandy roads; late-afternoon shadows grow longer. Jason circles a beach block and drives down Sea View Road, past his house. Already, it feels like only a memory.

More worrisome is that Maris' car isn't in the long driveway. Otherwise, he'd have parked at the curb, knocked on the door and asked her to talk on the front porch. Just for ten minutes, even.

Instead, Jason keeps driving.

But it's when he sees the stone train trestle ahead that an odd feeling hits—this leaving, this driving *away* from his gabled house by the sea.

A house he'd once thought he could never leave.

A house he'd believed held every answer his life might ever need.

And one week ago, he left it behind.

Now he does it again, headed for his new home. A temporary one, at Ted Sullivan's cottage twenty miles down the coast.

Driving past Nick on guard duty, Jason doesn't stop. Doesn't roll down his window and bullshit for a few minutes. Just waves and drives on through the cool, shaded stone tunnel before leaving Stony Point and turning onto Shore Road.

His SUV is quiet. Windows up, a/c on. He passes bait shops and golden saltwater marshes. Lines of people stand at the take-out windows at a local seafood joint. So much is the same, but so much is different—in only one week.

Just then, he spots Celia's car approaching from the opposite direction. She's headed to the trestle. She'll drive beneath it in a different frame of mind than his. Will park at her little shingled cottage with some relief, Jason imagines. He gives a wave and lightly beeps his horn as they pass each other on the winding beach road.

～

What was she thinking? There's no telling how many times that question ran through Celia's mind on the long ride home. And there's no other answer than she wanted to see something of Shane's life, in Maine. Wanted to see where he landed all those years ago, when he left Stony Point.

Well. See it, she did. He'd been home less than a day when the sea called. When the ocean beckoned. The lure, to Shane, is irresistible. It was apparent in the way he threw his packed duffel aboard ship. In the way his crew welcomed him. In the way he'd wasted no time getting back on the water.

Celia saw it all. Saw it as she hurried across the docks, hoping for just a few minutes with him at that point. A coffee, maybe. Some words, a touch, a smile. She saw it as he settled in on deck, laughing and shaking hands with the crew. He was utterly comfortable aboard ship, amongst the stacks of lobster traps strung with rope and buoys. At ease beside the hydraulic hauler ready to lift pots from the sea. At home in the thick salt air; in the spray of the ocean.

She saw his world—and the hold it has on him. The sea is where Shane belongs.

There was no convincing herself otherwise, the whole drive home. Not when she kept a steady speed on the highways, not when she stopped to give Aria her bottle and some fresh air. Slowly, each hour ticked past until—finally—she exited the highway in Connecticut. The thing is? Passing Jason on Shore Road now and returning his friendly wave assures Celia of one thing. Of something she hadn't realized even early this morning.

It assures her that as much as Shane is where he belongs, so is she. A relationship can never work between them.

"*It's all for the best*," she says to herself. Says it with a glance at her rearview mirror, all while imagining the fishing village of Rockport far, far behind her now. Yes, it's for the best that Shane's lobster boat was pulling out, Celia thinks. He didn't even see her. Doesn't know anything about the impulsive trip she'd made. She was simply caught up in a moment, an idea, a hope. He'd given her an out, after all, when he recently told her to come to Maine if things ever got to be too much in Stony Point. And the thought of everyone gathered today at Mass and brunch, well, it *did* feel like too much. So she went where there were no prying eyes. No whispers behind shingled walls. No questions. No judgments.

On top of it all, she lied to Elsa, texting her some cover-up about being in Addison today because her father had car trouble. *Lied* and said she was helping him out.

Far from it.

Instead, after driving to Maine and back in one day purely to see Shane—*and* spending too many hours on the road—Celia feels the distance. Her poor daughter fussed for much of the ride home, too, after being strapped in her car seat for so long.

"Oh my gosh, what would we have gotten ourselves into?" Celia asks aloud.

But she knows. Now she is well aware of what would've come from seeing Shane in Maine.

Nothing.

Packing up her baby and food and the car this morning would've amounted to nothing. Shane's life is clearly entrenched there, on the docks, at the edge of the Atlantic.

"*Foolish, foolish,*" she whispers with a slight shake of her head. At least no one here saw what she did.

So with some relief, Celia takes in the *Connecticut* sights on Shore Road. The take-out seafood joint doing the business. People sit at every outdoor table there, beside a saltwater marsh. Its sweeping grasses are golden; the water, blue. She sees the bait shacks, the weathered cottages, the beach shoppes—and is glad for the familiarity of it all.

Especially for the stone railroad trestle ahead, when she takes the turn off Shore Road. Sure, anyone who leaves does so with one of three things: a ring, a baby, or a broken heart.

But what about those arriving? Those turning *in* to

Stony Point? She drives through the short tunnel, then stops to talk to Nick standing guard. Smiles when he taps at the car's back window and waves to Aria. And finally, Celia drives the sandy beach roads she's come to call home.

After passing the painted bungalows and summer shanties, her gingerbread guest cottage comes into view. Its golden cedar shingles and little front porch have never looked sweeter. And the diamond-shaped stained-glass window glimmers in the low, late-day sun.

What happens then is this: Her breathing comes easier. With a salt-air sigh, Celia pulls the car into her driveway and gets out. But she momentarily closes her eyes against some powerful emotion that suddenly wells up. It surprises her, the way hot tears sting her eyes. She fights them, though, squeezing them back and pausing for a long second. Then, and only then, she leans into the backseat and unstraps her baby.

"Nobody ever needs to know where we went today," she whispers to Aria as she lifts her in her arms. *"It'll just be our secret."*

five

Late Sunday Afternoon

SHOULD SHE, OR SHOULDN'T SHE?

Maris wavered on the question all day. But her conscience got the best of her, so she decided to do it. To make the trip. It'll only take an hour to get there. She packed a few things in her car, drove beneath the trestle and heads to Addison—forty miles away. It's her hometown, the place of her childhood.

But still, the ride isn't easy.

Because here's the catch. Here's the truth that had her waver all day. She's not in Addison for herself. Not here to cruise the quiet streets and see the colonial home where she grew up. There'll be no fond reminiscing today. No, she stays steady on her course straight *through* town, passing older Federals and English Tudors set in the shade of towering maple and oak trees. The day is hot, even now. Crossing some railroad tracks, she continues on through a newer housing development. The homes here are more modern, and have smaller yards. Children's bicycles dot the driveways; someone's mowing the grass.

Still, Maris keeps driving. Finally she picks up the turnpike, where there are no trees, no green lawns offering relief from the summer heat. Instead, this busy four-lane thoroughfare is lined with warehouse stores and gas stations and fast-food restaurants and simmering parking lots. She keeps driving until about a mile before Hartford, where she slows and pulls onto the shoulder of the road. After a moment, she opens her window, shuts off the car and just sits there. The hot engine ticks. Cars fly past, one with a radio blaring.

Then, quiet.

Before getting out, Maris looks around. To the left, a large cemetery covers a sloping hill. To the right, beyond an immense parking lot, a strip mall houses a discount store, grocery store and other small shops.

Lastly, she looks ahead to a stretch of pavement just past a traffic light. To the spot where, ten years ago, a car collided with two brothers on a motorcycle—and Neil Barlow died.

Taking a long breath, Maris gets out of her car, walks around to the passenger side and lifts out the large happiness jar she'd made earlier. Her window of time to do so was limited. But she knew she could walk the beach right after Neil's Mass, when everyone would be at the diner for brunch. No one would spot her strolling along the Stony Point driftline, basket in hand. Spending a quiet hour beachcombing and thinking of Neil, she'd collected golden sand, pretty pieces of seaweed, driftwood, sea pebbles and shells. When her basket was full, she sat on her deck at home. There, with waves splashing out on the bluff, she decorated a jar with her sand and seaside finds. For a finishing touch, she lifted one perfect seagull feather from the basket and tucked it into some burlap wrapped around the Mason jar. Neil's journals are all bookmarked with random gull feathers of silver, white and gray—each one noting special passages. So *her* feather commemorates the thoughts and images in his journals that Maris uses to shape their novel.

Holding that jar now, Maris walks over weedy dry grass to the turnpike's curb. It's been three years since Jason brought her here. Three years since he told her that to know him fully, she had to see where the accident happened. His roadside words that day were painful. Beneath the hot summer sun, she'd winced when he told her that Neil's Harley-Davidson was stopped at the traffic light when Ted Sullivan's car came up behind them. Out of nowhere. How later they'd learn that Ted had a heart attack at the wheel—with his foot on the gas.

Parked at the bleak spot where the accident happened, Jason repeated details of the fatal collision. His voice dropped low; his eyes were serious.

A whirlpool of roaring grew louder ... deafening.
Not one second of time to ditch the bike and run for cover.
Took the force of Neil's weight fully on my back.

40

The impact bending me over enough that his body flowed like a wave over my head.
Neil airborne; the motorcycle spun incessantly.
My jeans hooked onto something twisting up my leg, keeping me attached to the bike.
Ripping pain burned through my leg.
Sight and hearing stopped working.
Thrown to roadside brush. Then, nothing.

She looks to that patch of scrubby grass where Jason landed when he was thrown from the bike ten years ago. She could actually put her happiness jar *there*, as much as at the spot where Neil died. Because Jason's alive, after all. The reminders of life's goodness that she bottled inside her burlap-wrapped jar might help him. Yes, she'll put it there.

When she takes a step toward that patch of roadside grass where he once lay, critically injured and unconscious, she stops. A sudden motion gets her to freeze, drop her eyes closed for a moment, then turn. When she does, she sees Jason standing at the curb, off in the distance.

⁓

Jason made the trip. He doesn't do it every year, but something about today got him to visit the crash site, the memory. After everyone witnessed his life unraveling at brunch, coming here was his way of escaping it all. His way to think only of Neil, and time, and summers gone by. So after stopping at Ted's cottage, feeding the dog and washing up, Jason hit the road.

But he never imagined Maris would be at the turnpike, too. In his mind, once she walked out of the church, she was done with him.

Done with his troubles.

Done with his memories.

Done with his ghosts.

So it's a surprise to see her standing right there, on the one small piece of earth that changed his entire life. Instead of her navy church outfit, she wears a cropped white blazer and an olive tank top over utterly distressed and shredded denim cutoffs. Her hair is pulled back in a low twist, and she has on large sunglasses.

He walks to her now. Turns up his hands, looks briefly away to fight a knot of emotion, then looks at her again as he nears.

The walk, quiet except for the occasional passing car and the sound of his footsteps on the pavement, takes on new meaning. It's no longer about Neil.

Being here is about them. After all he and Maris have been through in recent weeks—facing the past, and Shane, and lies and secrets—it feels like this is the crash site of their marriage now, too. They can piece it back together. Or else they'll put flowers down, talk a bit, let memories drift off in the hazy summer air ... and walk away from each other.

"Maris," he says, stepping off the road and joining her on the dry grass.

She gives him a sad smile. On the ground beside her,

there are a few hydrangea branches heavy with blossoms and tied together with twine.

"I brought flowers. And this," she says, holding up a large happiness jar. "*For Neil*," she whispers.

Jason only nods then, as more cars drive by. He and Maris are so close to the road, he feels the hot wind of movement when the vehicles speed past. It's noisy, too, with the sound of car engines, and tires on the pavement.

"It's just that," Maris goes on, "I wasn't sure where to put the jar."

"Well." Jason looks to the road, to the spot where his brother took his last breath. Then he turns to Maris. "Can I see?" he asks, reaching for the burlap-wrapped jar she holds.

Maris gives it to him. "I picked up some things on the beach earlier. Things that made me think of Neil."

Jason raises the jar. She'd nestled seaside trinkets in sand surely scooped off Stony Point's beach. Sand that meant the world to Neil. Anything about Stony Point did. Seashells lean in the jar; beach pebbles edge the glass.

"I got the sea fern off the rocks, where Neil liked to sit." Maris steps closer and points out the bits of seaweed she'd placed in the jar. "There's a little sea lettuce, too."

Jason looks from Maris, to the jar. He's sure every sea-smoothed stone, every piece of frosted sea glass, every seaworn shell, is attached to some memory she has of Neil. There's a note in there, too. A piece of stationery folded into a small square. Jason can only imagine the heartfelt words Maris penned. He touches the white seagull feather tucked into the burlap outside the jar.

"*Neil used feathers as bookmarks.*" Maris' voice comes softly to him—so soft, he's not sure if she actually spoke, or if he's hearing her thoughts.

As they stand there, traffic picks up beside them. A truck roars past, blowing some gritty road dust their way. Again, Jason looks to the pavement where Neil died. He also sees the patch of scrubby grasses where *he* landed after being thrown from the bike. Where that one day suddenly went silent and dark. This summer, that same dark feeling snuck up on him again, no matter how hard he fought it.

But this jar, Maris' happiness jar made special for Neil, it lifts Jason's heart—as much as it breaks it. "Are you sure?" he asks, glancing at the jar again.

"About what?"

He looks at Maris, but can't really read her beneath her dark sunglasses. "Are you sure you want to leave this here?"

"I was *going* to. For your brother."

"But ..." Jason hands the jar back to her. "It'll go to waste here. Someone will take it, or smash it. And ..." Again Jason glances to the street right as two cars drive by. "It's really personal, Maris. I mean, you walked the beach alone, thinking of my brother." He takes a long breath. "And I'm not sure—"

"Jason."

He briefly takes off his own sunglasses and swipes an eye.

"I thought that, well ..." Maris pauses when an SUV speeds past, beeping its horn at them as it does. "Jason, do *you* want the jar? I can leave it with you."

He says nothing. All he can manage is one last look at the street on this ten-year anniversary. One last look at where he last saw, heard and felt his brother, alive. Then he looks to Maris right as a pickup truck rumbles along.

"Jason?"

"We should really get off the road here," he says.

Maris is quiet for a long moment. Maybe she's thinking a sad goodbye to Neil. Or silently praying a few words for his spirit.

"Can we go somewhere? To talk," Jason adds, then just stops. Stops and looks at his wife standing there, roadside.

Maris brushes a wisp of fallen hair off her face. "Bella's?" she asks.

six

Sunday Evening

MARIS DRIVES THROUGH THE SOUTH End of Hartford, with Jason following in his SUV. They pass brick-front bakeries, pizzerias and clothing boutiques. Tables spill from cafés under the shade of sloping canopies. It's a perfect summer evening to dine outdoors.

But they don't.

They don't need outdoors—with tables of people crowding all around them. With sounds of traffic. What she and Jason need is the cool, dark interior of Bella's Ristorante. They need the comforting aromas of lasagna and fresh-baked bread. They need a candle flame flickering low inside a red glass globe on their tabletop.

By the time they park, walk inside and are seated in a padded booth, Maris knows. They also need the hushed quiet here. It gives them space to talk. So while Jason lifts a carafe of wine and fills two goblets, she sets Neil's

46

happiness jar on the table, then slips off her white blazer. Which is when she notices Jason's fatigue. There are shadows beneath his eyes, whiskers on his jaw. The day, never mind the summer, hasn't been easy on him.

"How was brunch?" she asks while lifting her wineglass.

"Something to get through."

"Jason. Come on."

He takes a swallow of wine and sets down his glass. "No, it really went that way. Didn't help that Trent set up a last-minute interview for me tomorrow. I'll be on *Today's New Englander*, that show out of Boston."

"Wow, that's a big deal! Congratulations."

"Yeah. After the public TV station there picked up season one of *Castaway Cottage*, Trent scheduled the Q and A. He sent them promo pics for the talk, snapshots and footage from Stony Point. Now I just have to show up." Jason glances at his watch. "And prep for it later. Back at Ted's."

"So you're driving to the station in Massachusetts tomorrow?"

"No." Jason takes another sip of his wine. "We're meeting up and filming over in Essex. At that historic inn there. The talk will be broadcast live, probably midmorning."

"I'll watch for it," Maris says. Then, nothing. She just opens her menu and scans the dinner choices.

"Oh, who am I kidding," Jason admits. "It's not stress for an interview that derailed the brunch. It's that without you there? Everyone pretty much saw my life, and our marriage, coming undone." He slowly turns his glass on the table. "Which wasn't how I wanted to honor my brother today."

"What *did* you have in mind?"

Jason's words, they come quietly. Maris only listens when he talks about paddling through the marsh with Sal last summer on this day. They'd spent a few hours in a place Neil loved. Jason slides Neil's happiness jar closer then, and looks at the shells and stones inside it. He goes on to say how this anniversary's conflicted him in recent years. He's not sure what to do with it anymore, this annual twenty-four hour block of time when life simply stops for him. "That beach walk you took today? Sounded nice," he says, setting Neil's jar aside again.

Before Maris can respond, they're interrupted by their waiter, who approaches with a pad and pencil. "Good evening, folks. Ready to order?"

Jason opens his menu and drags a finger down the selections. "What's the Sicilian-style chicken?" he asks.

"Chicken breast in a sauce with capers, vinegar, olives, celery and mushrooms. Orzo on the side."

"No," Jason says, glancing at the menu. "Let me have the cavatelli primavera, instead."

"White sauce, or red?"

"White."

"Very good. And for you?" the waiter asks Maris.

"Just an appetizer. The hot eggplant salad, please."

When the waiter collects their menus and walks away, Jason asks Maris, "That's it? You don't want a dinner?"

Maris only shakes her head. "So tell me more about brunch."

"It was the usual. You know, with everybody there. Not much to tell, really. Other than I was getting grilled. The questions, they didn't stop. *Where's Maris? Is she coming? Working under deadline? On her way?* It all made for an uncomfortable morning." As he talks, their waiter sets down a basket of warm bread with a plate of foil-wrapped butter tabs. "And after bluffing my way through it all, *and* thinking about Neil today, I'm feeling a little lost right now," Jason explains while unfolding the red-and-white checked cloth covering the breadbasket.

"And injured." Maris points to the side of his forearm, where a bruise shows beneath his pushed-up chambray shirtsleeve. "What happened?"

"It's nothing," Jason says with a glance at the bruise.

"Nothing? Looks pretty bad to me."

Jason spreads a tab of butter on a warm bread slice. "Well, I was out of sorts ... being in an unfamiliar cottage. And rushing around in Ted's the other day, I hit myself on a door." He bites into the bread then.

"Okay." Maris butters a slice of bread for herself. "So what do you hope to accomplish staying there, twenty miles down the coast? If you're out of sorts, bruising yourself. Where's it leading?"

Jason sets down his bread and sips his wine.

"Nowhere, right?" Maris asks before he has a chance to give her a line.

"Listen. I left home—"

"*And* me. You left me, too, Jason."

He pauses, then nods. "I left for a lot of reasons. One of which was to give you space to take care of your past. Especially after I walked into that shack the night Shane was there with you. It was a pretty charged space, inside those four walls." Jason takes another swallow of his wine. "You ask where my staying at Ted's is leading? Let's turn the tables, Maris. It might help you to understand why I left. Because if I didn't walk into that shack when I did, where would *that* situation have led?"

"I told you nothing happened."

"That doesn't answer my question."

"Well, I *have* sorted things out with Shane."

Jason sits back in the booth. Sits back and draws his knuckles over the raised scar on his jaw. "Sorted things out. Which means?"

"It means I gave Shane his old engagement ring back— and *not* to appease you. But I didn't just drop it off. We met, Jason. Shane and I talked for a *long* time. We talked about the past. Reminisced about ... I don't know ... summer afternoons when I'd sketch fashion designs on the docks in New London. The times when I'd sit there at an old picnic table and embroider waves and stars on denim. He'd return from a lobstering trip and we'd while away the hours together. That's the kind of relationship we had. *Easy.* So the way I'd left him, all those years ago? It was wrong on so many levels. And it bothered me, to this day. We talked about that, too."

Jason, still sitting back in shadow, quietly asks, "How exactly did you leave him?"

"Over the worst phone call of my life." Maris picks up her bread and pulls off a piece of the crust, but eats none of it. "I broke up with Shane from the old Stony Point payphone by the creek. It was a freezing cold winter day, with the wind blowing off the water. Problem is, the call was cut short when I ran out of coins, and that's where it all ended—a broken engagement, our relationship. And it hung unfinished like that for fifteen years, because we never spoke again, Shane and I. Not until this summer. Not one word. Think about that, Jason." She drops her voice to a whisper. "Just *think* if I were to walk out of here right now ... and that's all we saw or heard from each other, for fifteen years."

⌒

"Point taken," Jason barely says after a long silence.

"Good."

He nods, and sips his wine. Around them, in their old familiar restaurant, paintings of piazzas and olive orchards hang on the golden walls. The lighting in Bella's is dim. A candle flickers in a red glass globe on their table. Everything familiar, yes. Except for the talk. The talk has them feel like strangers, as Maris explains a difficult end to her relationship with another man.

"An unfinished phone call? No, that's *not* your style, Maris," Jason says. "And I get it now. How it came back to haunt you this summer." He keeps his voice low and serious. "But all that still doesn't *change* what happened in the shack. There was some leftover emotion between you two that night. Desire, regret? Love? I don't know. What I *do* know is that you two were ... It looked like I walked into an affair."

Maris sits back while the waiter delivers their food. He sets the steaming plates on the table, asks if there will be anything else, and quietly leaves when Jason tells him, "No."

But Maris doesn't miss a beat. No sooner does the waiter turn his back than she defends herself. "It wasn't an affair," she insists, her voice as low and serious as his. "It was a *moment*. Yes, Shane and I had a moment. An emotional one." She picks at her hot eggplant salad. "A *charged* moment, maybe. But that's all it was." She lifts a forkful of her meal and takes a bite. "So you can stop doing with Shane the same thing you do with phantom pain in your missing leg," she says around the food.

"And what would that be?"

"You know." Maris sips her wine. "When the phantom pain's bad, you displace it with another pain. Like when you wrap a scalding towel around your thigh."

"And you're saying I do the same thing with my life? And our marriage?"

"Yes!" Maris stabs at a few peas and a piece of garlic on her plate. "Is it easier for you to wedge Shane between us than to face what's really bothering you, Jason? Because doing that, using Shane like that, it's not fair. But it feels like that's exactly what you *are* doing this summer, ten years after the wreck."

While raising a forkful of cavatelli, Jason's hand stops midway to his mouth. "You're mad," he says, setting down his fork.

"I am." Maris looks away before speaking. "Because Shane and I aren't the real problem here."

"Maris—"

"Neil's gone, Jason. You *have* to accept reality now. He's *dead*. Ashes to ashes. He's a *ghost*." She grabs up her napkin and dabs at her eyes. "Blaming your emotions on me and Shane, walking away ... it's not going to bring Neil back." This she nearly whispers. The candle in its red globe flickers between them. Their food is barely touched.

"Maris. I'm *telling* you I didn't leave because of my brother." Jason shakes his head in frustration. "I left because of *you*. I was giving you space to handle your past with Shane. To settle it. To get it to a good place for *everyone's* sake—us included," he adds, turning up his hands in defeat. There'll be no reaching across the dark table and holding Maris' hand. None of his thumb stroking the soft skin of her wrist. Nothing romantic tonight, in their old familiar place. No looks; no whispered affections. Instead, there's this. "I don't know what more you want from me," Jason says. "What do you want me to say to change things?"

The air is thick between them. Those paintings of piazzas and olive orchards on the walls don't work their magic; don't lighten the mood. Jason drags a hunk of bread through the sauce on his plate. All the while, he's waiting for Maris' words.

But none come.

After a few quiet seconds, he looks at her. Her fingers toy with the beach jar she'd made for his brother.

"What do I want you to say?" she repeats, reaching for her wineglass now.

"Yes."

Maris sips her wine, then shrugs. "I want you to say, *Help me through this.* I don't want you to run, but to say, *We've both made mistakes. We're in this together, you know.*" She stops, picks up her napkin again, and this time pats her mouth. "Tell me, *We'll get through the highs and lows. Always.*" She adds that pivotal word from their wedding vows before slipping into her cropped white blazer and gathering her small black purse and keys. "But you won't."

"Wait. You're leaving?"

"And how does it feel, Jason?"

"Come *on.*" He shakes his head, watching her from across the table.

Maris loops the gold chain strap of her purse over her shoulder. "I met with Shane this week. I *returned* his ring. We talked and came to grips with things. With the past."

"Where? At those same docks in New London?"

Maris gives a small laugh. "At the *laundromat,*" she says. "I took care of the past so that—in *your* words—it wouldn't hunt me down." Leaving Neil's beach jar on the table, she slides out of the booth, stands and turns back to him. "I fixed my life, Jason. Let me know when you fix yours."

seven

Early Monday Morning

ELSA RUSHES OUT OF HER office. Her *office*! It's still hard to believe. She has her very own office at her very own Ocean Star Inn. It's really happening. Her dream is coming true. Holding a bulleted checklist, she hurries to the kitchen to switch on the coffeepot for when Celia gets here. She also lifts her handy-dandy spritzer from the counter and gives her window-side herb pots a drink. A few sprinkles on each plant will suffice. That done, she sits at her marble-top island and reviews the day's itinerary:

> *Confirm arrival of inn's first Saturday guests.*
> *Check that kitchen is stocked.*
> *Finalize first official Ocean Star Inn Sunday Dinner Menu.*
> *Verify rowboat is prepped for marsh rides—sun canopy, oars, life vests.*
> *Order new chalk for sidewalk inn-spiration messages.*

Finally! Finally, her inn by the sea will open its doors. It's what Elsa's wanted to do since she arrived at Stony Point two years ago. That first day here, she'd kicked off her sandals, wiggled her bare toes in the dewy grass and just sensed it. A change in her life was imminent.

It might have taken two years, but here it is. Oh, if there's one thing Elsa always knew, it's this: The best place to start over is somewhere by the sea. *And this is proof*, she thinks while reading her about-to-open inn checklist.

Reads it, that is, until a sharp knock sounds at the main entrance door. So pushing her leopard-print reading glasses to the top of her head, she leaves the checklist behind and hurries down the hallway, past the reception desk, beneath the Mason-jar chandelier—and opens the door. An unfamiliar mail carrier stands there holding a stamped-and-labeled business envelope.

"Oh! You're not my regular guy. Where's Ernie?" Elsa asks.

"Has the week off for vacation. I'm covering his route." The mailman glances at that envelope he holds. "Is there a ... Mrs. *DeLuca* here?"

"Why yes! That's me. How can I help you?" Elsa steps outside onto the glorious summer day. The sun is shining; birds are singing; the sky is blue as can be. "Here, have a seat on the porch swing. Ernie usually sits and chats a little."

"That won't be necessary. Just need you to sign for this." The mailman hands her the envelope.

"Oh, okay. Well, this looks interesting." She slips on her

reading glasses and gives the envelope a good scrutiny. It's large and *very* official-looking, with its serious labels, and a return-address insignia, and hefty postage, and a stamped message declaring it *Certified*. Most importantly, it's *Elsa's* name and address appearing on the front-and-center label. "And where do I sign?" she asks.

"Here." The mailman gives her a pen and points to the appropriate blank line on a form attached to the envelope.

"I wonder what it could be," Elsa muses while writing her signature. She looks up at the waiting mailman and hands the signed envelope back to him. "Did I win something, maybe?"

"Don't know." He finishes his transaction and returns the envelope to her.

Elsa takes it, flipping that one piece of mail from front to back, twice.

"Any questions, I'm sure there'll be contact information in there." The mailman tips his uniform cap before walking down the front porch steps and heading back to his truck parked at the curb.

Elsa watches him go for only a second. This mystery delivery is too intriguing to ignore, so she sits on the porch swing and opens the envelope, right there. As her finger slips beneath the flap, she wonders what on earth would be sent to her via certified mail.

"*There's only one way to find out,*" she says to herself, then pulls out the papers. There are several, starting with the cover letter. She quickly scans that letter, then returns to the beginning to carefully reread it.

And to think this *must* be a mistake.

Slowly, she reads each detailed line, starting with her name. Okay, so yes, this *is* intended for her—no mistake there. At one point, she glances out toward the street, as if the mailman might have some further assurance for her. Some clarification. But he's long gone. So she shuffles through the handful of papers behind the letter, each one neatly typed and stamped and dated.

"*Oh no!*" Elsa quietly exclaims while thumbing through each sheet. "This just cannot be." Sitting back on the swing, she dreads what's to come. Not only that, she also feels utterly defeated by this terrible news. Adjusting her glasses, she reads the cover letter one more time. Certain phrases truly alarm her: *regret to inform you ... no physical changes ... detailed statement ... comprehensive plan ... additional threat ... lasting impact.*

This simply can't be happening to her. Not now. Not at all! "Oh my God, what will I—"

"Good morning, Nonna!" a singsong voice calls out then.

Elsa looks up to see Celia pushing Aria's stroller along the inn's front walkway. In the bright sunshine, Celia wears a tank top and frayed black shorts, her fedora tipped low on her head. "Oh. Celia," Elsa says. She quickly presses her official-and-detrimental papers into their envelope—grabbing up one page that falls to the floor—then rushes down the porch stairs to give Celia a hug.

"Anything interesting?" Celia motions to the stuffed envelope clenched in Elsa's hand.

"What, this? No. No, just routine paperwork." With that, Elsa lifts Aria out of her stroller. "Hello, my little love," she murmurs, all while her thoughts are going a mile a minute in another direction entirely. A very *worried* direction, so contrary to the sweet bundle of granddaughter in her arms. How will she *ever* deal with this news? *Well*, she thinks while kissing the baby's cheek, *it'll just have to remain a secret for now.*

"I hurried back from Aria's walk because it's almost ten o'clock, Elsa. Your text message said Jason has a TV interview this morning?"

"That's right! You were at your father's in Addison yesterday, when Jason announced it at the brunch." Still managing to clutch her official envelope, Elsa puts Aria back into Celia's arms and turns to the door. "Let's go inside. Coffee's brewing, and I have the TV on for us."

"Upsy-daisy, Aria," Celia says as she climbs the porch steps to the inn. "We'll go watch your godfather now."

eight

Minutes Later

MARIS ISN'T SURE. EITHER THERE'S something about window seats, or there's something about sisters. Because this is where she always lands when her life hits rough seas—on her sister Eva's kitchen window seat. Everything always seems like it'll work out when she sits there mulling things over. Today, sunbeams shine through the window and onto the wood floor. Beside her, fresh-cut black-eyed Susans and wisps of tall beach grass spill from a crystal vase on the mahogany pedestal table. Best of all? Outside the window where Maris sits, the marsh spreads beyond Eva's yard, and so the scent of the sea wafts into the kitchen.

"I'm really glad it's your turn to host our weekly coffee," Maris says as Eva sets a tray of warm pastry on the table. "What *are* those sinful-looking treats?"

"Peach cobbler muffins," Eva tells her before turning off the oven.

"But you just got back from Martha's Vineyard. When did you bake these?"

"I didn't. I bought them at a farm stand." She puts a muffin on a plate and hands it to Maris. "I'm too upset to even *think* about baking. I mean, how could things turn so bad, so quickly, between you and Jason?"

"I don't know." Maris bites off a piece of the crumbled, streusel muffin top. "There's been this perfect storm of situations, and we're just not seeing eye to eye."

"And who's right? Who's wrong?"

"That's the problem, Eva. Who knows?"

"Well, at least you saw him last night. Did *anything* come from having dinner at Bella's?" Eva turns on her countertop TV, then pours a mug of steaming coffee and hands it to Maris. "Will Jason be back home soon?"

"Not sure." Maris holds her coffee close while thinking of their dinner the night before. A touch of sea breeze comes through the window. Finally, she looks to Eva sitting at her antique kitchen table. "But I did let him know that I fixed things with Shane—"

"Wait. You talked to Shane, too? When did this happen?"

"Last week. On Sunday."

Eva drags her chair closer to where Maris still sits on the window seat. "I swear, I'm *never* going away again. How will I ever catch up on your life?"

"I'll catch you up, right now. When I left the restaurant, I told Jason I took care of my past. That I fixed my life." Maris sips her coffee. "And when I walked out, I told him to let me know when he fixes his."

"Oh, Maris. I hate to see you guys like this."

Maris, well what can she do? Not much more than shrug. As she does, the opening music begins for *Today's New Englander.* "Look," she says, pointing to the TV. "It's about to start."

They go silent at the intro to Jason's interview. Panoramic scenes of the Connecticut shoreline fill the screen. There are tranquil harbors and winding boardwalks. Stately oceanfront homes rise on bluffs; shingled seaside shanties are nestled on sandy beach roads.

Maris gets it, right away. The intro gives flavor to all that is Jason Barlow's world. All that might influence his architectural vision, his work and *Castaway Cottage.* She continues to watch. Rowboats are anchored in marshes edged with sweeping grasses; people fish off narrow piers. There are take-out seafood shacks and historic inns—one of which is the location for Jason's live interview. He sits with the show's host, Raymond Nyes, in the inn's darkly paneled dining room. The room is serious, masculine and shows its age. Framed paintings of historic steamships cover the walls; antique ship lanterns and long wooden oars hang from the ceiling; a massive brick-front fireplace is unlit.

Maris sees it all, but especially Jason now. He sits across from Raymond at a square wooden table. Their chairs are simple—brown padded seats with striped upholstered backs. Simple, somewhat nautical and perfectly suited to the interview. Glasses of water are on the table. Portable lighting is angled above them; microphone stands are nearby.

"*Castaway Cottage*, CT-TV's new cottage-renovation series, seems custom-made for renowned architect Jason Barlow," the host begins. "His forte is restoring beach houses in the coastal Connecticut community where he's lived his entire life."

While the host talks, a few more photographs—these ones, personal—pan across the screen. One picture is a distant view of Jason's home on the bluff. A family portrait, then, from when he was a young boy. In it, Jason stands at the water's edge with Neil and Paige in front of their parents. They all squint against the sun; a sea breeze lifts their hair. Another portrait, this one of Jason working at his drafting table in his barn studio. His hand rests on a sketch. Maddy lies on the floor beside him.

"Jason calls seaside Stony Point home, residing there in his family's old gabled cottage," Raymond says, "with his wife, Maris."

Which is when the next photograph fills the screen. This picture is of Jason and Maris sitting side by side on the boardwalk. They're completely at ease as Maris leans close. She has on her straw cowboy hat; Jason's sunglasses are hooked on his shirt collar. The picture is from last summer, when they had an early Sunday morning coffee by the sea. Nick happened by and grabbed the shot.

And it's the last photograph to air. Now the camera turns to the two men seated at a dark wooden table in the historic inn. Behind them, wall sconces glimmer. That camera lens captures the moment in real time, panning around the richly paneled room.

But more importantly, this is it—Jason Barlow unveiled for all of New England to see.

Maris, perched on the window seat, draws up her knees and watches Eva's countertop TV. Jason is finally shown in close-up. His dark hair is slightly disheveled and needs a trim. A few days' whiskers cover his face. He wears black chinos and a long-sleeve button-down folded back at the cuffs. The silver chain of his father's Vietnam War dog tags is visible beneath his collar.

But nothing—not makeup, not the lighting—can conceal the faint shadows under Jason's dark eyes. He clears his throat and shifts in his chair when Raymond talks about the Stony Point landscape of homes: from the grand shingle-style to classic painted bungalows to tiny weathered beach boxes.

"A recent recipient of the prestigious Connecticut Coastal Architect Award," Raymond continues, "I'm happy to have Mr. Barlow as our guest on *Today's New Englander*." He extends his hand across the table. "Welcome, Jason."

"Thank you," Jason says while returning the handshake. "I'm glad to be here."

But he's not. Maris sees it. "*Eva*," she whispers.

"What's the matter, hon?" Eva asks.

"I'm not sure I can watch this."

"Why?" Eva looks from the TV to Maris. "He's doing good. Give him a chance."

As Eva says it, the host is talking to Jason about his

weathered home on the bluff. He asks Jason if an environment becomes a part of who we are after spending much of a lifetime there.

"It does. Without question," Jason asserts. "Your thoughts, and awareness, even your body, grow in tune with the *pulse* of a place."

"I can see that," Raymond says. As he does, an image fills the screen. Maris recognizes it—the wall of Jason's completed cottages, each massive photograph framed and illuminated in his barn studio. "All of your renovations seem imbued with a breath of salt air," the host goes on. "Looking at them, I sense the sea."

"Appreciate that, Ray. That's always my intent."

"Now how about your wife. Maris?"

Jason nods.

"Is she a part of Barlow Architecture?" As Raymond asks, the same boardwalk photo of Maris and Jason briefly fills the screen again. "Does she have a hand in the business, too? A partner, maybe?"

"No. Not in the business." Jason sits back and takes a long breath. "Maris was a denim designer for many years, bringing a casual beach vibe to her fashion lines. So she's as tuned in to the coast, the sea, as I am." He draws his knuckles along the raised scar on his jawline. "But she *is* a partner, in a different sense. Maris is the love of my life, and I couldn't pull off what I do without her. Her support, and insights ..." Another pause comes then, one that Raymond does not fill. It's a visibly uncomfortable moment as Jason is suddenly at a loss for words. He sits forward in his chair and leans on the armrests. His gaze is downward as he clears his throat again. "My wife's pretty amazing," he finally says with the briefest smile. "I'm fortunate to share my life with her, beside the sea."

Maris feels it all along, a burning in her eyes as she fights stinging tears. Because Jason's navigating this interview, yes. But *she* sees what's in the long pauses ... in his shadows. Much of it stems from their dinner yesterday, when she gave him nothing. Not even some hope. She blinks back those damn tears when Jason can't even sustain that one brief smile. Can't *hold* that second of happiness. He tries. Oh, that shows on his face, that effort in the pained moment of silence before he continues talking. Shows for all the viewers to see. It gets Maris to abruptly set down her coffee cup—nearly spilling it on the window seat.

"What's wrong?" Eva asks.

"I have to go." Maris quickly stands and grabs her tote.

"But ..." Eva glances to the TV screen, where Jason's recovered his composure. He's segueing his talk to a safe thought—to the way cottage style evokes everything his clients want in their lives: sandy beaches, gentle Long Island Sound waves, swaying dune grasses, evenings on old boardwalks. They want to see all that in the *structure* of their beach homes.

Maris doesn't wait to hear more. To see more of the pauses that will surely come, the looks that say more than Jason's words. Not here, she can't. Not under her sister's watch. She rushes out of the kitchen, through Eva's living room, toward the front door.

"Maris!" Eva calls out from behind her.

Maris stops on the front porch. Oh, she knows. She was no help to Jason at dinner last night, in their favorite Italian restaurant. It's obvious why he's fatigued on TV. Why he's clearing his throat, folding his arms. Hesitating. She gave him *nothing* to help him through this. Not a practice run, asking him likely interview questions in their booth at Bella's. Not a good-luck hug. Bad enough his life was under scrutiny yesterday at brunch. There, he at least knew everyone.

Today? Today the whole East Coast is watching.

The whole East Coast is seeing that, yes, Jason Barlow is lost.

"I have to go," Maris says to Eva, right before hurrying out the door.

⁓

With the proliferation of raccoons here this summer, Cliff types at his computer, *it is important that we make our homes and yards less favorable to them. Please note and adhere to the following Raccoon Control Guidelines.* After centering a raccoon graphic on the newsletter article, Cliff continues typing.

REMOVE ALL FOOD SOURCES:
-Bowls of pet food and water at night
-Overloaded bird feeders

Well, he has neither pets nor bird feeders. So he wonders if the scratching noise he's been hearing beneath the Stony Point Beach Association trailer can even be a raccoon. He walks over to one of the trailer's sliding windows and takes a look outside. Nothing. No sign of any animal at all.

But what there *is* a sign of is mail. Someone flipped up the red flag on his mailbox. Checking his watch, Cliff first returns to his desktop computer and pulls up the live-streamed episode of *Today's New Englander*. The host, Raymond Nyes, is just introducing Jason, so Cliff puts up the volume to better hear it as he heads outside to grab whatever's in his mailbox. The day is warm, the sun bright as he hurries down the trailer's metal steps. Finally opening the mailbox's creaking lid, he finds some netting tied up with a piece of twine.

"What the heck …"

But he doesn't have to say more. Because in that one second, he recognizes what the netting is wrapped around. Will wonders never cease! It's his lost lucky domino. He unties the twine and removes the talisman, giving it an instant flip before reading the note there, too.

I really needed the luck, Commissioner. Sorry if you lost any.
—Shane

"What?" Cliff looks down the street, as if he might see Shane driving off. As if Shane just *now* delivered his lucky domino this Monday morning. Which is impossible, because Shane left Stony Point on Saturday. "Son of a gun," Cliff says, rereading the note. "Shane Bradford *stole* my domino! Right from under my nose." After another glance to the street, he folds the note back in the netting and hurries inside for Jason's interview.

On his way up the trailer stairs, though, a motion catches Cliff's eye. "*Shoo!* Go home now," he tells some neighbor's white cat as it scoots out from beneath those steps. The cat must be searching for whatever animal's been making its home under there, too.

But hearing Jason's voice carry outside from the interview, Cliff doesn't hang around to see the cat off. Instead, he goes inside, swings the trailer door shut and sits at his tanker desk. For a better look, he adjusts the livestream to full-screen on his desktop computer. The interview's well underway, with Jason sitting at a square wood table in a paneled room. The first thing Cliff thinks is that he looks tired. His arms are folded across his chest as he leans back in his chair.

"Talk to us a little bit," the host is telling Jason, "about the renovation in the pilot episode of *Castaway Cottage*."

"Good luck, Jason," Cliff says, giving his newly returned domino a flip before setting it on the desk.

"That would be the Ocean Star Inn—a project very personal to me," Jason begins. As he does, before-and-after images of Elsa's inn flash on the screen. The structural differences, seen in this way, are striking. "Elsa DeLuca, who purchased the cottage in a run-down state two years ago, is a relative of my wife. But my own history with the old place influenced the redesign as well."

When the trailer door suddenly inches open, Cliff looks over just as that same white cat bumps its head into it and runs inside. "You again?" Cliff asks, realizing that finicky door didn't close tightly before. And now this!

"Hey!" he calls over, rolling back in his chair to keep an eye on the sneaky feline darting across the room. "Out!" Cliff gets up and follows the cat to the filing cabinet in the corner. "Out you go, my friend."

But he can't reach the cat, which has slunk behind the cabinet. "Come on, kitty," Cliff quietly says, leaning closer. "Here, kitty, kitty." When he reaches a hand down to where the cat's hiding, a white paw shoots out from behind the filing cabinet, then quickly retreats. The whole time, Jason's interview is blaring from the computer. The TV host, Raymond, is digging deeper in his talk. He asks why a back room at the Ocean Star Inn was left unchanged in the reno.

Cliff looks from the hidden cat to the computer atop his tanker desk. Problem is, he can't get back to that interview until he keeps this rascally feline occupied. So he opens the accordion-style door to his apartment concealed behind it. There he finds a small can of tuna and forks it into a bowl. After setting the food down near the filing cabinet, Cliff fully closes that pleated door blocking off his living quarters. This way, he can watch the interview without having to keep an eye on that wandering cat.

First though, he opens the outside trailer door all the way so that darn cat can eat, then scoot back out to wherever it came from. And by the time Cliff sits at his desk again, the

TV host is asking Jason how he started his business: "You teamed up with your brother. Neil Barlow?"

"I did. Neil was on board from the get-go. Every potential cottage reno was a coup to him. Even if it was just a little job, doing over a porch," Jason says, an easy smile coming to his face. "I'd have to rein him in sometimes. Tell my brother, you know, maybe *another* firm might win the bid. But Neil wouldn't have it, which I kind of dig. That attitude alone kept clients at our table. That confidence." Jason stops then, takes a long breath and draws his hand along his jaw. Some thought of Neil shut him down a notch. "There was no better partner," he says now, his voice low.

And that's it. The slightest shrug, a quick looking past the host then back at him.

Cliff watches as some change drops over Jason. His awkward silence gets Cliff to lean closer to the computer screen, all while shaking his head.

⁓

Kyle's got only one TV in the diner, mounted behind the counter. He doesn't turn it on much. Usually only bad weather or breaking-news headlines will get him to switch it on for his customers. Or a tight sports game will do it.

Monday morning, Jason's live interview on *Today's New Englander* is the biggest news to hit these parts in some time. So the TV's on, every stool at the counter is occupied, and several folks at the tables have turned their chairs to watch.

Kyle and Lauren stand behind the counter and watch, too.

"That your friend?" a woman calls out from a table.

Kyle looks at Jason on-screen. Other customers join in, shouting questions across the diner.

"Yeah, isn't that the guy who sits here Monday mornings? Has a cruller?"

"That's the one," Kyle says.

"What's his name? I recognize him."

"Jason," Kyle answers. "Jason Barlow." But shit, he's seen Jason look more recognizable than he's looking today, that's for sure. His face is drawn. Shadowed.

"So how were you two as business partners?" the show's host, Raymond, asks Jason now. "You and your brother."

"Well, I'm the architect. Draw up the plans, the designs to suit the property owners' wishes *and* zoning technicalities. And Neil? He was the carpenter and historian. He's the guy who valued the structural and personal *history* behind these old places. My brother built our vision, nail by nail. You know, back in the day, a true beach cottage had barely a foundation, no insulation. And as a way to avoid any cottage teardowns, Neil would convince the owners to lift the structure, build that necessary foundation, insulate the walls, match the shingles. He wanted the renovated places to retain their historical character."

"So fill in the timeline for us. Ten years ago," the host says then, "you were both in your twenties. And your business was on the cusp of taking off."

"It was."

72

"When things changed."

On the TV screen, Jason takes a long breath. "I'm not sure if *changed* is the right word." Another uncomfortable pause comes as he shifts in his chair. "Ended might better suit the situation."

"Ended?"

Silence, then, "Yeah."

"How so?"

"Ten years ago, I lost my brother. He died in a motorcycle accident."

"The same one in which you lost your leg?"

Jason only nods. Nods and obviously fights some emotion as he looks briefly away with another deep breath.

"That's a strong take on things. On the state of your business. That it *ended*," Raymond presses. "Because Barlow Architecture is still intact, no?"

Again, Jason nods.

And still Kyle watches.

"It *is* intact," Jason's saying. "But the business as it was *then*? It ended. That accident shut the door on Barlow Architecture for a long time. I had to focus on recovery— learning to walk with a prosthesis, managing my pain and outlook. Sometimes just making it through one day was a challenge." Another pause, this time with Jason clenching his jaw, or biting down on his lip to hold back. "I rebuilt it since then. My life *and* the business. But not before closing shop and working with a big firm in Hartford." He leans a forearm on the table, looks to the floor, then at the show's host. "Driving home one afternoon, I realized something.

Doing that kind of corporate work in the city … designing businesses, and office buildings? Neil wasn't a part of my daily *thoughts* anymore. And it felt like I was losing my brother all over again. Until I went back."

"Back?"

Jason nods. "Back to my humble beginnings. Took on a random side job renovating a cottage porch. And there was Neil. In the design. This was our gig, man. And that little porch reno brought him back, in a way. So one cottage at a time, I rebuilt Barlow Architecture. For myself, *and* him. From the bottom up."

"That's really commendable." Raymond tips his head with a caring smile. "Do you ever wonder what Neil would think now, seeing how far you've taken the business? Taken your architecture in all the coastal homes you've designed since?"

"Yep." Then, silence as Jason tears up and swallows some lump in his throat.

"Wow, look at that," a man at Kyle's diner counter interrupts. "Your friend's upset. They should just cut to commercial or something."

Kyle hasn't *stopped* looking. Live TV is doing Jason in. His face is ashen and struggling to maintain composure.

"I mean, we're talking coveted awards," the host goes on. "*And* you've secured a cottage-reno TV show. That's big stuff."

"It is." A moment passes. Jason crosses his arms and gives Raymond a tight smile, obviously because he can't get out any words. Raymond nods and kindly smiles back—

seemingly giving Jason the space to get himself together.

"Neil …" Raymond finally nudges him. "Think he'd be proud of how far you've taken this brother venture?"

Jason nods, then briefly closes his eyes and draws his hand over his mouth, his jaw. "I owe him this much," he manages, his voice hoarse now.

Raymond leans his elbows on the wood table. He looks Jason straight on. "What do you mean, *owe* him?"

"Go to break, for Christ's sake," Kyle suddenly yells out. "Ask a different question!"

Instead the camera comes in closer to Jason.

"*Why* do I owe him?" Jason asks.

"Right. It's an interesting choice of words," Raymond notes. "That you *owe* him."

Jason skirts the question. His voice cracks. He says something about Neil being *all in*, no matter what he did. Jason draws his hand along his face again. Looks down at the table, nodding, buying a desperate second or two—as if he's trapped.

But here's the thing. The answer that's trapped him *is* visible on his face. No words necessary. Oh, the camera catches it all.

Jason *owes* his brother because *he* lived—and Neil didn't.

"It's not right," Kyle says quietly to Lauren in the now-silent diner. "Just not right."

~

In Elsa's kitchen, Aria coos in her bouncy seat atop the marble island. Soft felt animals spin in a mobile hanging above her. Celia hears the baby, but doesn't look over. The windows are open in the kitchen, too. Warm sea air drifts in. Elsa's mentioned in the past that she believes her herb pots thrive in the garden window because of that salty air. Her little plants seem to drink it up.

So the room is peaceful. There's the rhythmic buzz of cicadas outside. And birdsong comes in: a robin twittering; a raucous seagull cawing. Celia sits on a stool beside Elsa, but neither looks to the open windows.

For the past half hour, their conversation has stopped. They've looked only at the TV screen as Jason spirals in this live interview. It's *his* voice that overtakes Elsa's kitchen.

His voice that's gone hoarse.

His voice that his throat has closed up on.

His voice that says in tone alone everything he's been feeling this pivotal summer.

Celia's heart drops for him.

Beside her, Elsa takes a biscotti from a plate and holds it uneaten in her hand.

Celia lifts her coffee cup, but slowly sets it back down without sipping any. She does something, though. She swipes away a tear, and slightly shakes her head.

~

Jason knows.

Oh, does he know.

He bombed that interview. He tried—Lord knows he tried—to salvage some of it. He deflected certain personal questions. Steered the talk to the latest *Castaway Cottage* project: the Fenwick cottage. Mentioned the secrets in its walls, and how that last-standing cottage on the beach survived every hurricane that's barreled up the coast. He even spoke of Carol's grandfather going missing at sea back in the sixties, and how the Fenwicks hope to honor him in a redesign.

But once the damage was done, once Jason struggled to keep an emotional grip, the sound bites were had. He can just imagine them. *Sand, Sea and Sadness.* Or, *Castaway Cottage Host Loses It On Air.*

Finally, it was over. He shook hands with Raymond Nyes and made his exit.

Leaving the dark interior of the historic inn now, Jason squints into the bright summer sunshine. It's hot out, and few cars are in the parking lot this early in the day. On his way to his SUV, he turns on his cell phone. And it starts.

Text messages from Eva.

One from his sister, Paige.

The phone rings, too, then goes to voicemail. It's Kyle.

His producer, Trent, calls.

Trent texts.

Texts again.

Matt texts with a go-for-a-brew invite, obviously trying to calm Jason.

There's a missed phone call from Mitch.

A phone call from Cliff.

It just doesn't stop.

Jason crosses the parking lot, gets in his SUV and looks

at his phone once more before tossing it on the passenger seat.

The *only* call he'll pick up is the call that's sure as hell not coming.

The call from Maris.

nine

Monday Noontime

MARIS NEVER HAD TO PRAY for Jason Barlow before. He's always been a rock for everyone. Until now.

In St. Bernard's Church, she stands at the bank of flickering candles. Only a handful of them are burning, seven or eight. Most of the white votives are unlit. The candle stand could almost be a gauge, she figures, to the priests here. A way to tell if the parishioners are doing okay. If few candles are flickering, not too many people are praying for help, or praying to ease some troubles. So judging from the candles now, these late-August days are sweet for many.

Maris drops a few dollars in the offering box before reaching for a taper. The first time she'd ever lit a candle for someone was only two months ago, at Aria's christening. That day, Jason explained, *You light the flame with thoughts of someone, here or gone. When you light the candle, it shows*

79

your intention to say a prayer for that person. When Maris then held her burning taper to a wick, she'd prayed for her mother beside the candle's flickering light.

Here she is again, lowering a burning taper to a candlewick—three rows up, on the left side. Today, she thinks only of Jason.

After momentarily bowing her head, she leaves the candle stand and sits in a nearby pew. Unlike at yesterday's Memorial Mass, the church is vast and empty. The stained-glass windows are tilted open to the summer day. The wood pews are cool to the touch. The space, calm.

This is the church where she and Jason had their wedding two years ago. She'd committed herself to him and their marriage, right here. In her personal vows, she spoke of words Neil had penned in an old leather journal. He'd written about the waves of the sea ... and how they're always there. *Always.* Maris then vowed to be by Jason's side, always.

And now? Now her marriage is crumbling. When Jason needed her yesterday—when he *admitted* he was lost—she could've done more for him. She could've taken his hand across the table at Bella's. Could have driven with him to Ted's cottage, helped him pack and convinced him to come home.

He would've agreed to; she just knows it now. He was almost *looking* for that when they sat in a dark booth—the lighting dim; the wall beside them, deep gold; Jason's words, quiet.

But Maris didn't do it.

Didn't let him in.

Didn't bring him home.

Instead, she left him there to find his own way back. To dig himself out.

Maybe she was right to do so, maybe not. Some questions have more than one answer, depending. But after leaving Eva's earlier this morning and going home to watch Jason's interview alone, the problem is this: Maris feels as lost as Jason. So she kneels in the pew and bows her head. Any words she whispers seem pointless.

But they're all she has. Words, hope, some faith that she'll find *her* way, too—back to Jason, back home, back to Neil's unfinished manuscript, back to who she wants to be. Because Maris has never felt this unmoored.

There's no better proof of that, too, than when she walks out to the church parking lot. Instead of leaving, she can't get any further than her car—upon which she leans. In the bright sunshine, her world is spinning; traffic is passing. There were no answers here, at church. No prayers to guide her. No thoughts to lead her.

Now she doesn't know which way to turn.

But there's someone who *would* know. Someone on the outside, looking in. Standing at her car in the afternoon sunlight, Maris realizes her only hope comes from this unlikely person—who just might have an answer for her.

So she lifts her cell phone from her purse and pulls up the number. When her call goes to voicemail, she leaves a brief message. Her quiet words feel like her *own* prayer, really.

"It's Maris," she says. Cars drive by on the street behind her. The church casts a shadow on the parking lot. "I really need to talk with you. I'll be home later tonight, if you could call me then. Please."

ten

Early Monday Evening

THIS IS WHAT ELSA FEELS like today: a spinning top.

It's as if someone unwound the string on her life this morning when that certified letter was hand-delivered to her door, and she hasn't stopped spinning since. From reading and rereading the surprising papers in that envelope, to watching Jason's emotional interview, to having lunch with Celia and Aria, to an afternoon of busyness at the inn—including making difficult phone calls and *attempting* to reach Maris—Elsa's pivoted, twisted and twirled from one thing to another.

And now, this.

A reminder dinging on her cell phone for this evening's meeting she nearly forgot—a business meeting with Mitch Fenwick and his daughter, Carol.

The problem is Elsa's outfit. It's just too casual. She'd spent the afternoon wearing a white tank top over a pair of paint-spattered cropped jeans. With no time to spare, she hurries to her bedroom for an easy fix. A matching white crochet sweater dropped on over her white tank top will do it. The loosely stitched sweater is light and airy, perfect for an hour or two on a seaside deck. And a pair of jeweled flip-flops dresses up her outfit, just enough.

Lastly, Elsa grabs a sandy-gold scarf and loops it around her neck while hurrying down the hallway to the kitchen side door. She steps outside, and just like that spinning top, dashes across the lawn toward the inn's secret beach path.

~

In the fading sunlight, the dune grasses seem to whisper summer secrets as Elsa winds her way through the path. Once on the beach, she slips off those leather-and-jeweled flip-flops and walks barefoot in the sand. Oh, and doesn't that do the trick. After a few steps in the soft, still-warm sand, she finally stops.

"*Breathe, Elsa*," she whispers, then inhales that sweet salt air. As she does, her eyes drop closed, her muscles unknot and she begins to relax. Standing there, she feels a change this late-August night. The days are shorter, evenings cooler. Though only slightly today.

At last, Elsa walks along the beach toward the imposing Fenwick cottage. The setting sun casts waning light, and lazy waves lap at shore. As she strolls the sand with her sandals looped through her fingers, Elsa takes in the sight of the horizon. It's like an artist swept red, pink and lavender paint along the edge of the sea.

"Ahoy there!" a man's voice suddenly calls out.

Elsa turns to the last-standing cottage on the beach. Someone's up on the deck. It's Mitch Fenwick, leaning his arms on the railing and looking down at her. He wears a short-sleeve button-down over tan chinos rolled at the hem. A well-worn safari hat is on his head.

"Oh, Mitch," she says, veering his way as she loosens her scarf. "Hello!"

Mitch walks to the top of the deck stairs and waits for her there. "Glad you could make it tonight."

Elsa stops to put on her sandals at the bottom of those stairs. "What a spot you've got here," she says while joining him on the elevated deck. Because if Elsa thought the evening horizon was beautiful on the beach, from this higher vantage point? It's like she's standing on the deck of a ship and facing the entire deep blue sea. "The view is gorgeous."

"That it is," Mitch says beside her.

The thing is, when Elsa glances over at him, he's looking right at *her*. Looking at her and tipping that safari hat of his. But only for a moment. Only until they walk the wraparound deck and see it all: that muted horizon, and the pink-tinged sand of sunset, and the rocky ledge at the end of the beach where the guys like to fish.

"These must be the beach binoculars I've heard Jason mention." Elsa stops at the black pedestal base and leans close to the swivel top.

"Here, give them a whirl." As he says it, Mitch drops a quarter into the unit.

"Don't mind if I do." Elsa looks through the eyepiece. Slowly she turns the silver binocular top to scan the length of the beach, then aims the viewfinder far out over Long Island Sound. Gazing through the lens, you'd think the earth simply drops off at that lavender horizon. "Jason just knew, didn't he?" she asks while stepping back from the binoculars.

"Knew what?" Mitch nudges up his safari hat and takes a look through the binoculars himself.

"How perfect those would be here."

"I guess his brother helped him decide."

"Neil?"

Mitch straightens and nods his head. "Jason found a photograph in one of his brother's scrapbooks. Apparently Neil took a picture of someone beside beach binoculars years ago … at some *mystery* beach. So," Mitch says, patting *his* binoculars, "that's where the idea for these came from. Neil Barlow, actually."

"I'm not surprised," Elsa quietly says. "Jason always finds connections to Neil in his work."

Mitch motions to the cottage then. "Well, shall we begin, Elsa? I'll give you the grand tour of the old place, pre-reno."

With that, Mitch opens the slider and they step inside. He steers her first to an enclosed porch, where Elsa draws her hand along the dried-out wood of the windowsills. The furniture in the room is as sparse as the weathered window frames. She walks around graying lobster-trap end tables and faded wicker chairs until Mitch beckons her to a far wall.

"Check this out," he says.

Elsa walks closer to a framed picture hanging on the wall. The image is of a towering wave rising over Stony Point Beach. Several cottages on the sand, including Mitch's, are in that monster wave's direct path. It's a violent picture, actually, of a churning sea meeting terra firma, head-on.

"Hurricane Carol," Mitch says from behind Elsa. "Took down all the cottages left on the beach except for the very one you're standing in."

"Dad!" Mitch's daughter says from the porch doorway. "You tell everybody that story!"

Elsa turns to Carol. She's standing there wearing a black tie-front sleeveless blouse over cutoff denim shorts. When she walks closer with a heavy step, Elsa notices the black lace-up leather ankle boots on her feet.

"Nice to see you, Elsa," Carol says, shaking Elsa's hand.

"Carol? Like the hurricane?" Elsa looks from Carol to that photograph.

"You got it." Mitch nods at the framed photo. "My wife and I named Carol after that particular storm. We hoped our daughter would be strong, and willful too."

"Dad, that's enough." Carol motions to Elsa. "Come on. I'll give you the rest of the tour."

And she does. Carol and Mitch both do. They walk from room to room in the rambling beach home. The windows are open, and a vague briny sense of the sea pervades the cottage. In golden lamplight, Elsa glimpses a white living room anchored with a large fireplace and rough-hewn mantel. The sofas and chairs are coastal chic, upholstered in faded blues, whites and greens.

"I see you like the classics," Elsa notes when she stops at built-in shelves filled with beautiful old hardcover books. *"Gone with the Wind. Walden."*

"Those are Dad's," Carol explains. "He collects illustrated editions."

"I use them for my work too, Elsa. I'm an English professor over at the university," Mitch tells her.

"Really, now! I didn't know that."

Mitch nods. "I just asked Jason if he could add a suitable office somewhere in the cottage. A spot to grade papers, do some research and writing, right beside the sea."

All of it—the rooms, the snippets of talk—it intrigues Elsa. There's something about this last-standing cottage on the beach, some sense of its survival, which commands one's attention.

They continue on, with Elsa remarking that she hopes not *too* much demolition will happen. Mitch and Carol assure her that demo work will actually be minimal. Strategic areas will be altered, and other areas only updated. They walk through the kitchen next. Its wide-planked floor is painted gray. Shabby white cabinets and dark butcher-block countertops frame the space. In the adjoining dining room, a dimly lit white chandelier hangs over a white-painted table.

But it's what's *on* that table that gets Elsa to veer closer. There's a large scrapbook open to old photographs. "Your family?" she asks without taking her eyes off the images.

"Yes. We're selecting pictures to display on the rowboat Jason's having restored for us," Carol explains. "It's being turned into a shelf unit."

"Would that be the boat your grandfather went out in, searching for little Sailor?" Elsa asks.

"It is! And it means the world to us that we have it back," Carol says as she thumbs through faded photographs on the table.

Elsa glances at the photos, too. But what really grabs her in this sprawling cottage are the endless windows. They're everywhere. Every wall seems to be wrapped in them. She hasn't seen such an expansive view of the sea since being at Bagni Sillo on Italy's Ligurian coast. The view tonight leaves her sadly nostalgic.

Mitch must notice how she's drawn to the sweeping sight of Long Island Sound. "Let's get back outdoors and catch that amazing sunset," he says, leading Elsa through a kitchen slider.

Outside, tall rope-wrapped glass jars hold flickering candles on the deck's patio table. Tin-can wildflower bouquets are scattered atop the deck railings and table, too.

"Your cottage is lovely *now*," Elsa declares as she pulls out a seat there. "When Jason is through with it, it'll be a showstopper."

"Oh, Jason." Carol slowly sinks into a chair beside Elsa's. "Did you see him on TV today?"

Elsa only nods.

"He okay, Elsa?" Mitch asks as he sits across from her at the table.

She takes a quick breath. "It's a long story, and the most

89

I can say is that he's really had a hard summer."

"He seems to be running on fumes lately." Mitch sits back, leaning on one of the chair's armrests. "Hate to see him like that."

"I hope he's all right," Carol says then as she moves aside a tin can of flowers. "The cameras will be rolling soon."

"Yes, they will." Elsa takes that as her cue. Really, she's not comfortable talking about Jason like this. It feels too personal. So she pivots. "And *Castaway Cottage* production is about to resume, no? Which is why I'm here." She sits up straight, crosses her arms on the patio table in front of her and looks to both of them. "So I'd like to get started giving you some on-camera pointers!"

"Perfect. Except I hope you don't mind, Elsa," Carols says while suddenly standing.

"Mind?"

"That I have to leave, just for a few minutes. But go ahead and start, because my dad needs the advice more than I do. He's *really* camera-shy."

Elsa turns to Mitch. "Seriously?"

"Oh, he is," Carol assures her. "I have to run over to Scoop Shop and pick up an ice-cream cake I ordered. It's such a warm evening, it'll be nice to have some outside tonight." She walks around the table and pats her father's shoulder. "Be back soon," Carol says before walking her booted feet across the deck to the stairs. "And Dad," she calls out. "Pay attention to Elsa's advice!"

The evening is humid. There's a pale mist in the glow of twinkle lights strung along the patio umbrella spokes. And in that evocative light, the deck goes suddenly quiet. It's the type of quiet when, the more Elsa tries to think of something to say, the more she freezes up.

So she quickly looks for something—*anything*—to talk about and motions to a few large deck pots brimming with lush plantings. "Who's the gardener?" she asks. Yes, anything, *anything* to break that unexpected silence.

"That'd be Carol," Mitch tells her. "Every plant has a purpose. She's got some lavender. And marigolds." Mitch twists around in his seat and points to a nearby ornate black pot. Clusters of spiky purple flowers grow from green, featherlike foliage. "And that one there is catnip."

"Catnip? You have a cat inside?"

"No. No pets. All of those plants—the lavender, marigolds *and* catnip—actually keep away mosquitoes. It's Carol's natural method of pest control."

"That's a great idea. I'll have to try that myself. And these," Elsa says, reaching for a tin-can vase of wildflowers on the table. "Carol's, too?"

Mitch nods, but says nothing more. He just leans back in his patio chair, lifts a sandaled foot to his knee and crosses his arms over his chest.

Elsa looks from him to the canned bouquets. Each tarnished silver can holds a mix of white Shasta daisies and orange tiger lilies. There are black-eyed Susans and white phlox and purple coneflowers. The stems are bunched and loosely tied with twine, then set in old tin cans of water.

They look just like a tin-can bouquet Cliff surprised her with earlier in the summer. "Your daughter has quite the charming green thumb," Elsa says, inhaling the flowers' aroma. When she sets the can down, she slides it away. And hesitates. And gives a quick smile. "So! I understand you want advice for being on camera."

Mitch draws a hand along his goatee. "That's right. Something about being in front of that lens gets me to clam up." He sets his safari hat on the patio table then, before sitting back again.

"Okay," Elsa says, pulling in her chair. And doing something else, too. She's noticing Mitch's wavy, fading-blond hair now. And some metal pendant hanging from a rawhide choker he wears. "*Well*," Elsa begins, shaking off her observations, "I've been through the whole TV ordeal. And don't kid yourself, filming *will* be an ordeal. But very much worth it. And I'm better able to help if you first tell me a little about yourself and your daughter."

When Mitch does, Elsa's relieved—for one reason and one reason only. His talking forces her to stop her prattling. So she listens as he tells her that he's a Southern transplant, hailing from South Carolina. And that his wife, Kate, passed five years ago. And how he enjoys being a professor at the college a few towns over.

"Any other children?" Elsa asks.

Mitch nods. "My boy's out yonder in the Pacific Northwest. He's in his thirties, like my daughter. Haven't seen much of him since Kate died. So this summer at the cottage? It's just me and Carol. The flower lady," he says, pointing to one of the cans of summer blossoms.

"Carol ... who insists that you're camera-shy?" Elsa squints across the table at Mitch. "But you're a college professor. Which means you *do* frequently talk in front of people."

"I do. But it's not like being on camera." Mitch glances around, then stands. "If you'll pardon me for a sec," he says before going indoors. A moment later, he returns holding a notebook and pen. "I'm not usually the student, but I'm ready to take notes tonight." Sitting again, he clicks his pen. "Shall we start over?"

"Of course." Elsa sits back in her seat and takes in the view of the beach. Which brings to mind her first tip. "Number one. You'll often be filming outside. To eliminate squinting, try to align yourself so that you're not facing the sun. And ... and no sunglasses! Viewers want to see your eyes. They connect that way."

"Interesting," Mitch says while writing *No sunglasses*. "Got it."

Elsa looks at him across the patio table. Like herself, he seems to be in his mid-to-late fifties. And she notices how he's comfortable in his own skin, with a unique style all his own—like that leather choker he wears. It shows beneath the open collar of his button-down canvas shirt. "A very important second tip? Wear your natural clothes," Elsa says as she considers his. "They'll reflect the *real* you."

Mitch sits back in his seat, notebook in lap, and jots a few words.

"*And* you'll be most comfortable," Elsa tells him.

"Wardrobe—natural." He looks over at her. "Good."

"As for number three? Drink plenty of water to stay hydrated. You won't get a frog in your throat that way. And if you do, I can tell you from experience that the croakiness will *only* get worse with Jason and his producer standing on the sidelines staring at you—arms crossed, with no expression."

"Jason does that? Kind of stoic-like?"

"Oh, he turns into a real media mogul when the cameras are rolling. But," Elsa says with a shrug, "it *is* his show, after all. So be sure to hydrate!"

Mitch laughs, saying, "Water, water," as he writes the words.

"And number four is paramount. I mean it's *imperative*. You must try to *physically* relax. Anxiety really shows, for instance, in tense arms." Elsa stands and steps away from the table to demonstrate. In her white crochet topper, she first rigidly throws both arms skyward. "Some people pose trying to *look* like they're having a *great* time. *Tsk, tsk.*" Then she shoots her arms downward—fingers splayed. "You see?" she asks, moving closer to where Mitch sits. "Every stress in my life would be laughingly apparent in that body language."

"I'll say. True mark of an amateur in front of the camera?"

"Absolutely. Tense hands are always a dead giveaway. So maybe find a prop to lean on, if that helps."

"*Relax arms,*" Mitch whispers while writing.

"And, you know," Elsa says while moving closer to the

deck railing. "Talk *with* your hands sometimes. Jason taught me that one." As she says it, Elsa moves her hands freely … loosely. "Thoughts, well they just … *flow* better when your hands are … *helping*," she says, demonstrating by sweeping one arm to the side.

And abruptly inhaling a sharp breath when her hand brushes across the old dried-out deck railing—and a nasty wood sliver slips deep beneath her skin.

eleven

Monday Evening

CAN YOU CHECK AGAIN?" CLIFF asks into the phone. He's sitting at his metal tanker desk in the Stony Point Beach Association trailer. But he's not alone, that's for darn sure. Nope, a shy, four-legged tenant seems to have moved right in here. As Cliff talks to the animal control officer, that timid feline gently bats at a crumpled ball of paper before darting back behind the file cabinet.

"Sorry, Raines," the officer is saying. "All's been quiet."

"No reports of lost cats? *Nothing?*" Cliff waits as the officer clicks through a few computer screens. "Well, okay," Cliff finally tells him. "But listen, if anyone calls looking for a white cat, send them my way, would you?"

Once Cliff hangs up, all official resources have been exhausted. He grabs a pencil and crosses off the phone numbers of the animal shelter, animal control and two local veterinarians. "Nothing, nothing and nothing," he says.

Now he's left to his own devices. So he prints a few copies of a *Found* flyer he designed after grabbing a partially blurred photo of that elusive cat. Still sequestered behind the file cabinet, the feline has made its own corner office there.

"Well, you're going to need food until I find you a *real* home," Cliff calls out on the way to his kitchenette. At the counter, he scoops the last of some tuna fish into a cereal bowl. Sitting in shadow behind that cabinet, the cat watches his every move. Cliff can't miss it peeking out as he sets down the tuna.

Finally, after stuffing those freshly printed flyers into a folder and lifting his key ring off the desk, Cliff heads out. He doesn't have far to go. Just a short ride—under the train trestle and a left into Scoop Shop's parking lot. Figures he'll kill two birds with one stone there tonight—pick up his regular ice-cream order *and* buy some cat supplies.

Once inside the little convenience store, Cliff scans the aisles for pet items. There they are, two rows back. He hurries over and grabs a few cans of food, a package of dry treats and a disposable litter tray. All of it should tide over that vagabond cat for a day or two. Right as Cliff gets in line, a familiar woman in her early thirties walks in. She's got on a sleeveless blouse and denim cutoffs, not to mention scuffed leather ankle boots. When she nods to him while taking her place in line, he recognizes her. It's Carol Fenwick from the cottage on the beach.

"Oh, Commissioner!" the clerk at the register calls out. "Your order's all set," she says while heading to the freezer case.

Cliff glances back at Carol, then to the clerk. "Let this young lady go ahead of me. I've got a lot to ring out," Cliff says, raising his cat supplies.

"Well, *thank* you," Carol tells him while walking to the register. She talks to the clerk, who lifts a massive ice-cream cake out of the glass-front case and sets it on the counter.

"*What?*" Carol asks with a quick laugh. "I didn't order that! There must be some mistake."

The clerk checks her written order. "Extra large?" she confirms. "It says here you ordered extra large." She turns the paper for Carol to see.

Carol bends close, squinting at some order she must've phoned in. "No," she says, pointing to the paper. "No, no. I'd asked for extra *crunchies*, not extra *large*. The chocolate *crunchies* between layers. On a *small* ice-cream cake. This is only for three people!"

"Well, our mistake," the clerk admits while scrutinizing the scribbled phone order. "And store policy states if it's our mistake, the item is yours. *Free!*" She gives Carol a smile and nudges the supersized ice-cream cake her way.

"Free?" Carol asks.

"Free!"

So Carol hefts up the box of cake, turns and shrugs to Cliff, then shoulders open the door.

Cliff watches her go before proceeding to the register, where the clerk is retrieving his ice cream from the freezer. He sets down his cat items and pulls out his wallet.

"Here you go," the clerk says from where she's bending into the freezer case. "Cappuccino crunch with a side of hot fudge. One or two spoons today?"

"Just one."

"Oh!" The clerk sets his white bag beside the cat supplies. "You got yourself a cat, Commissioner?"

"No, not really. A stray's been hanging around. Might have to bring it to the shelter if no one claims it. But I have some *Found Cat* flyers," he says, pulling a few from his folder. "Was wondering if you might tape one in the store window?"

The clerk looks at his photograph of the cat. "Aw, cute little thing, isn't it? All white, too!" She takes a handful of the flyers. "We'll put one in the window and leave a few right here, at the register."

"Appreciate it," Cliff says while pulling his prepaid store card from his wallet and swiping it. Taking his bags then, he heads outdoors to the summer evening. Surely someone will recognize the cat on his flyer. Everyone from Stony Point stops in at Scoop Shop for ice cream, or a loaf of bread, or rolls of paper towels in the general store section.

Walking to his parked car, Cliff whistles lightly. Mission accomplished. First, his cat poster will be hung. And second? With Carol picking up her order ahead of him, his daily ice-cream run is still secret—safe from the prying eyes and eavesdropping ears of folks he knows.

⁓

On the way to his car, Cliff passes Carol in the parking lot. She's struggling to maneuver that three-foot-long cake box into her tiny golf cart with hefty all-terrain wheels. Anyone can see there's no way that box will fit.

"Aren't you Carol?" Cliff asks, coming up beside her golf cart. "Carol Fenwick?"

Carol looks up from her box-finagling. Her long bangs sweep partially over her eyes; her face is flush. "Yes, that's right."

"I helped with your grandfather's rowboat excavation," Cliff reminds her.

"Oh, yes." she straightens while balancing the tottering box on her golf cart. "Commissioner ..."

"Raines. Cliff Raines. Do you need a hand there?" He hitches his head to her oversized, jumbo cake.

"It just won't fit on the seat *or* in the side basket. I don't know *how* I'll get it to the cottage."

Cliff looks past her golf cart to his car. He motions for her to follow him. "Bring it here, we'll put it in my trunk."

"Are you sure?"

"Of course. I'm headed back and can drop it off at your place." As he says it, he pops his car's trunk and unlocks the doors. After setting his take-out ice-cream bag on the front passenger seat, he quickly helps Carol set her cake box in the trunk. Through the clear plastic box top, he sees that the white cake is dotted with chocolate sprinkles and edged in blue-raspberry swirled piping. "I'll meet you at your cottage?"

"This is *really* nice of you, Commissioner. Not sure how I ever would've gotten that cake home otherwise."

Problem is, Cliff's not sure now how his *own* ice-cream

order will last the trip. So he gets in his car, cranks the a/c and directs a front vent straight at the passenger seat, where his bagged order sits. Then, and only then, he accelerates out of the parking lot, guns it beneath the trestle and speeds along to the Fenwick cottage.

~

The beautiful summer sunset is lost to Elsa. Now all that matters is a slice of wood lodged beneath her skin. *And* the person maneuvering it out.

Using his thumb, Mitch presses the skin on Elsa's finger. He leans close at the patio table and raises a pair of tweezers with his other hand.

"*Ooh, ooh,*" Elsa nearly whispers, pulling back.

Mitch stops, then looks up at Elsa. "Don't worry. These are sanitized. I dipped them in alcohol inside." With that, again he lowers the tweezers to the embedded sliver in her finger. "I can *see* it," he says, his face close to her hand. "But I need to get the tip out, just a smidge."

Elsa nods. "Okay. But our meeting …" she manages, watching as Mitch's thumb nudges one end of the sliver. "I feel so bad, interrupting it with this mini-minor catastrophe."

"Nonsense. Time enough for all that other business later." Mitch shifts her hand and with the tweezers poised above it, presses at that pesky sliver again.

Elsa quickly inhales through pursed lips when a small sting shoots through her finger. "You know, maybe I'll just take care of it at home, Mitch. I don't want to be a bother."

"Bother?" Mitch sets down her hand. "Not at all. And I don't want an *infection* setting in, with that slab of timber beneath your skin. But the sliver's a tad too deep, and I *don't* want to hurt you." He stands and drops the tweezers in his button-down shirt pocket. "I reckon the situation needs some salt."

"What?"

"You wait there," he says with a nod, then goes inside through that scraping slider screen.

Which gives Elsa a moment to take a breath and sit back. *And* feel warm enough to whip off her silky scarf— which she tosses on another chair. While waiting for Mitch then, she tries to relax and notices the sun sinking toward the horizon. All the while, she also hears tap water running inside. Minutes later, Mitch returns with a saucer of warm water and a container of Epsom salt. He sets it all on the patio table and sits beside her again. Inches his chair a little closer, too.

"This will really help?" Elsa asks. "Salt?"

"Absolutely." Mitch mixes some salt into the saucer and gently stirs it with a spoon. "It's a tried-and-true remedy." He takes Elsa's hand then, gently, and sets her fingertips in the warm saltwater mixture.

"*Oh, what a day,*" she whispers, mostly to herself. Every incident of this particular Monday flashes through her mind in a bulleted list, starting with the news in her certified letter, followed by Jason's emotional interview. Then there were the difficult phone calls she began making *because* of that letter, and now this—injured, seaside. Her finger throbs.

But the funny thing is that the rest of her body unknots as her fingers soak. And as Mitch's voice soothes, and as the skin of her hand feels his light touch. His closeness, his ... well, his *way*. All of it—after the day she's had—all of it has the effect of a massage on every tense nerve, every tight muscle in her body. With a long breath of sea air, she goes with it. Goes with the sudden relaxation washing over her.

"You okay?" Mitch asks, an easy smile on his face, his eyes watching hers.

"That feels better already," Elsa says, lifting her fingers from the saucer.

"Uh-uh." Mitch's hand covers hers and presses it into the warm water. "Let it soak for a good ten minutes." He softly pats the back of her hand. "The sliver will swell up from the salt, and then I'll get a firm grip on that nasty lil' bugger."

"Ten minutes? Let me set my phone timer." Elsa twists around for her purse.

"Heavens, no." Leaning on his chair's armrest so that his arm brushes hers, Mitch nods to the violet sky streaked with red, far over Long Island Sound. "We'll just watch that big ol' sun sink into the sea, which should just about take up those ten minutes."

Elsa looks out at the water. The way the wispy clouds streak across the violet-smeared sky, you'd think you're being granted a secret glimpse at heaven. Gentle waves lap onshore, just below the deck. The salt air grows richer with each darkening minute. A slight breeze touches her upturned face. It's the most peaceful ten minutes she's had in a week.

"*Okay*," Mitch finally whispers while sliding a rope-wrapped candle closer. "Hate to break the reverie, but the sun's dropped low enough." He takes hold of Elsa's wrist and pats her fingers dry with a napkin. "Let's try again," he says, lifting the tweezers from his shirt pocket.

And it worked—that water-soaking.

Because this time, Elsa's fine.

This time, she doesn't resist.

Doesn't pull back or gasp.

She just listens to that ... that *voice*. And takes in the sight of Mitch up close, with that fading-blond hair, and that shadow of silver whiskers. And ... well. And feels his touch on her hand.

"Here it comes," he says, pulling back on the tweezers. But he stops suddenly. "How am I doing?" he asks, looking at her again. Their faces are inches apart with Elsa bent close to watch, and with Mitch bent close to maneuver the sliver. "Any pain?" he quietly asks in the warm summer air.

Elsa only shakes her head. Though she doubts Mitch knows it, she *can't* talk. Heck, she's not even *thinking* of that silly sliver anymore. All she's aware of is Mitch's touch on her wrist. And his low voice, dripping like sweet honey. Oh, if ever she's been lulled, it's right now—with the horizon deep red, the sea mist rising, the waves sloshing on the sand.

"Little bit at a time," Mitch says, his voice getting quieter with each word. "*Easy ... does ... it.*"

Elsa feels the gentle tug at her slivered hand. Mitch pauses and looks at her for a second—a long one, in which neither speaks—then gives the slightest nod before raising the tweezers. "Got it!" he says. "You're good as new."

⌁

There's no mistaking the late-August sun. Once it starts its descent, it goes down fast. So by the time Cliff parks behind the Fenwick cottage on Champion Road, the evening light's turned dusky. He remembers when he was a boy— little Sailor—this kind of misty illumination scared him. It got him to look twice into the beach shadows; had him turn his head at whispering dune grasses; had him hurry home to his cottage across the street here.

After opening his car's trunk now, he looks over his shoulder at the silhouette of the grand cottage-on-the-sand. That one place, more than any other, holds his biggest secret. Here, in *his* mind, Cliff will always be little lost Sailor—for whom Gordon gave up his life over fifty years ago.

"Do you need a hand?" Carol asks after parking her golf cart behind him.

"No, I'm good. I'll carry it in for you." Cliff lifts out the massive ice-cream cake box and follows her along a sandy path around the cottage. "Having a birthday party tonight?"

"Not a party." Carol glances back at him. "More of a

casual get-together. Sort of like a business meeting, I guess." She walks past the side of the cottage, with Cliff following close behind. "That lady who owns the new inn here? She's giving me and my dad pointers for our *Castaway Cottage* filming. You know," Carol goes on, "tips to loosen up in front of the cameras."

"You mean, *Elsa*? Elsa DeLuca's here?"

"Uh-huh. She's out on the deck. With my father."

"I know Elsa," Cliff says, throwing a look up at the raised deck.

"In that case, stay for a slice of cake? Lord knows it's more than we can ever finish."

"No. Thank you, anyway," Cliff says, glancing back at his idling car—which is keeping the a/c blasting on his take-out ice-cream bag. "But I've got somewhere to be," he tells her. Just then, they round the corner out of the dune grasses and onto the sand … the deck staircase rising before them.

～

"*Cliff?*" Elsa stands and walks to the top of the stairs. "Is that *you?*" she asks, squinting into the darkness as a man holding a cumbersome box climbs the steps.

"Yes. Yes, I'm giving Carol some assistance."

"Whoa!" Mitch says from right behind Elsa. "We'll be feeding the whole beach with *that* ice-cream cake."

"I know. It's *huge*, Dad." Carol steps onto the deck behind Cliff. "The shop made a mistake with my order, so it ended up being free. And when I bumped into Mr. Raines, he was nice enough to deliver the cake—which would *never* fit into my golf cart."

"I should say not!" Mitch declares just as Cliff sets the bulky box on the deck table.

"I'll grab us some napkins and plates," Carol tells them while opening the slider and going inside the cottage.

"Mitch?" Elsa's voice cracks as she asks, so she discreetly clears her throat. "Do you know Cliff?"

Leaning on the deck railing, Mitch looks over at Cliff. "I think we may have crossed paths here, why yes."

"Cliff." Elsa motions him closer. "Clifton Raines, he's the beach commissioner. And he's my, well ... um," she says, clearing her throat again. "I guess you could say ... He's my—*neighbor*. Yes, that's it," she says with a decisive nod. "My neighbor."

Mitch draws a hand down his goateed jaw while squinting through the evening shadows at Cliff. "Believe I saw you Sunday. At Jason's brunch," he says. "And wait. You were at the rowboat recovery, am I right?"

Elsa watches as Cliff first raises an eyebrow at her, then turns to Mitch. "Yes, I was there. Good to see you again," he says, shaking Mitch's hand. "Didn't get a chance to say much that day, what with the excavation and all. Glad the boat's back home."

"Safe and sound, finally. What an operation that was, getting that old beaten-down vessel out from beneath the sand and carrying it through the path from Little Beach."

"Felt like a funeral procession," Carol adds as she

107

nudges the slider closed with her booted foot. She heads to the patio table and sets out plates and spoons.

Cliff nods. That's it, just nods, Elsa sees. It's apparent he's a little uncomfortable in this moment that's somehow turned awkward again.

"Commissioner?" Carol drops a hefty slice of ice-cream cake onto a plate. "You sure you won't stay and enjoy some? It's the least I can do to thank you."

"No." Cliff looks from Elsa, back to Carol. "I won't keep you from your ... meeting. But it's been good seeing you again, Carol. Mitch." He turns and nods to Elsa. "Mrs. DeLuca."

"Cliff ... But, but ..." Elsa quietly says, taking a sudden small step before stopping just as suddenly. And looking from Carol, to Mitch, to Cliff leaving. By the time he gets down the deck stairs and turns onto the path leading behind the cottage, oh does Elsa know. There's some funny vibe in the air, leaving her feeling like she's caught in the middle of something. She glances over the deck railing just as Cliff gives a wave, rounds the corner of the cottage and heads onto the road—where his car is parked beneath a lone streetlight.

twelve

That Same Evening

LIKE THE PERSISTENT SUMMER HEAT, Jason's day never let up.

Until now.

In the guest bedroom, he's finally changing out of the button-down from his TV interview this morning. Feels like a year ago. When he pulls on an old concert tee, a text message arrives.

Will you be around tonight? I want to stop by and talk.

"Now what," Jason says. After agreeing to the visit, he goes downstairs and walks into the living room just as Maddy slinks off the sofa. Slinks off Ted Sullivan's brand-new, driftwood-gray sofa. "Hey! What are you doing on the couch?" Jason asks as the German shepherd drops her head and barely wags her tail. She knows better and *always* sleeps in her own dog bed—which Jason forgot at home when he left Stony Point over a week ago. He goes to the couch and brushes his hand across a cushion. "*Argh*, Maddy! It's covered in fur!"

But when Jason turns to figure out where the vacuum cleaner might be, he sees more. Work papers are scattered on the coffee table. His calculator and tablet are there, too. His sweatshirt is tossed over the top of a club chair. Dregs of coffee fill the bottom of a mug on an end table. A pile of his dirty laundry totters in a basket on the dining room floor.

"Company's coming. We've got to straighten up, Maddy," Jason tells the dog. First he scoops up the basket of cargo shorts and tees, carries it to a laundry room off the hallway and drops the clothes into the washer. On his way back, he checks a hall closet for a vacuum cleaner and for once, gets lucky. He hauls an old canister vac to the living room, plugs it in and hits the foot switch. The vacuum roars to life—sounding like a train blowing past and getting Maddy to rush closer. Jason maneuvers the powerbrush around the room and wonders why it is that cottages always have ancient, cumbersome vacuum cleaners. As he pulls the clunky canister behind him and gets the floor somewhat cleaned, the dog drops low on her front legs and gives a bark at the noisy machine.

"Move," Jason tells her, then lifts the roller brush to the sofa cushions and sucks up the dog fur embedded there. "Not acceptable," he scolds over his shoulder as Maddy drops her head again and slinks away. As she does, Jason's foot hits something beneath the couch. "Oh, no," he says, shutting off the vacuum and pulling out a slipper. It's an expensive canvas-moccasin type, utterly chewed to shreds. The canvas hangs in strips; teeth marks cover the thick suede sidewall; pieces of the soft interior fabric dot the floor.

"Madison!" Jason calls out. The dog is slunk down beside the club chair and won't meet his eye. "These are Ted's very good slippers! From MaineStay." He takes the slipper to the dog and lowers it to her nose, which gets her to turn her head away. "Do you know how much these cost?" he asks, giving the destroyed slipper a shake. "What am I going to do with you?"

Nothing, right now. Because by the time he puts away the vacuum, grabs his sweatshirt and dirty coffee mug from the living room and goes into the kitchen, he has only minutes to finish cleaning up. Minutes to load the dirty plates and cups from the sink into the dishwasher and wipe off the gray-swirled marble island top. In his rush, he nearly topples the burlap-wrapped happiness jar Maris made for Neil yesterday. He catches the jar before it falls, though, straightens the seagull feather tucked in that burlap and returns the jar—intact—to the counter. Back at the kitchen sink then, he splashes a few handfuls of water on his face and neck, grabs some paper towels and dries off.

Which is precisely when he hears someone say his name.

～

Celia can't help it, the way she deeply inhales the salt air that is somehow more pungent here at Sea Spray Beach. Stronger.

Wilder, even. It reminds her of the air in Maine yesterday. She still can't believe she did that. Drove all that way to see Shane for a chance at—*what?* She shakes off the thought.

Now, after parking in Ted Sullivan's driveway and lifting Aria from the car seat, she carries her up the deck stairs. Flickering lanterns are scattered on a wide railing and small tables. There's a large teak deck table, too, with twinkly lights strung from the umbrella spokes. A massive white conch shell sits on the table beside a pad and some papers. Celia steps on the deck, walks past a grilling station and pauses at the open slider. Recessed lighting illuminates the kitchen inside; a round white table sits in a windowed nook; a planked, hardwood *ceiling* is edged with cream-colored cabinets. Jason stands at a stainless-steel farm sink, his back to her as he cups his hands beneath the running tap and rinses his face. She watches him through the slider screen for a few seconds before speaking.

"Jason."

At the sound of her voice, Jason turns to her. He's holding several paper towels; his skin is damp at the hairline. "Hey, Celia," he says while dabbing at his whiskered face before shutting off the faucet. "You made it." When he tosses out the paper towels, his dog rushes over to the slider. Jason takes her by the collar, opens the screen and joins Celia outside on the deck.

"It was a quick ride," Celia says. She steps back and shifts Aria in her arms. "Not much traffic tonight." When Jason gives her a light hug, she quietly tells him, "Thanks for having me."

"No problem." He turns to his goddaughter then and pats her tiny hand. "Hi there, Aria," he says. "You're up late, no?"

"She slept in the car on the way here. Didn't you, sweetie?" Celia brushes Aria's face as the dog hovers around them. Her tail's wagging, ears alert, as she prances on the deck.

"Do you need help carrying anything up?" Jason asks. "Baby gear?"

"Yes, actually." Celia gives him a warm smile, steps closer and gently places Aria in his arms. "Would you hold her while I get us the pizza from the car?"

"Pizza?"

"Just a snack I picked up on the way."

After Jason sits somewhat awkwardly at the teak deck table, and the dog inches beside him to sniff at the baby in his lap, Celia leaves her tote on the table and heads down the deck stairs. She grabs the pizza box and a sweater from the front passenger seat, and a portable bouncy chair from the trunk. By the time she's maneuvered it all back on the deck, Jason is having a deep, one-sided conversation. The baby is mesmerized as he explains how he renovated this cottage. Jason's voice is low and serious; the baby's eyes watch his face. Beside them, the dog sits with her head tipped, also watching this man-with-baby exchange.

"You have a rapt audience," Celia says while setting the pizza on the table.

"I'm not sure anyone's ever been as interested in my work."

While Celia puts her lacy cardigan on over her tank top,

Maddy circles around the table. "Hey there, girl." Celia pats the dog's head just as Aria squeals at the sight of the German shepherd. "You keeping Aria entertained, too?"

"Maddy's *very* curious about this new little visitor," Jason says while turning Aria to better see the dog. "This person stealing all my attention now."

After arranging the bouncy seat on the table, Celia reaches over and takes Aria from Jason. "Babies have a way of doing that," she softly says, kissing her daughter before settling her in the baby chair.

"You okay with sitting outside?" Jason asks. "It's not too damp for Aria?"

"No. This is nice. The salt air will do her good."

"Okay, then," Jason tells Celia before heading inside with Maddy. "I'll get us some plates. Be right back."

While they're in the kitchen, Celia walks to the edge of this large deck and looks across the street to the beach. Sweeping dune grasses feather the view. In the evening light, she sees that the beach reaches along a straightaway length of the coast. Unlike Stony Point, there are no curves in this coastline, no patch of woods at the end to protect it from the open Sound. This beach is more ragged; the waves, stronger. Celia closes her eyes and feels a breeze touch her skin, but turns when Jason comes back out carrying a few dishes topped with napkins and flatware.

"I was surprised to get your text," he says while putting down the dishes before settling Maddy off to the side with a few dog biscuits. "And that you wanted to meet. Did you find the place okay?"

"I did." Celia walks over and sits on a cushioned chair at the patio table. "Your directions were good."

"So you've never been to Sea Spray before?"

"No. And you'd think, oh, another Connecticut beach. They're all the same, right?" As she says it, Celia hears those distant breaking waves. "Which couldn't be more wrong."

Jason sits across from her and passes her a dish and napkin. "My brother used to say beaches are like snowflakes. No two are alike," he tells Celia while then gathering up some work papers on the table. "I was going to do rough sketches out here for the Fenwick project. An added-on design request came in."

"Your clients can do that? Even once you've finalized plans?"

"In this line of work? Nothing's ever final. Mitch emailed me that he wouldn't mind an office in that big old cottage now. So let me get these papers inside, out of the way."

While Jason's in the kitchen, Celia sets a slice of pizza on her dish. The dog is at her side again, ears straight, trying to have a look at Aria. "*You can say hello later,*" Celia whispers to Maddy. "*After we eat.*"

When the slider screen opens, Jason returns with glasses and a carton of orange juice. "My food options are a little sparse. Haven't been to the store much."

Celia bites into her pizza slice. "I get it," she says around the food. "Being alone and doing it all?"

Jason nods, then reaches for a piece of pizza. "What've we got here?" he asks, setting the slice on his plate. "Breaded chicken topping?"

"And zucchini."

"Ha. You're like Elsa. Pizza's okay as long as it's with a salad, or loaded up with veggies?"

"Pretty much." Celia pours two glasses of orange juice. "And I figured that living out here by yourself, you might need some vegetables."

"You'd be right," Jason agrees, lifting the pizza slice. "So, like I said. Your text caught me off guard." He takes a bite of the cheesy pizza. "Everything okay?"

"With *me*?"

"With you and the baby."

"We're fine, really." Celia sips her juice.

"Is it someone else, then? Maris?"

"No, Jason. No." She gives him a small smile. "It's *you* that I'm actually worried about."

"Me?"

Celia fusses with a ruffle on Aria's plaid romper, then pulls a string of beads from her tote. She gives the teething beads to Aria to hold. All of it buys a few seconds to get her thoughts together. Finally, she turns to Jason again. "*Everyone* is worried about you."

"Everyone?"

Celia only nods. But she does something else, too. She sees that the day's beaten Jason down. It shows. He hasn't shaved. His hair is wavy with the sea damp here on the deck. His clothes—the same dark pants he wore on TV and some concert tee he's since changed into—are wrinkled from whatever the hours entailed after that live interview. An interview that apparently took its toll on him.

Jason says nothing as he sits back, pizza slice in hand.

"The whole gang saw you on TV today," Celia tells him. "I did, too. And ... oh, Jason."

"Eh. It was just a bad interview."

"I wouldn't call it *bad*. Emotional? Maybe. A little raw?"

"Fair enough. God knows I could've done better. But some of those questions ... Man, they came at just the right time, you know? It's been a tough couple of weeks."

"No kidding."

Jason sets down his pizza slice, turns up his hands. "But ... it is what it is." Again he picks up the pizza slice and takes another bite. "So if you're here to check up on me for anyone—Elsa, Maris—you can tell them I'm okay."

"I'm not here for anyone else. As a matter of fact, no one even *knows* that I'm here. So it's our secret."

"Seriously?"

"Seriously. I'm just here as your friend." Celia gives him another slight smile. She picks at her pizza, too, having a small bite, wiping her mouth with a napkin. "And actually?" she continues. "I'm not here to *check up* on you."

The evening quiets. Aria coos and shakes the string of beads with her fisted hand. The dog laps water from a bowl at the deck railing.

"Okay, Celia." Jason takes a long breath. "What gives?"

And what her noticeable pause does is this: It heightens everything. Jason living alone. Everyone's worry about him. The conflict in his marriage with Maris. It even heightens some anger Celia hears in his question.

"Listen," she says, moving aside her plate and leaning

her arms on the teak table. "Last year, when I packed my bags and left Stony Point? I thought I was done there. Losing Sal so suddenly like that? It was too much to face at that little beach that held all my memories." She reaches across the table and squeezes Jason's hand. "But one night, *you* drove to Addison. You knocked on my door and *convinced* me to come back."

"I remember."

"And I'm here to do the same for you."

"Celia."

"No, hear me out." She pauses. Fusses with Aria, touches the baby's hair. "You can't deny to *me*, of all people, that grief for your brother isn't *part* of why you've isolated yourself out here."

He sits back and crosses his arms.

"Jason. It's the same reason I moved away last year." Celia raises an eyebrow. "And this summer's the ten-year anniversary of Neil's death. Don't tell me you're not feeling *some* expectation to close the chapter on that part of your life? On that loss? You're not feeling a pressure to ... *move on?*"

"Okay. Okay, sometimes. Sure."

"Well, listen. We *don't* move on, Jason. We don't. So don't you ever think that." She touches a tarnished lantern glimmering in the evening light, then looks at him across the table. "What we do is we move *forward*. Move forward *with* our memories, our experiences. Our love. *With* Neil, or Sal. If anything, they're more a part of who we are *now* than ever before."

Jason looks at her, then gets up and walks to that deck railing. The one facing the sea. Oh, did he know when he renovated this cottage ... Celia wonders. Did he know how necessary that contemplative spot would be? For Ted, poor Ted. For himself.

Jason eventually turns to her in the evening shadows. He takes another long breath. Drags a hand through his unkempt hair. Shakes his head. "As simple as that?" he finally asks, his voice tired. "I'm supposed to just ... move *forward*? With everyone aboard? Meaning the spirits?"

Celia nods, managing a smile, too. Because yes, Sal will always be on board. No matter what. And of *course* Neil will be for Jason. "Simple as that," she tells him. "And don't overthink it."

Jason draws a hand along the raised scar on his jaw. A moment later, he returns to the table and sits again. Not saying anything, he reaches for another slice of pizza and this time, cuts a piece. Cuts a piece and stabs it onto his fork. Finally, he looks at her across the table. "Thank you, Celia. Thank you for that."

"Please, Jason. Please know you're *not* moving on, and leaving your brother behind. *Neil moves with you*," she insists. "Anyone who loves you will understand that. So no more worry. No struggling with any final goodbyes."

"No."

"Promise me?"

Jason hesitates, then raises his fork to his mouth. After chewing, and drinking a long sip of his orange juice, he nods. "Promise."

119

"Okay, good. So that's settled." Celia grabs another slice of pizza. "Which leaves one *more* issue to settle—you and Maris."

Jason considers Celia. Her auburn hair is down. She wears a lacy cardigan over a tank top and frayed black shorts. Her baby is ever in her sights as she reaches over and fusses with Aria's clothes, her hair. Touches the baby's hand. Picks up the beads Aria drops. Celia is immersed in her own life—yet is *here*.

"Me and Maris?" Jason repeats. "That's kind of personal, Celia."

She gives a short laugh. "You've obviously been away *far* too long now. Have you already forgotten where home is?"

"What?"

"Stony Point? Because believe me, *nothing's* personal there."

Well there's no denying that, so Jason lifts his orange juice in a toast. Does something else, too. He actually unloads on Celia. Somewhat. But while killing that pizza together, he vaguely tells her how situations spiraled this summer. How he never saw some things coming, either. And that as much as he's moved out, it also feels like Maris *wants* him out now, too. So he just doesn't know what to do.

"The more Maris and I talk, the more time goes on," he

says, "it seems like the summer is just this brick wall we can't get past. Shane. And their engagement. And my own demons that Maris got a good taste of recently."

"You know, I've seen Shane this past week." Celia lifts Aria out of her bouncy chair and sets her in her lap. She turns the baby so she can watch the German shepherd standing close, sniffing at Aria's arm, her hair. "We talked, Shane and I," Celia admits then. "About a lot of different things. And if there were something between him and Maris, I'd tell you straight up, Jason. As your friend."

"And there's not."

"No. There's nothing between them now. Not one thing. Shane and Maris have a history, and that's all it is."

"History."

Celia nods.

"Appreciate that, Celia. But from my end, things are a little more complicated."

Celia says nothing. She simply holds Aria—and watches Jason.

So in the damp sea mist, he goes on. The best he can, anyway. "Honestly? What it feels like, in the midst of everything, is that we really lost our way this summer. Maris and I. And that scares the hell out of me."

"You lost your way?"

"We did."

Celia pauses before standing with Aria. She bounces her a bit, lets her baby breathe the strong salt air here. Finally, she turns to him. "Lost your way," she slowly repeats, her voice restrained now.

"Yes."

"Well. You're a fortunate man, Jason Barlow. Because you still *have* Maris in your life."

Saying nothing, Jason leans back in his chair. Celia's sudden anger surprises him.

A quiet second passes before she reaches down, picks up her tote from the table and slings it over her shoulder. "So you *find* a way back to her," she tells him then, her voice stern.

And Jason knows. Celia *can't* find a way back to Sal. He's been dead a year now. Her beautiful infant daughter will never lay eyes on her father. Will never see his loving face. Never hear Sal whisper, *Sorridi!* Will never sit in an idle rowboat out on Long Island Sound with him and listen to stories of his childhood in Italy. The hole in Aria's life is already huge.

Jason uncomfortably walks with Celia down the deck stairs to her car. He waits while she buckles Aria into her car seat. When Celia turns and notices the mottled bruise on his arm, he lies to her about bumping into a door.

He reaches into the car, then, strokes Aria's cheek and whispers, *Goodnight.*

Squeezes Celia's hand and thanks her for the pizza and visit.

Only nods when she repeats, "Find a way back, Jason."

thirteen

Monday Night

MARIS HAS A SECRET.

In Jason's absence, she's getting a new kitchen. In fact, she spent much of the afternoon at a kitchen-and-bath design showroom. And brought much of the place home with her, it seems.

She sits at the kitchen island now. Spread out before her are samples. Hardwood floor samples. Backsplash tile samples. Countertop granite and quartz and marble samples. Every stone type, in every neutral shade of white and sand and gray and blue. Speckled, veined and solid. You name it, she's got a sample lined up on her old laminate-top island *and* the entire counter, too. It's like assembling a puzzle—move this piece here, edge it with this complementary color, that contrasting shade. She walks away and looks at them from a distance. Leans subway tiles up against her plain walls. Would they go with

123

light granite, dark floor? Or dark quartz with a whitewashed wood floor. Then there's wood-look flooring tiles, which would be very durable—holding up to sand *and* Maddy's wet paws.

And don't forget the cabinets. They're old, but not original. So should she replace them? Or repaint? Probably paint, because there's not enough time for a total gut. But a facelift is definitely in order.

Regardless, the appliances are all going. Refrigerator, stove, dishwasher, microwave? Out, out, out, out. No question there.

Again Maris shuffles through the countertop and backsplash samples. Monochromatic would be nice, too. Sleek. She can go with all silvers and light grays. Oh, her mind spins with the options. She's actually relieved when her cell phone rings—though it requires walking through a maze to reach it on the kitchen table. Carefully, she steps around, past and over clusters of tri-samples scattered about: cabinet door colors butted against flooring samples, with squares of marble on top of them.

Finally reaching her phone, Maris sees it's Ted Sullivan returning her call from the church parking lot earlier today.

"Ted," she says into the phone as she sits at the table. "I'm glad you got my message."

"I just got in, Maris. I hope it's not too late to talk."

"No, this is good," she says, glancing at the array of tiles and hardwoods fanned out across the room. "You caught me at a good time."

"It's Jason, isn't it?"

Maris gives a sad smile. That's Ted, through and through. Tuned in to Jason like no one else. "It is, Ted. I would never interrupt your travel plans otherwise. But it's that important. Do you have a few minutes to talk?"

"Now?"

"Yes."

Ted takes a quick breath. "Maris. You know Jason is really important to me. So why don't we meet in person? It'll be better that way, instead of over the phone."

"What? You're still here in Connecticut?"

"I am."

"But I thought you were away. There was a wedding—"

"Maris."

"And your anniversary cruise?"

A long silence comes then.

A silence when Maris can just picture Ted shaking his head, no. "Ted?" she quietly asks.

"We're still at home, my wife and I."

"You *are*?"

"Yes. Not at the cottage, of course. At our year-round house, inland a ways. So can we meet to talk? Maybe have an early coffee tomorrow?"

"Could you come here?" Maris asks. "To my house?"

"At Stony Point?"

"Yes. It's the big gabled cottage at the end of Sea View Road."

"Okay. Okay, that'll be fine. About nine? Nine-thirty?"

"Perfect. Oh, and Ted? If you should talk to Jason in the meantime ... I mean, you know, if he calls you for something? Please don't say anything about this."

"You have my word."

There's something about Ted, about his tone, which has Maris hang up the phone with some hope. Because let's face it. Space and time away from Jason gave her no answers. Church earlier gave her no answers.

So maybe Ted Sullivan can. He's the man who saw Jason last, after all—right before Jason left home, left her.

Maris gets up and considers the mess of her kitchen. She'll have to move all these granite and marble pieces, and backsplash tile samples, and flooring planks to the dining room. That way she and Ted can have coffee tomorrow in the kitchen, or maybe outside on the deck. So she lifts the wood planks first. But when she's setting them down beside the buffet in the dining room, her phone rings again.

Carefully, she rushes back to the kitchen—trying not to trip on the samples strewn on the floor. Before the call can go to voicemail, Maris lunges past blocks of marble leaning against a kitchen chair to grab her cell phone off the table. Ted must've thought of something, or maybe wants to meet somewhere else.

"Oh, I'm here! I'm here," she says, breathlessly beating the voicemail. "Was there something else you needed?"

～

You find a way back.

Jason can't get Celia's words out of his head. He heard them, loud and clear.

And she's right; he knows it. That's why he couldn't sketch much more once she left—every rendering of Mitch's added-on office trashed. It's why he couldn't watch a TV program. Why he found himself roaming from room to room in Ted's cottage, as though he was looking for something.

Turns out, he was. A way back.

So he starts, and calls Maris. But he's thrown by her immediate greeting on the phone.

"Oh, I'm here! I'm here," she says, sounding rushed. Winded, even. She was obviously talking to someone moments ago, judging by her words. "Was there something else you needed?"

Her voice is close in Jason's ear. Though the question clearly isn't meant for him, he can damn well answer it.

Is there something else he needs? Yes. Now more than ever in his livelong life. For one thing, he could use his left leg back.

And his brother, too. Yes, he needs Neil back. Needs him in the business collaborating on their work, and living close by. Needs to just talk with him. What he wouldn't give to have a beer on the bluff together.

Time, too. Way too much time has been lost in the mire of this summer alone. Even a few minutes back could get Jason kneeling in gratitude.

Hell, sure would be nice to have his father back, too. Dad and all his sea lore. His war stories. His way. That loss is deep.

How about having his whole life back, in general? Just

127

the routine of it. The normality of getting through his mornings without thought. Get back to multitasking and emailing and texting while having a coffee and breakfast. Have his own shower back—with a stool in it. Have his twig-strewn driveway back. His living room chair. Bedside chair. His walks on the hard-packed sand below the tideline.

Yes, how about having his happiness back?

Oh, and one more thing. One that ensures all the rest.

He needs Maris back.

Instead of all that, instead of telling her what he needs, he says into the phone, "It's me, Maris."

"Oh. Jason? It's just, well … I thought—"

"It was someone else. I know."

"Well, yes." A pause, then, "How are you, Jason?"

"I wanted to ask you a question," he says without answering hers.

"Okay."

Another pause, this one his. "You said something yesterday. At Bella's. And it stayed with me."

"*I* said something?"

"Yeah. You said that you fixed your life. That you sorted things out with Shane. And your past."

"I did."

"But you said more. You said that you fixed your life, *and* to let you know when I fixed mine."

"Jason … It's not that—"

"No, please." Jason stops her. Takes a long breath. Closes his eyes. There's nothing to see. He doesn't want to see right now, anyway. He wants only to hear. "Maris," he says then. "It's going to take some time, but I'd like to start."

"Start what?" she asks.

"Fixing my life."

"Fixing your life?"

"Yes."

"How, Jason?"

"For starters, I'd like to ask you out on a date." His eyes tear up with that, not that he'll let on.

"What? Are you serious?"

"I am," he quietly says. "Because I want to get to know this girl I never knew. The girl sketching denim designs at harbor docks. The girl who could sit at an old picnic table for hours, stitching ... and ... waiting for someone she loved."

When he stops then, Maris is silent. Not a word comes through the phone. Nothing. Not a noise from the house. Not the old refrigerator kicking on. Not the slider scraping open. Not the jukebox playing or dishes clattering as she empties the dishwasher. Nothing indicating what she was doing when he called.

So Jason does it. Hard as it is, he breaks the silence.

"Are you free tomorrow night?" he asks.

fourteen

Later That Night

THE BATHROOM FAUCET'S DRIPPING AND it's driving Kyle crazy. Because that one lousy, constant drip will keep him tossing and turning all night. So before getting into bed, he brings a piece of string into his en-suite bathroom. Right away, his blood pressure rises when he hears that *drip ... drip*. There's no way he's losing another night's sleep to it. So he ties one end of the long string to the faucet and carefully threads the other end down into the drain.

The result comes instantly. Instead of his leaky tap sending random drops of water *drip-dripping* into the sink, the drops silently slide down the length of string and into the drain. No drips, no dribbles, no tiny splashes. Just beautiful quiet. Already he breathes easier and heads to bed. There he folds down the blanket and gets under the sheet, then props his pillow and sits back against the headboard.

Before picking up his cell phone, he first checks his alarm clock on the nightstand. And listens to the sounds of his family.

"Lights out, Ev," Lauren tells their son from out in the hallway.

"One more page?" Evan's voice carries to Kyle.

"Okay." Lauren turns into their bedroom and calls back, "But just one." While taking off her robe and laying it across the end of the bed, she says to Kyle, "I talked to my mom. She'll be here first thing tomorrow so I can cover for Stacy waitressing."

Kyle looks up from his phone. "Okay, good. I'm doing it, then."

"Doing what?"

"Sending a group text for a boardwalk meeting in the morning."

"Tomorrow? What about work?"

"Rob's opening the diner. Because I can't wait any longer to clear the air with everyone."

"About Shane?" Lauren stands at her dresser and takes off her rings.

"Yeah. It's time." Kyle starts typing a text message. "Shit," he says while sitting in bed and plucking at the keys. "I was *so* wrong about the whole situation with him. And now I have to eat my words in front of the gang." He deletes a phrase on his phone, then resumes plucking out his message. "I hope they don't hate me, but damn, I hate *myself* right now."

"Oh, don't say that."

"Ell. I turned everyone against my own brother all those years ago."

Lauren brushes her hair while watching him in the dresser mirror. "At the bonfire?" she asks.

Kyle nods. "I can't believe I had them all burn his name. Hell, I guess I was so friggin' mad at the time."

"Understandably, Kyle. It was a misread situation."

"And a costly one," he says as he deletes some words, adds more.

"It's late." Lauren gets under the sheet and sits beside him. She wears her navy satin nightshirt; the fabric feels cool against Kyle's leg. "Do you think anyone's even up?"

"Of course they are." He looks toward the open window and listens to the slow chirp of crickets. The night is still enough that he even hears the soft lapping of small waves on the bay across the street. "No one can sleep in this God damn peaceful paradise," he says while typing again. "Didn't you see how Jason looked on TV this morning? He must not have slept in a week. What a wreck."

"I hope he's all right. He was really there for us after the vow renewal fiasco."

"I left a dinner on his stoop a few days ago. At Sea Spray. But other than that, I got nothing. Barlow's just not talking." Kyle types another line, then backtracks and deletes again.

So Lauren takes Kyle's wrist and tips his phone to better see it. "No, Kyle! Put the date in all caps." She points to his phone's screen. "They don't even read. They just skim!"

Kyle fixes the date, then adds a subject line. *Boardwalk Meeting.*

"Tell them to be prompt, because we'll have to get to the diner." Lauren leans close, pointing to the screen. "And to maybe bring a coffee if they want. We'll spring for a box of doughnuts or something. For refreshments, yeah. Food always gets them there. They don't care what it is as long as they can dunk it into coffee."

"Food *will* be served," Kyle says while typing.

"No, don't make it all formal-sounding like that. Set it up like Elsa does. Clear and to the point. And *short*—to hold their brief attention spans." Lauren grabs the phone and quickly types a few lines of text. "Remember. The important stuff goes in all caps." In a minute, she holds the phone out to him.

Kyle looks at the phone screen and reads the message aloud:

PLEASE COME: Boardwalk Meeting
WHY: News to Share
WHEN: Tomorrow Morning, 7:30 AM
WHERE: Stony Point Boardwalk
BRING: An Open Mind + Coffee (pastry will be served)

"*Open mind?*" Kyle asks, scratching his bare chest. "Do we really need that part?"

Lauren pats his arm. "You're going to need all the help you can get, hon."

"Okay. The message is good, then."

"I'll put in their names and hit *Send.*"

When Kyle hears the *whooshing* sound of the text message being sent, he takes the phone from Lauren and sets it on the nightstand. All across the Connecticut seaboard, he imagines the cell phones separately dinging—right at *this* very second.

Jason's phone somewhere in Ted Sullivan's cottage.

Maris' phone at the Barlow house on the bluff.

Matt's phone in his state police cruiser.

Eva's phone in the recesses of the Gallagher house on the marsh.

Elsa's phone at her soon-to-be-opened Ocean Star Inn.

Celia's phone in her gingerbread guest cottage.

Vinny's and Paige's phones dinging in unison as they watch the late news.

And Cliff's phone giving a warbled chime in that tin-can trailer of his.

This is it, Kyle thinks. He right away shuts off his own phone before their instant responses keep him up like that dripping faucet. Switches off the bedside lamp, too—relieved his mea culpa is initiated, at last.

fifteen

Early Tuesday Morning

EVERYONE'S IN FULL-ON GOSSIP MODE for his boardwalk meeting. Kyle can tell as he approaches with Lauren. Their friends are huddled close to each other, voices hushed. In his workout gear, there's Matt cooling down beneath the shade pavilion. Looks like he already jogged a couple of miles. Eva's sitting beside him, dressed like she'll be showing a house this morning. She's leaning into Maris, who's looking over her shoulder to the parking lot. Celia's off to the side, wearing her fedora and a long sundress. Her hand gently pushes Aria's stroller on the sandy boardwalk planks, back and forth. Back and forth.

Which Kyle assumes the gossip is doing, too—ping-ponging back and forth as they debate why they've all been summoned.

That assumption's confirmed when everyone turns at

the sound of his and Lauren's footsteps. Their questions fire off right away.

Eva: *Is this something about your vow renewal?*
Matt: *Setting a new date, maybe?*
Celia: *Hope it's good news, Kyle.*
Maris: *Or are you arranging a group gift for Elsa? For the inn's grand opening?*
Eva: *Wait, Maris. Do you think Jason will show up here today?*

Kyle just sits himself down in the shade, too, and takes the box of muffins Lauren's been holding. Before he can even say anything, Nick approaches in his security guard uniform—khaki button-down shirt with black epaulets over matching black shorts. Nick jumps right in to Eva's question about Jason.

Nick: *The dude's been at Ted's for over a week now.*
Matt: *What are you doing, keeping tabs on the guy?*
Nick: *Listen, one of the perks of being a guard? I witness every Stony Point secret coming and going under that trestle. So keep that in mind.*

Kyle sets the box of muffins on the boardwalk bench, but looks over at the others when they go quiet. Something's got their attention, and it's Elsa and Cliff. Their heated dialogue has silenced all.

"*That's* how you introduced me to Mitch Fenwick last

night?" Cliff is asking as they cross the boardwalk. "As your *neighbor*? Is that what we are now? *Neighbors?*"

"We *could* be called that, Cliff," Elsa assures him.

"Do neighbors spend the night? Do neighbors keep a duffel with a change of clothes at each other's house?" Cliff shakes his head and is quiet for a few steps. "Of all the cockamamie …"

"What are you two arguing about?" Matt asks as he stands, grabs onto the seat-back and stretches his arm muscles.

"Oh, it's a little disagreement." Elsa squeezes beside the others beneath the shade pavilion and peels the lid off her take-out coffee.

Maris leans over and asks past Eva, "About what?"

"Nothing, really." Elsa sips her coffee. "It's just that Mitch Fenwick and I had a business meeting last night. On the deck of his cottage—"

"What?" Eva looks from Elsa, back to Maris.

"A *business* meeting?" Maris presses her aunt.

Elsa takes an indignant breath. "Yes! A business meeting about filming for *Castaway Cottage*. I was at the Fenwicks' to talk to Mitch and Carol. And … and Cliff came up with an ice-cream cake."

"Wait," Lauren jumps in. "You're losing me. For your business meeting with the Fenwicks, *Cliff* brought dessert?"

"Yes. Well, no. You see, *Carol* ordered an ice-cream cake from Scoop Shop. But they made it way too big … And I guess it wouldn't fit in her golf cart? So then, well then Cliff saw her there at the shop and offered to deliver it in his car.

And … well … Oh, it's a long story," Elsa adds while turning distractedly to Cliff. "What was I supposed to say, Cliff? That you're my *boyfriend?*"

Cliff walks closer and sits beside Elsa. "Boyfriend is certainly better than *neighbor*," he tosses back while opening his thermos and pouring a cup of coffee. "Especially since I've been wooing you for a year now. Doesn't that count for anything, Mrs. DeLuca?" he asks while also motioning for Kyle to hand him one of his boxed muffins.

"Blueberry, chocolate-chip or lemon-poppy?" Kyle asks.

"Lemon-poppy," Cliff says, then turns to Elsa. "I mean, *neighbor?*"

"Clifton. I'm in my late fifties," Elsa reminds him as the muffin is passed along. "And the term *boyfriend?* That ship has sailed."

Cliff rips off a piece of the lemon-poppy muffin and dunks it in his coffee. "We can change that right now, if I get down on one knee." He motions his now-dunked muffin piece to the silent crowd watching him go at it with Elsa. "We have plenty of witnesses."

Elsa slaps his hand away. "Don't you dare." Promptly standing, she takes a chocolate-chip muffin before sitting between Maris and Celia. She does one more thing, too. Elsa bends over and pats little Aria's cheek. "*Good morning, sweetie pie,*" she coos, then settles on the boardwalk bench and bites into her chip-laden muffin.

When Lauren nudges Kyle, he looks at her. "*What?*" he whispers.

"You better start. They're getting too distracted," Lauren quietly tells him. "And a little out of control. I mean, Cliff's so riled up, he didn't even fine us for breaking an ordinance—no food on the beach!"

Kyle looks at the gang. They *do* seem on edge today. There are no long sighs as they sit back and watch the gentle waves break. No smiles as they inhale that sweet salt air. No heads tipped up, eyes closed, as they soak in the morning sunshine. Regardless, it's now or never. Time to eat his words and hope for the best.

So Kyle stands and thanks everyone for coming. He's wearing his work clothes—a black tee over black pants—and feels warm. But his outfit is also an out, once he's done here. Those work clothes are an excuse to hightail it to the diner. To pots and pans and spatulas and standing behind the big stove. Alone, cooking, with no finger-pointing, no prying questions.

As he begins talking now, Jason steps onto the boardwalk. He's got on an open denim jacket over a black tee and olive shorts. The jacket sleeves are shoved up; the shorts rolled at the hem. From the looks of him, he's also headed to work soon—some job site, or the TV studio in Hartford. Jason grabs a spot beside Cliff, who shakes his hand and tells him the pastry is beneath the shade pavilion. Jason glances past him to the boxed muffins, then sits back, sips a coffee he brought and nods to Kyle.

Kyle nods back to Jason, then paces the length of the boardwalk where everyone sits, sips, dunks, eats, whispers and nudges whoever's beside them. It's hard to tell if they're even paying attention. There's one way to find out, though, and that's to get right to it.

"This is a difficult talk, and I hope you'll bear with me," Kyle begins then. "Because I'm announcing something really important today."

"What is it, Kyle? You look a little pale," Celia mentions as someone's cell phone dings.

With his hands clasped behind his back, Kyle continues to pace the boardwalk. "It's about something that happened fifteen years ago, Celia. You weren't here then," he says, turning to Elsa, too. "Neither were you, Elsa." He also nods to Cliff and Nick. "But I guess you're all a part of this now." As he's talking, someone's cell phone loudly dings again. But Kyle keeps going. "I made poor choices back then. Choices about my brother, Shane. The worst of it happened around a bonfire one summer night, up at Little Beach."

As if the interruptions can't get any worse, Eva proves otherwise. "Kyle, hang on," she says while grabbing a napkin and blueberry muffin from the box and scooting down the boardwalk to Jason. Kyle pauses, patiently—and silently—waiting for Eva to give Jason the food before hurrying back to Maris' side, in the shade. And motioning for Kyle to continue.

Right as Vinny arrives, trotting down the boardwalk and sitting near Lauren and that pastry box. "Sorry, Kyle," he manages while breathlessly lifting a muffin. "Oh, and Paige is home with the kids. She couldn't make it."

"That's fine." Kyle resumes his pacing, walking past

them all before sitting sideways on the edge of the boardwalk. Behind him on the beach, waves splash onshore. A seagull squawks as it swoops low. Finally, he goes on. "Today, I'm here to *explain* that situation involving my brother." Another pause then as the mysterious cell phone dings yet *again*, getting Kyle to look over in Elsa's direction.

When all quiets, he says the hardest words yet. "And I gathered you guys here today to do one more thing. To admit that I was wrong about Shane. Really, really wrong."

⁓

Again, Elsa's cell phone dings. It not only dings, but it vibrates in her tote. Then again, another two dings— quick—one after the other.

Celia elbows her. "*Get it!*" she whispers. "*It keeps interrupting Kyle.*"

Stuffing the last of her muffin into her mouth, Elsa digs in her tote for that intrusive phone. She swaps her sunglasses for her reading glasses, tips the phone away from the sun's glare and squints at the message. It's from Mitch Fenwick, telling her she left her silk scarf behind last night.

"*Gesù, Santa Maria,*" Elsa whispers, then reads several texts Mitch is sending.

So I'd like to return the scarf to you. Sure I can walk the few steps through the beach path to your cottage …

Another ding.

But, you know. It's so darn hot, and you're busy getting your inn ready.

Elsa drops her hand on her lap with a quick thought. Mitch texts the same way he talks. With well-placed pauses. She can just imagine the tip of his head, too. When another ding sounds, she looks at the phone screen and reads more of his easy chatting.

How about dinner at Dockside Diner tomorrow? My treat. I'll bring your scarf. Have a few more on-camera questions too.

With a quiet sigh, Elsa glances at Kyle as he's explaining himself. Then she looks at her phone again—sigh long gone. Because how bad does it look that she actually left her scarf behind at Mitch's? It's the oldest trick in the book! Mitch will think she left it on purpose. That she's *that* forward, trying to finagle another meetup.

"*Oh, no,*" she says under her breath.

"*Who is it?*" Celia whispers, leaning close.

"*What? It's ... It's just ... just the Chamber of Commerce. Yes.*" Elsa slightly turns away as if to block the sun's glare on her phone. But what she's really doing is blocking the screen from any roving eyes as she types back. "*Confirming the inn's ribbon-cutting,*" she lies to Celia while typing.

The thing is, Elsa plucks out a line far *different* from her lie—a line discreetly *accepting* Mitch's dinner invite.

But she notices something else, too. Everyone's gone silent. There's only the sound of the waves lapping at the sand. So she quickly finishes her text message and drops her phone and reading glasses back in her tote. "Sorry, Kyle," she says when she sees him still sitting there—arms now crossed—on the edge of the boardwalk. "I took care of it. Phone's off." With an apologetic smile, Elsa behaves now, giving Kyle her undivided attention.

sixteen

Minutes Later

THE MOMENT OF TRUTH HAS arrived.

Kyle knows it, feels it, takes it all in. And with every sentence he says from where he sits on the boardwalk edge, something happens. His breathing comes easier. Every admission is like an exhale—from his *I want to do right by Shane*; to his *You need to hear what I learned last week, shooting the shit with my brother one night*; to his repeating Shane's towline story, saying *Me and my brother's relationship snapped just as suddenly.*

"The day I drove to Maine after my father's funeral fifteen years ago, I was fixin' for a fight. I see now that much of that was grief, and Shane became my target. Instead of listening to him try to explain things—"

"Explain what, Kyle?" Matt asks. "You told us he *took* the whole estate."

"I did." Kyle hesitates, then stands and walks a few steps

144

on the boardwalk. The waves break on the beach; the sun is hot on his back. "Because some truths are hard to believe when you're young and full of yourself and think life owes you something. So when Shane told me there *was* no estate after our father died, what I *chose* to believe was my own illogical thought—that my brother left me high and dry and burned through our inheritance. Drank it. Gambled it. Blew it. Pawned it. Whatever. I also felt our father *died* on Shane's watch, living with him up north. And I blamed my brother for that, too." He pauses then.

Of course, that pause gives his friends time to get in some words; some questions; some groans.

What do you mean?

Your brother screwed you over, man. Didn't give you a dime.

So is it his fault, or isn't it?

Kyle doesn't answer. Instead he puts up a hand to stop them. "Please, guys. Let me finish." When they quiet, he continues. "We had it out back then, Shane and I. Duked it out, actually. Swung a few fists. Got a few bruises." He stops and is sure to meet everyone's eye before he says the rest. "But Shane was right. He *was* telling me the truth."

"Which is ... what?" Celia persists.

"That my father was actually destitute." Kyle swipes at a bead of perspiration on his forehead. He explains then what he learned only last week. That essentially their father was drowning in debt—in their mother's medical bills and a second mortgage. It was Shane who tossed him a life ring.

"So Shane *didn't* steal what you told us was rightfully yours?" Eva asks.

"No. There was nothing *to* steal. If my father didn't sell his house when he did, apparently the bank would've foreclosed." Kyle's voice is fatigued now. And that breathing that came easier a few minutes ago? It was short-lived. He can barely swallow around some lump in his throat. "Shane actually gave my old man the sweetest final months a guy could want, living on the docks at the edge of the sea."

"Are you *kidding* me?" Jason asks.

"No I'm not, guy." Kyle looks over at Jason, who's sitting further down the boardwalk bench. Jason leans forward, elbows on his knees, and raises his sunglasses to the top of his head. "I was wrong about my brother," Kyle says again. "Dead wrong. For all these years."

"But that day of the bonfire," Vinny presses, standing now. "We made a pact. You had us burn Shane's name, for God's sake. To vow never to even *say* his name again."

"And we *did* vow," Eva adds. "For you, Kyle. We believed you. That your brother truly did you wrong."

"How do you think *I* feel?" Kyle shakes his head with every ounce of regret he can muster. "Damn, it's all my fault."

The questions, and the accusations, they keep coming. They're barbed, and forceful, and constricting.

"You *shunned* the guy?" Nick asks. "For all this time?"

"Everyone makes mistakes," Elsa says then. "Misreads, misinterprets—"

"But still," Matt argues. "That's fifteen years ... gone. For *all* of us. Shane was our friend too, Kyle."

Kyle turns up his hands. "And I take full responsibility for the situation."

"Guys," Lauren says, standing beside Kyle now. "It *is* too bad it all happened. It's awful, actually." She looks from Kyle to each of their friends. "But it's *not* too late to fix things."

"If it wasn't for Lauren," Kyle tells them, "and the way she invited Shane to our vow renewal—"

"I still have you penciled in for a possible redo date," Elsa calls out. "Later in September?"

"We're not sure, Elsa," Kyle says. "Just not going there again. Maybe another time."

Lauren slowly nods. "We're so busy now. The kids will be in school. We'll see …"

"But what about *Shane*?" Nick asks. "Shit, Kyle. He's gone. And he's good with all this? With how you got a lot of people to turn their backs on him?"

"He is," Kyle admits. "*That's* the kind of guy Shane actually is. A bigger man than me. And I wanted to meet with you to set the record straight." When Kyle says it, he notices the way Jason just watches. "I totally messed up, believing something that wasn't even true," Kyle goes on. "And look what happened. I wronged my brother and turned you all against him. Now I'm asking for forgiveness." Kyle closes his eyes against stinging tears before continuing. "I'm sorry. So, so sorry. And I hope," he says, clearing his throat, "I hope you can all get past things and accept Shane into your lives. He *really* deserves no less."

"So are you going to start doing things with him? Brother things? Will you see him occasionally?" Maris asks.

Kyle takes a long breath of that salt air that's not doing any curing today, not by a long shot. "We have no definite plans, Maris." Kyle takes another breath. His chest feels heavy again. Eh, his whole life feels heavy. This didn't go as he'd hoped. "For now, I'm just taking down that darn wall between me and my brother."

~

Celia knew it. Didn't she just know? Ever since her rowboat ride with Shane, she knew. Knew Shane Bradford was a good person. She could tell by his way, his words. She knew enough to be comfortable going out with him—a pure stranger—in that boat at midnight, on the night of Kyle's called-off vow renewal. Her instincts didn't steer her wrong.

And now this.

Her heart breaks for Shane, especially. Because one talk between two brothers can't erase the hurt. Or the personal loss Shane has to feel. Can't erase the fifteen-year ripple effect cutting deep into all their lives.

So at this moment, she really misses him. Misses hearing Shane's voice, his careful words. Wherever he is out on the Atlantic, this still has to sting—this dark history at Stony Point. She remembers the night she'd slept with Shane. Afterward, they sat out on his cottage porch and he came up behind her. A heavy waning moon rose, leaving a swath of golden light on the Sound. Celia wore only Shane's long-sleeve denim shirt and sat on the half-wall. He stood behind her and unwound her braid. Even now her eyes briefly drop closed, remembering his touch. Remembering his words asking her to stay the night.

Sitting on the boardwalk this morning, she can't miss the ocean stars sparkling on Long Island Sound. Thousands of them float on top of the rippling blue water. Elsa says those ocean stars—celestial stars that have fallen to the sea overnight—grant wishes, too.

Oh, Celia has her doubts. Some things we just know can never be. But if she dared to make a wish on one of those twinkling sea stars, it would be this: that she could simply reach over and squeeze Shane's hand beside her.

⌒⌣

Cliff knows what it's like to be exiled.

He also knows what it's like to come back. He'd felt exiled from Stony Point for most of his adult life after a man named Gordon died searching for him. That happened during a hurricane over fifty years ago. Yet even now, Cliff can't shake his past as little lost Sailor—after all this time.

But he did it. He came back.

Shane did, too. He came back this summer after being exiled. And even though it turns out Shane's a good person, look at the turmoil his return stirred up. Too much. That turmoil nearly derailed a marriage; threatened friendships.

Divided the brothers yet again.

Which confirms to Cliff that his identity as Sailor must remain a secret. Only Jason and Maris know that one truth. No one else does, and it has to stay that way. The last thing Cliff needs is a boardwalk meeting announcing to everyone that he's the mysterious boy from the beach. Oh, no. After all these years, every painful detail of the day Gordon died would be magnified and somehow put on him to bear.

Sitting there on the boardwalk, Cliff pulls his lucky black domino out of his shirt pocket. Couldn't they all use a little bit of luck? He rubs his thumb over the domino's white-dotted pips. Across the sand, waves lap at shore; the sun beats down warm. Finally, he does it. Discreetly, Cliff gives the domino a toss—flipping it in the air this time for Shane Bradford. Poor guy.

Maris can't get one visual out of her mind—bonfire flames licking high at the sky. Fifteen years ago, the fire snapped and crackled and danced beneath the moon. Sparks flew like tiny burning stars. They were all in their twenties—the beach friends. Beside the fire, they looked like dark silhouettes shifting on the sand. That night, she'd reluctantly walked to the tall flames. As the bonfire burned, stinging tears burned her eyes. The heat of the flames felt warm on her skin.

And Maris did it. Sometimes the pain of doing so feels greater than the pain of breaking up with Shane. But she did it, that night. Her fingers were clenched around a piece of paper with Shane's name on it. She remembers the moment now—the moment she whispered, *Goodbye, Shane.* The words left her lips right as she tossed that slip of paper into the roaring fire. What it felt like was that the fire swallowed Shane whole. All their past, all their sweet memories—happy and sad—were burned to cinders.

Sitting on the boardwalk and hearing Kyle's story today? It doesn't change things. Doesn't change how on that long-ago night, Maris tossed a piece of her heart into that fire, too.

~

Was it only a few weeks ago when Jason got Lauren's text message? *Oh my God, Jason. Please come over.*

And he did, finding Lauren alone and in complete distress in her home on the bay. Jason sat in her kitchen. Lauren wore her two-piece wedding dress. Her fingers clutched a tissue. Her chignon was more undone than done. Running makeup smeared the skin beneath her eyes. When her emotion got her trembling, he'd wrapped her lace shawl over her shoulders.

Lauren and Kyle's vow renewal ceremony was over before it even began. All because of Shane Bradford's arrival. His presence unleashed a panicked chain reaction among them. Jason remembers how he tracked down Kyle that night. Talked him down, too. Brought Lauren to Kyle at their second-honeymoon cabin. Didn't make it home himself until the sun was practically rising.

Before all that, though, Jason saw Shane at Elsa's inn. Saw him standing on the inn's grand staircase, where Lauren had painted her seaside mural.

Jason *could've* said, *Hey, man. Long time no see.*

Instead, he looked Shane in the eye and told him to get the hell out of Stony Point.

Told Shane a week later to get away from his wife.

To leave Maris *and* Kyle alone.

Told Shane that no one in Stony Point wanted anything to do with him.

Now Jason looks at Kyle pacing the boardwalk. Perspiration beads on his friend's forehead and dampens his dark tee. His voice breaks as he admits *he* wronged his brother. Fifteen years of remorse show on Kyle's face.

So everything that happened these past weeks? All those damning words Jason sent Shane's way? It was all for nothing.

Turns out Jason was wrong, too.

～

Of course it wouldn't be easy. Kyle knew that even as he arranged this early-morning boardwalk meeting.

Of course everyone would see his story differently.

Of course doubts would be cast.

But Kyle never realized his admission would come too late. Fifteen years of shunning his brother, of everyone shunning Shane, left a scar among them.

"How can the guy not hate you all?" Nick asks, tipping up his security cap and looking at Kyle. "How could he have even gotten in his truck and driven here to see everyone?"

"Wait a minute, Nick," Lauren says. "Shane never imagined the whole gang would be here. He'd thought that Maris, Jason and Neil, Eva ... well, that we all went our own ways. And regardless, he never *knew* about the bonfire night."

"And he's not going to *ever* know," Kyle adds. "Why rub salt into the wound?"

"Don't forget, Nick," Lauren persists. "When I invited him to our vow renewal, I extended the olive branch. To make peace between the brothers. And ..." She looks from Nick, to Kyle, to every single person sitting on the boardwalk. "And Shane *accepted* that olive branch. He did!"

"And *look* at the welcome he got when he arrived," Elsa says, sadly shaking her head.

"Son of a gun." Jason runs a knuckle over his scarred jaw. "Our hostility must've thrown him."

"But, Jason. Elsa. We worked it out with him," Lauren goes on. "Me and Kyle. And it was because of *Sal* that I did it. That I gave Shane and Kyle a second chance. Because ... because Sal always said in his Italian way ... second chances were *molto speciale*?"

"Very special. I get it," Cliff agrees. He stands and shakes Kyle's hand, patting his shoulder, too. "Everyone needs a second chance at some time in their life. Everybody."

"Thanks, Judge," Kyle tells him.

Cliff nods and sits beside Jason again. Still, Kyle's uncomfortable with the fallout of his boardwalk confession. There's simmering anger, actually. Anger at him. And disbelief. *Skepticism.*

"Listen," Kyle says. He presses his arm to his perspiring forehead. "Okay, so ... you know. If I ever have Shane over for a barbecue or something, would you guys even come?"

Jason, Kyle sees it, tosses up his hands and sits back on the boardwalk bench without answering. Vinny, sitting near Celia, just shrugs.

"I would," Elsa says then.

After a quiet moment, Matt jumps in. "All right. Me, too."

Celia, holding Aria now, nods at Kyle. "Same here."

"Maybe make that barbecue for *next* summer, Kyle. Because we've had an emotional-enough summer already." Eva stands and gathers her purse and coffee cup. "Sorry, all. Really got to run. I have to show a cottage."

And just like that, with Eva standing to leave, the meeting breaks up. Suddenly everyone's talking quietly amongst themselves. And picking up their cups and napkins.

Vinny heads over and claps Kyle's shoulder. "I've got a professional development seminar to get to at the high school. But I'll run this all by Paige later," he says before leaving for his car.

Matt walks to Kyle and pats his back while telling him, "It's good, Kyle. You know, good you and your brother reconciled."

"Thanks, man. Thanks for coming, too."

"Anytime," Matt says. "I'm off to mow the lawn, then grab some sleep to cover the late shift tonight."

"I hope it works out for you, Kyle," Nick adds before he leaves to patrol the beach. "I always liked that Shane."

Slowly, they all scatter—going off to sell houses and write novels and prepare for inn openings and enforce beach rules and adjust blueprints and review history lesson plans.

Kyle lingers, sitting with Lauren beneath the boardwalk's shade pavilion. When Jason approaches Maris, Kyle overhears some of what they say to each other.

"I'll pick you up tonight?" Jason asks. Maris still sits on the boardwalk bench, and Jason stands beside her.

"No." Maris stands then, too. "No, I'd rather drive myself. I'll meet you there." With a quick smile, she turns to walk toward the footpath, home.

Before Jason leaves, he glances back at Kyle. "Later, man," he says, waving and heading to the parking lot.

Pick you up? Meet you there? Kyle's not sure he likes the sound of what just transpired between those two. Something's going down. But watching Jason looking beat and leaving alone, it sure doesn't seem good. Could they be talking divorce? Even signing papers—the way they're keeping it secret?

Goddamn secrets will undo this place. Whatever Jason's is, it has him looking battle-weary.

Which is how Kyle feels right now, too. Like he just fought some *psychological* battle, convincing them Shane *wasn't* an enemy among them.

But Kyle also feels like he lost. He's defeated. Lauren squeezes his arm before picking up the empty muffin box.

"It was a start," she calls over her shoulder on the way to a trash can. "They'll come around, you'll see."

Stepping off the boardwalk, Kyle slips out of his shoes at the water's edge and cuffs his black work pants. After taking a few steps into the shallows, he bends and splashes handfuls of the sea on his face. His wet hands run through his hair; he tips his head up to the hot sun.

seventeen

Tuesday Midmorning

JASON'S FATHER BELIEVED THAT THE sea speaks to you. It has its own language. Sitting on the boardwalk some evenings, Jason's explained this to Maris. *Listen!* he's said on calm nights when a quick, bubbling *swish* moved along the water's surface in the boat basin behind them. The *swish* was evidence of a school of panicked minnows. That same swishing sea also told them something else— that there was a dangerous presence *behind* those minnows. An aggressive blue or striper was on the hunt, driving the tiny fish into the shallows.

Or there were times she and Jason sat out on the bluff, and swells rolled in silently. You wouldn't even know they were there until those swells broke on the rocks below. And the frothy spray reaching right up to the top of the bluff? *More sea talk*, Jason would say. That hissing spray was the sea's announcement of not only the swells' presence, but their immense size, too.

Which means that oftentimes, the sea actually cautions you.

Today, Maris thinks the sea's being deceptive. The water's all blue sparkles and tiny waves. It's blissfully calm—serene, even—this late-August morning. Calm and serene, two feelings the furthest from the truth in her life.

So the sea today? If it speaks to you, it's telling lies, all lies.

She wonders what Jason would say to that. But he's not here—beside her on his father's stone bench on the bluff.

Instead, she decides to bring Ted Sullivan here for their coffee together. Sitting on the bluff's rocky ledge better suits their talk, anyway. So after Kyle's boardwalk meeting, Maris sets up a small table facing the Sound. There's a box of raspberry Danish there, and small dishes, too. A gray rock anchors a handful of paper napkins.

"Jason's father was a mason," Maris tells Ted now as they carry their coffee mugs along the narrow path from the yard to the bluff. "He made this bench when he came home from the Vietnam War."

Ted stops beside the bench. He takes in the view of Long Island Sound first, then turns to the bench and runs his hand along the stone top. There's a breeze here—there often is, far above the Sound. That salty breeze lifts Ted's silver hair and ripples the brown polo shirt he wears with khaki shorts. And when Ted squints against the bright sun, deep wrinkles line his leathery face.

"Jason said that after the war, his father wanted a place to sit beside the sea. Somewhere peaceful. And that he'd sit out here for hours, sometimes alone, sometimes with his sons," Maris continues. "His father convinced him and Neil that the sea would talk to you, right here. If you sit still long enough, it'll answer your questions."

"Wise man," Ted says. He cups his coffee and sits beside Maris on the bench. "My guess is that Jason sits here often."

"He does."

There's quiet, then. A brief silence as they both simply listen to the sea.

"I saw Jason's interview yesterday," Ted finally says. "On TV."

"Oh, Ted." Maris takes a long breath.

"It didn't seem to go well."

"No. It didn't. That's why I called you." She sips her coffee. "I'm worried about Jason, and you're my last hope."

"*I* am?"

Maris nods and hands Ted a slice of Danish and a napkin. "I was really surprised Jason went to see you last week. And I wonder if he said anything. Something that might help me to understand what he's doing."

"First, let me clarify, Maris. I *called* Jason that Sunday morning. Thought we could take a walk together on the beach. To remember Neil on the ten-year anniversary of his passing. So Jason only came to Sea Spray because he was invited."

"I didn't know that."

159

Ted bites into his raspberry Danish. He nods while chewing. "And we did walk the beach. And talk."

"Was Jason mad? That you could tell?"

"Mad?" Ted shakes his head. "No."

"Upset?"

"No. More ... tired. He mentioned it had been a hard month. And that Neil's loss felt fresher this summer."

"It's true. He's been struggling with that recently."

"But it's when I asked about *you* that he opened up," Ted says then. "He said you were both taking a breather. That you needed space."

"Which he apparently decided by himself. His leaving was news to me, Ted, when I came home from grocery shopping that day."

"Now that couldn't have been easy for you."

"It wasn't. And truthfully? It still stings."

"I'm sure. I *sensed* something was wrong right away. And I also told Jason if he took a breather? The distance could be hard to bridge. To which he said that distance lets you see things more clearly. He didn't elaborate, but I wondered what, exactly, he needed to scrutinize."

"It's complicated," Maris says. She sips her coffee while looking out over the bluff at the blue sea. That deceptively peaceful sea that isn't speaking to her today. "Someone came to Stony Point and brought some unresolved baggage with him—which compounded matters for Jason."

Ted nods. "Jason mentioned that, but I didn't press him."

"So let me see if I have this straight. He *asked* to stay at

160

your summer beach house?"

"Oh, no. No. He said he was looking for a short-term rental, maybe a local motel, or a cottage. And I did *not* like the sound of that. For too many reasons, Maris—one being that *you* didn't need to worry about his whereabouts. So I *insisted* Jason stay."

"I had no idea." She takes that in. "Well ... that was really thoughtful of you, Ted."

"He argued at first, of course. Didn't want to impose. But I convinced him, seeing as he knows the ins and outs of my cottage. He's in a safe place there."

"He is. Jason thinks very highly of you, you know. So I'm sure he appreciated your offer. But what about your cruise? Will you be leaving soon? Because he also mentioned you'd be away on an anniversary trip, and that's why the cottage would be empty."

Ted sips his coffee, sets the cup on the table and stands. He walks closer to the edge of the bluff, then turns and looks her straight on. "I'm going to let you in on a personal secret."

"A secret?"

Ted nods. "There was no cruise, Maris. Oh, my wife and I went to a wedding, but that was only one weekend. Since then, we've been home—a few towns inland—and giving Jason use of the cottage."

"Are you kidding? But—"

Ted holds up his hand to stop her. "I lied on the spot to Jason because I didn't believe he'd stay otherwise—especially if he thought his presence was keeping me out of my own cottage. And I feared that could mean trouble for him, if he left."

"You might've been right."

"Listen." Ted, still standing there on the craggy bluff, turns up his hands, then wrings them. "Maris."

A pause, then. And a decisive breath—she sees it.

"I'll let you in on a little more," Ted tells her. "More of another secret that you should probably know. It could help you understand *my* actions."

"What is it, Ted? You sound serious."

"I am. And this is something I'd rather Jason *not* know. It'd be too much." Ted returns to the bench and leans forward, elbows on his knees. "So you'll keep it between us?" he asks over his shoulder.

"Of course."

Ted still leans forward, but now? Now he looks only at that calm sea as he talks. "The day of the accident? It's *no* secret that I had a heart attack at the wheel. But what I don't tell people is that for a few moments, I was *very* lucid. The few moments before the impact."

Maris doesn't move. Doesn't talk. She just sits there and listens. There's only the sound of water sloshing lightly on the bluff. A seagull cries in the distance.

And then, Ted's low voice again. "I knew. In the throes of it all, what I was about to hit was very clear. But the pain, it prevented me from ... well ... people think I blacked out, and that was why the collision happened. I didn't. It's just that this horrific pain in my chest took over ..."

Another long pause. Maris watches as Ted drops his face in

his hands. After a few quiet seconds, his back shudders with a muffled sob. Oh, how many times can a heart break? Ted's. Jason's. Her own. She reaches out and pats Ted's shoulder. And waits then, as the sea, the blue sea, meets her gaze.

Ted's, too. He eventually drags his hands down his face, wipes away his tears. They still come though—random tears, another shaking sob.

But Maris sees what happens next. As Ted looks at that serene sight of blue, it must speak to him. He knows its language then, too. It's obvious. Because the vastness of that sparkling blue water calms him. Stops his tears, his shuddering breath. Brings him back from some awful inner torment.

"I knew," he admits now.

And she knows just what it is Ted knew. But she silently listens as he tells of the private burden he carries.

"I saw the traffic light getting closer. Christ, it was *red*, Maris. And I was about to drive into that motorcycle stopped there," Ted says. "I saw the moment of impact. The explosion when my world—Jason's and Neil's world—spun off its axis."

"Ted. I'm so very sorry."

Ted sits back. His hands are loosely clasped in his lap. His chest rises with each breath. His eyes, they're hooded. "I know exactly what Jason experienced because I was in the thick of it," he says, his voice fatigued. "Which is why I'd do anything for him. *Anything.* Anytime. Even lie to him. Anything to keep Jason's world intact."

So now Maris has this: Ted's unbearable secret. That secret—which she's sure Jason is unaware of—must make Ted's *life* difficult to bear at times. He was *not* unconscious during the accident; he saw, felt, heard the entire collision.

Maris knows something else, too. She's never going to find a heart of gold bigger than Ted Sullivan's. Knowing that Ted and his generous heart are a part of Jason's life, it gives her what she'd prayed to get from Ted: some hope.

Enough hope to get her to her writing shack once she thanks Ted for stopping by, and after she promises to stay in touch with updates, and hugs him goodbye.

Approaching the old fishing shack, Maris can still picture where it was *before* Jason had it towed here: on that remote, untamed beach beyond the point—where dune grasses grow wild; where waves crash; where gulls swoop low on wind currents. The shack still holds some of that wildness in its faded silver shingles and chipped trim paint. Inside, the air's musty. It's been closed up for a few days, so she leaves the door open. Sunshine streams in, turning dust particles into spinning stardust over the waxed hardwood floor.

Maris stops and looks back outside toward the bluff and that calm blue sea—a sea *not* deceptively calm, after all. Today it seemed to be calm solely for one man. For Ted Sullivan. To help him through a few painfully re-lived minutes. Maris could cry for him as she crosses the shack's room, passing dusty jars of shells and sea glass on a small table; touching a salt-coated hurricane lantern on a shelf; turning the pewter hourglass to get the sand dropping to the lower bulb.

164

Finally, she sits at her work area. Some of Neil's manuscript is stacked beside her laptop. The pages are old and warped by the sea's close dampness. Behind Maris, outside that open shack door, the calm sea assures her now. She lifts the manuscript pages and flips to an early unfinished passage, then finds where she'd retyped it onto the computer. Yes, here it is. The part when one character watches a woman on the beach. There's some unresolved issue between them, building in intensity.

"Building right along with the storm," Maris says as she lifts her fingers and begins typing.

~

Standing on the deck, he watches the woman walk the beach. Beyond her, the seawater is surprisingly still; the waves, few. It's the sky that's actually warning them. Its yellowish-gray hue is ominous.

But the water? Glass.

So he has time to join her on the beach. He slips off his boat shoes, cuffs his shirtsleeves and hurries down the deck stairs.

"I saw the letter."

Those are the first and only words she says when he catches up with her. It takes her a moment, a few seconds of the two of them walking side by side and not speaking.

"On your dresser," she adds then.

"Meaning?" he asks as they walk along the driftline.

"I read it."

Her words get him to stop. The damp sand is cool beneath his bare feet. And Long Island Sound before him? It's as silent as he is while

165

watching her continue to walk along the shore.

"It wasn't meant for you," he calls to her. "That letter."

So she stops, too, and turns to him. She wears a beaded headband over her straight dark hair. A crochet vest hangs open over a pale blue tank top; a wide leather belt is buckled over her low-slung jeans. And her eyes? They brim with tears.

"I read it anyway." She steps closer, brushing a wisp of hair from her face. "What are you going to do?" she whispers.

He shakes his head. Looks away, out at that steel-still sea. At that strange-colored sky. And back at her. His foot kicks at the sand. "I'm going."

"What?" she asks. Her face drops. And those tears still press at her eyes.

"It's not what you're thinking." He steps closer.

Just then, before he can say more, cold seawater sloshes over his bare feet. Even his jeans get soaked. So he jumps back when he sees that a sudden wave rolled in. Or more like a swell. Noiselessly, the crestless wave unfurled and reached far onto the beach. So he quickly looks out at the Sound. What he sees now is as ominous as the sky. Well spaced-out swells approach shore—silently—as though rolling in for a sneak attack. Oh, the sea's held that secret well.

But it's out now, its secret. And there's no stopping what's to come. Those ominous swells leave an odd feeling in the pit of his stomach.

"Look." He nods to the sea. "Hurricane's coming. Won't be long now."

～

Maris glances over at the pewter hourglass. The sand grains still fall. Several minutes are left, enough time to finally close out this unfinished early passage of Neil's.

And so, ever aware of that telltale sea beyond the bluff, she continues to type.

eighteen

Late Tuesday Morning

IT DOESN'T HAPPEN OFTEN, BUT sometimes life stops you in your tracks. Stops you and changes everything. Oh, doesn't Celia know it. Things happen that take your familiar days and flip them. Turn them on edge so that you lose your footing, good or bad. Good? Having sweet Aria in her life. As good as it gets, most definitely. Celia regained her footing after that pregnancy and her life's all the richer for it. Bad? Losing Sal. That one ... as dark as it gets. Her life was not only turned on its edge, but sent spinning, too. It took a long time to recover her balance. But she did. Life has been relatively smooth sailing lately.

And now, this. Life stopping her in her tracks at the very moment she pulls a letter out of her mailbox.

A letter from Shane Bradford.

Standing there in the bright sunshine, she flips the envelope from front to back to front. Her fingers slide

168

across the handwriting spelling out her name, her address. At the same time, Aria fusses in her stroller. Celia had taken her for a long walk after Kyle's boardwalk meeting, and the baby is ready for her late-morning nap now. Lifting Aria out of the stroller, Celia looks from her daughter to that darn envelope she also holds.

Actually, she's not even sure she *wants* to open it. To read whatever words Shane penned to her.

Not sure she wants to know whatever message he sealed in a small, plain envelope and somehow sent state-through-state down the coast.

What would be the point? He's there. She's here. He's out on the Atlantic Ocean. She's living in a gingerbread cottage behind a beach inn—hundreds of miles away.

So open the envelope? Or toss it?

Her mind is made up when she turns the key in the door and steps inside her cottage. Because that's when she realizes she hasn't stopped smiling. Not for one second since reading Shane's name on the return address.

Okay, so open the envelope she will.

But the moment has to be just right—quiet, with no distractions. A moment when she can almost *hear* Shane's voice saying the words as he wrote them.

So first things first. After dropping the envelope and her tote in the kitchen, she takes Aria to her room and changes her diaper. All the while Celia whispers sweet nothings, telling Aria that they'll read a book later. And asking the baby if she hears the buzz of cicadas outside. Afterward, she holds Aria close and rocks her for a few minutes. Her daughter loves this routine, one when Celia hums a lullaby and leaves a kiss or two on her soft cheek. Once she settles Aria in her crib, she bends close, whispering, "*Sweet dreams, love.*" Still the baby's drowsy eyes watch her; her tiny fisted hands move. So Celia winds up her music box, then goes to the window. She tinkles the seashell wind chime hanging there, draws the shade and tiptoes out of the room.

Okay, there's another order of business waiting, too. Back in the kitchen, Celia grabs her cell phone from her tote. Sitting at the table, she texts Elsa.

Putting Aria in for morning nap. Will be there after lunch to set out rooms' hospitality baskets?

It doesn't take long for Elsa to answer—she's so good about getting right back to her when it comes to the inn's opening. Celia reads the return text.

Come by a little later on. Have surprising number of business calls to make first.

Perfect. This'll give Celia some uninterrupted time. Time enough to open one particular letter from Maine—a letter somehow sent from a lobster boat.

But when she takes that letter with her to the living room, it's with some trepidation now—smile faded. She's actually a little afraid of what she's about to read. Funny how as she sits on the sofa and holds the envelope, it feels like all six-feet of a particular lobsterman is standing in the room, leaning on the doorjamb. Oh, she can just imagine Shane—arms crossed, tattoos covering his skin, newsboy cap tipped low—daring her to open that envelope.

Quickly then, she slips her finger beneath the flap and

does just that. Opens the damn envelope. What she notices right away is how short the letter is. It only fills half a notepad page. She looks at the slant of Shane's distinct cursive and reads the first line.

I saw you, Celia.

Instantly, her hand holding the letter drops in her lap. Her eyes fill with surprising tears, too. *My secret's out*, she thinks. *He knows I was in Maine.*

Then she reads more.

On the docks. You and Aria standing there in the sunlight. Really sorry I missed you, but glad you came. Hope you're both okay, too.

Talk soon—
Shane

And yep, sitting in her cozy cottage and holding one little note in her hand, there it goes again—life takes her day and flips it. Flips it but good.

Or, this time, Shane Bradford flips it.

nineteen

Late Tuesday Afternoon

YOU LET ME KNOW IF you have any questions. Or want to adjust the designs," Jason tells his clients. The couple stands with him in the front yard of their shotgun-style cottage at White Sands Beach. Normally he'd review their preliminary drawings at his barn studio, where he'd engage the software on his large desktop computer to illustrate his vision. Where his clients can study the massive framed photographs of Barlow Architecture's completed beach cottages. Those pictures hang illuminated on the wall—like his own personal renovation gallery.

But Maris has made it known that unless he's *living* at home, his studio is off-limits, too. Oh, he reads her loud and clear. Since *he* left, he can also deal with the fallout.

So for the past hour, Jason walked his clients through their partially-demo'd cottage. He unrolled blueprints on their kitchen table. He pointed out architectural details on his work tablet. The couple's aesthetic preferences were also noted, as were budget parameters.

Standing outside the cottage's front door now, Jason advises them, "It's a helluva lot easier to make any changes at this stage, before plans are finalized." He shakes their hands then, saying, "So study the renderings, top to bottom. Next time we'll select materials. Windows, doors, fixtures. The works."

After getting in his SUV, he gives another look at the tired cottage. Its brown wood siding is tinged black from the damp sea air. Exposed wood shows through streaks of paint on the trim of the tall front window, and a shutter hangs loose. One thing's for certain. This cottage will be unrecognizable when he's through with it.

As he drives off, Jason wonders exactly how many cottages he's worked on over the years. How many bungalows, shanties, Nantucket-styles have transformed beneath his architectural pen? Have taken new shape with added gables and lofts and peaks? How many beach homes has he renovated, updated and fixed over time?

Right now, though, it doesn't really matter. Not as he's about to see Maris. No, right now? She's all that matters. Because if he doesn't fix his very *life*—never mind the cottages—he knows.

He knows he'll lose her.

⌒

Okay, so Celia's not one to lie. And she *didn't* lie. After spending the afternoon helping Elsa set out hospitality baskets for this weekend's inn guests, Celia did something else. First, she asked Elsa to babysit Aria. Then, when Elsa asked her where she had to go, Celia didn't lie. She merely circled around the truth.

That's right, the truth. Celia said there was something she needed to mail at the post office today. Truth, all truth.

The part of the truth she circled around and did *not* reveal was that she had to mail a letter back to Shane Bradford, right away. Because there's just no room in her life for indecision. For toying with possibilities. For attempting a long-distance relationship. Celia needs calm seas, both for herself and for her infant daughter. Especially now, with the inn about to open and fill her days to the brim.

Oh, if ever Celia imagined her late-summer days as a movie, she supposes one title would do: *The Nowhere Affair.* Because that's where her time with a tenacious lobsterman led—nowhere. Why think otherwise? Best to put the brakes on any more life upheavals. Heart upheavals, too. She's had more than her fair share in the past year alone.

Another truth? She hasn't even written Shane's return-letter yet. So on the way out Elsa's door, Celia grabs inn stationery and an envelope from the reception desk. By the time she drives to the post office, she's sort of thought out her words, her kind tone. Because the last thing she wants to do, regardless, is let Shane down, or hurt him in any way.

The problem now is that it's late, and it's important her letter go out in today's mail. It'll put an end to things before they even get started. Sitting in the post office parking lot, she checks her watch. She has only minutes to write, address, seal and stamp the message that will sadly—yes, sadly—close a door. Close a door on Shane's, *Talk soon.*

Sadly … because wouldn't she just love to talk soon? Wouldn't she love to take a long beach walk and listen to Shane's voice beside her? But what's the point? It wouldn't be fair to either of them.

Oh, sometimes doing the right thing just isn't easy. She knows that for sure as she puts pen to paper while sitting in the car. With a few jotted lines, she tries, *tries*, to lightly brush off any connection between her and this lobsterman suddenly in her life. Tries to suggest they simply got caught up in a moment these past two weeks.

With only minutes to spare then, Celia seals the envelope and rushes into the post office for a stamp. What's surprising, though, as she puts the stamp on the envelope, is this: her heavy heart. Suddenly uncertain about the words she's sending north to a mailbox on the Maine docks, she doesn't leave her letter with the postal clerk at the counter. Instead she brings it outside.

And right there on the sidewalk, in the late-afternoon sunshine, she takes a long breath while holding that letter close.

Her note, yes, it's filled with the truth. All truth. She penned no lies to Shane. Which isn't to say she didn't circle around some deeply personal truths kept private. Truths about how regretful she *really* feels sending this letter. About how difficult it is. About how Shane makes her smile. He just does.

175

And oh, she also circled around some truthful *if onlys*. If only their situation were different. Their addresses closer. How sweet the rest of this summer might've been.

But that's not the case, and so—still holding the envelope—Celia knows one more truth. This is for the best, this clean break.

Damn it, she thinks while swiping at sudden tears. Then she opens the mailbox outside the post office and drops Shane's secret letter inside.

⁓

Their first married *date* is an hour—and Jason's nervous. Because he's not sure he and Maris technically ever even dated. A few years ago when they reconnected, it was more like they just fell into step with each other. Beach friends for all their lives, they were suddenly … a couple. And living together. So he's pretty darn rusty at all this dating stuff.

Which is why, fifteen minutes later, he's standing, confused, inside Maritime Market. He'd walked right past the farmers' market tents outside. No prepared meals there—just fruits and vegetables. Now he glances into the store's skylight café, where folks are sipping iced organic coffee and nibbling on raw banana ice cream or vegan pudding. Nope, nothing there, either. So he ventures past to the take-out aisle.

And hits the jackpot.

But he has to hurry. A small crowd peruses several

ready-packed picnic baskets. It's no wonder, too. In this heat wave, no one wants to cook. The baskets are flying off the shelf. So Jason manages a quick look. Pickings are slim, though, forcing him to think fast. One basket's label reads *Table for Two*—which sounds nice for his date. Inside the picnic basket are two flatbread chicken sandwiches with pesto-mayo and provolone cheese, a container of organic potato salad, two locally grown peaches and even dessert— slices of cheesecake with strawberry topping on the side. Plates and cups are included; plasticware is wrapped in paper napkins; there's even a red-and-white checked cloth to set out on a picnic table.

"Perfect," Jason says to himself.

After paying, he walks out into the hot summer evening—basket hooked on his arm—and plans one more stop for a bottle of wine to sip, dockside.

twenty

Tuesday Evening

NEAR THE NEW LONDON DOCKS, Maris spots Jason right away. He's at a picnic table on a small grassy area. The table is in the shade of a maple tree on a gently sloping hill. Beyond, tall green reeds edge the bay where the narrow docks reach out into the water. The docks are old, their planked wood gray with age and sea-damp. Maris hasn't been here for years.

But today's different from years ago.

Today, it's do or die.

Today's intent is for her and Jason to find their way back to each other. From a distance, she watches him. He's dressed casual in a short-sleeve chambray shirt over dark shorts and is lifting plates out of what looks like a picnic basket. He sets the plates down and scrutinizes them. Quickly he repositions them, putting one plate on either side of the table so that they'll eat facing each other. Next,

178

he stops. Looks out at the water view. Leans to the right. Then looks at the dishes again, moving one back to *his* side of the table so that they'll sit side by side instead.

Maris can't help but briefly smile. Yes, they're that kind of couple—always by each other's side. Side by side on the Stony Point boardwalk with morning coffee. Side by side beneath their beach umbrella. Even on their very first date three years ago at a take-out seafood joint on the Sound, they were at each other's side. They leaned on a railing after dinner and looked out at the dark waters. She remembers Jason telling her that night that there's nothing like being at the water to put life into perspective.

If only, Maris thinks.

Now, Jason's sitting at the picnic table. His back is to her as he arranges plastic forks and knives, then looks out at the scenic view. She does, too. At this dusky hour, a few sailboats and some lobster boats dot the harbor. The view has a pastel feel to it, all soft and smudged around the edges.

Finally, she approaches Jason from behind. After a brief hesitation, she quietly sits beside him at that one little table and gives his hand a squeeze.

∽

"Maris." Jason holds her hand for a long second, then reaches for the cups in the basket. He sets them down and pauses before fussing with the plastic forks and knives. "I don't really know how to do this."

"Do what?"

"Date. Having a hard time, actually."

"Well." Maris slides her fork closer. "I guess we start a date with small talk?"

"Small talk." Jason pulls the wrapped flatbread sandwiches and potato salad from the basket. One sandwich on her plate, one on his. "Okay," he says. Meanwhile, Maris is opening the lid on the potato salad container. "So, I'm working on something different, a new project. Just came from there."

"Which one is it?" she asks.

"That little shotgun cottage over at White Sands."

"Didn't you recently sign it on?"

"I did. But it's a challenge meeting some of the clients' requests, with the way the rooms are stacked back to back."

Maris only nods as she unwraps her sandwich and sets it on her plate.

"I saw Mitch earlier, too," Jason tells her. "I guess he gave Elsa a tour of his cottage yesterday. And he thought you might also like to take a look at it." Jason unwraps his own sandwich. "You know. To help you with writing Neil's novel. Kind of like research."

"Sure."

"If you see it in its current condition—before the reno—maybe you can bring some original details to the book." When she says nothing, Jason bites into his sandwich while looking out at the harbor. A few boats are moored to the old wooden docks. The water is calm, its slight ripples hardly moving. "Give him a call."

"I will." Maris scoops a spoonful of potato salad onto

her plate. "So ... I saw your interview on TV yesterday."

Jason takes the potato salad spoon and helps himself to a hefty scoop. "I figured as much," he says. "It wasn't an easy talk."

"No."

"Never saw some things coming."

"I was actually at Eva's and had to leave once you choked up. It was painful to watch, Jason," Maris says as she eats a forkful of the potato salad.

"I probably should've cancelled."

"Cancelled?"

"Yeah. I've been exhausted lately—mentally, physically. Hell, with Shane rolling into town, and Kyle's tanked vow renewal. Our own marriage issues. Not to mention the show's gone into high gear with a media blitz *and* with demo on the Fenwick property about to begin. Was way off my game in that interview."

"You feeling better now?" Maris asks.

He slightly nods, chewing a mouthful of sandwich. "Eh, you know. But afterward? Thought for sure I lost my job hosting *Castaway Cottage*. That the station would just pull me from the show." As he talks, Jason notices the horizon fading to violet over the harbor. "The interview was a train wreck, and I blew it." He pauses, shakes his head and whispers, "*Shit*."

"What did Trent say?"

"Trent?" Jason reaches for the bottle of wine and pours some into their cups. "He loved it."

"He *did*?"

181

"Yep. Thought the Q and A was raw. Painful, even. And that, get this, viewers eat up all that drama."

"No way!"

"Oh, yeah. He said the whole thing was great for ratings—at my expense."

Maris shakes her head with a small smile, then sips her wine. "That's Trent for you. He says it like it is. And you *know* he really respects you, always taking you at face value."

Jason does know that. Trent's never asked him to change his ways. Not once.

Neither has Maris. She's always taken him at face value, too—his leg issues; his occasional nightmares; flashbacks; some emotional swings. So a lot is riding on this date, because Jason *doesn't* want to lose her. The thought of that has kept him up plenty of nights recently. He drags a knuckle along his whiskered jaw. It's quiet between them now as Maris eats her sandwich and looks out at the harbor. He does, too. A couple of lobster boats are docked there. And a few cabin cruisers, further out.

But between Maris and himself? Silence, and not the easy kind.

〜

"Honestly, I'm surprised you wanted to meet *here*." It's the only thing Maris can think to say, breaking some sudden silence between them. "Especially with my history with Shane at these very docks."

"Which I'm accepting, Maris, by being here. I really am."

"And I'm glad for that," she says, moving her plate aside.

"Speaking of Shane." Jason takes a swallow of wine. "How about Kyle's talk this morning?"

"On the boardwalk?"

Jason nods.

"What'd you make of it?" Maris asks.

"I don't know." Jason drags the last of his sandwich through what's left of the potato salad. "I guess nobody knew what to make of it, the way things fell apart at the end."

"But it's sad, really. The two brothers, separated all this time?"

"And it was for nothing, that's the worst part." Jason finishes off the rest of his sandwich then. "It sucks, actually," he says while chewing.

"You going to talk to Kyle about it?"

"Eventually." Jason wipes his mouth with a napkin. "But tonight, I'm here to talk to you."

"About me and Shane? That's why you picked this spot?"

He shakes his head. "No. Asking you here, to the docks? It's about meeting the girl you described to me Sunday at Bella's."

Maris sips her wine. "I'm listening."

"That college girl you told me about? Embroidering on denim right here? She seemed to be someone I'd never met. She sounded ... new to me." Jason lifts a small, insulated container out of the picnic basket. He opens it and sets out two slices of cheesecake. "So tell me something about

183

yourself," he says while spooning strawberry sauce on her slice.

"What?"

"Tell me about that girl. The one who spent hours sitting in this very spot."

She's quiet at first, trying to grasp what's happening between them—this first-date introduction. While Jason drizzles sauce on his cheesecake, Maris samples hers. After a mouthful, she begins. "I used to sketch, it's true. Right here. And sometimes sitting on the docks down there. Waiting for Shane."

Jason nods while forking off a hunk of cheesecake. "Denim sketching?"

"Kind of, in an early form for my own designs. Using pastels, or charcoal, I'd pose sketched figures near the water. On the dock. Aboard a boat."

"Tell me more."

"Well, I wore a straw cowboy hat against the sun, like I still do. And the drawings just flowed right out of my hand. Lobstermen coiling rope on these very docks were channeled in rope accents I'd bring to my blue jean sketches—in a side stripe, maybe. Or at the hem."

"Inspired by the view, then? The salt water?"

"Not exactly. Here it was the sounds that did it for me."

"Sounds?"

"The bell buoy. Seagulls. The creaking docked boats. It was all a soundtrack to my fashion sketches. My background music, I guess, that would get me in such a creative zone."

"I never knew that."

"Well ... now you do."

And that's how it goes. They finish their dessert and have another glass of wine. The sun sets beyond the harbor. The slightest crescent moon hangs low in the twilight sky as the two of them sit side by side at a hillside table overlooking the docks.

～

Jason listens. That's all, just listens and gets to know this girl all over again. Learns more about what she thinks and feels, all as stars begin to shine in the darkening sky.

In a quiet moment, Maris brushes the mottled bruise on his forearm. "This isn't getting any better?"

"No. It'll take time." He doesn't let on that it's still painful to the touch, or that his fall from bed last week still frightens him.

"Maybe you should put something on it."

"I'll be all right," Jason tells her. He reaches over, picking up their plates and wrappers and plasticware.

Maris helps, too, folding the tablecloth and gathering empty food containers until their picnic basket is all packed up again. "Okay, then." She pulls her keys out of her shoulder bag. "Well," she says, jangling those keys with a glance toward her car. "This was a good idea. This date."

"Wait. Before you leave." Jason hooks the basket on his arm and looks out at the night harbor. Lights shine on some of the boats now. Copper dock lamps mounted on wood pilings illuminate the planked walkways.

He does something else, too. For the first time tonight, he really looks at Maris. At her dark silky hair, tucked behind an ear. At her white breezy open-stitch sweater, flowy over a navy tank top and cropped skinnies—tie-dyed at the frayed hem. At her long necklace of white stones and beads. Pure Maris. Any other time—a month ago, a year ago—they'd walk to the docks right about now. Sit on the edge of one and dangle their feet over the water. Whisper. Kiss.

"Listen," Jason says instead of all that. "Since we're getting to know each other again, there's something I want to show you. Because there's a side of me *you* don't know, either."

"Are you serious?" Maris asks, lifting her purse.

"I am." Carrying the picnic basket, he starts across the grassy area and heads toward his SUV. "Come on," he says over his shoulder.

"Where are we headed?" Maris calls after him.

"You'll see."

"Jason!"

He stops and waits for her to catch up. Reaches out and touches a loose wisp of her hair. "*It's a secret,*" he whispers.

twenty-one

Ten Minutes Later

NEVER BEFORE HAS JASON FELT this way, driving to Stony Point. Anxious. Uneasy. A little sick. That's how bleak—maybe even lonely—his secret feels.

He opens his window for a breath of salt air, but it doesn't do any good. He glances in the rearview mirror, too. Maris still follows behind his SUV.

Was this right, he thinks, *doing this?* There's no telling what she'll say. How she'll react. If she'll understand.

Driving the winding Shore Road, Jason tries to put it all out of his head.

Late-evening shadows grow long beneath the dusky sky. But just beyond the bend, he can still make out the railroad trestle. He turns beneath it, barely waves to the guard on duty and takes the first right. It's a street unsuited to the beach community. The dead-end road seems like it belongs in a campground, or lake area, with its pine trees and

187

winding rock walls. The train track embankment runs along a portion of the street. Wild brush grows beside parts of the road. Some of the homes are dark timber, with long front-porch overhangs. Lichen-covered boulders hulk on front lawns. Other than the salt air, there's little sense of the sea on this street.

Jason parks in front of a tiny cottage at the far end of the road. The cottage is lost among overgrown trees and shrubs. Raw wood shows through the peeling paint. The windows are cloudy with dust and salt from the beach air. He sits there until a car's headlights approach behind him. When the car door opens and Maris gets out, so does he.

"Jason?" she asks, walking along the gritty road. "Your secret's *here*? At Stony Point?"

He leans against his SUV and nods to the dilapidated cottage. "Right there," he says.

"*What?*"

"It's a lot to take in, I know. But let me explain."

He watches as Maris can't seem to help it, the way she steps onto the weedy front yard. She brushes aside tall grasses before veering onto a stone walkway—the stones broken, or missing, or unevenly tipped. Which is where she stops.

Jason catches up to her there. "It was the end of a hot day, ten summers ago," he tells Maris in the fading light. What he wants to do is reach out for her hand as he talks, but he can't. Instead, he crosses his arms over his chest. "After drawing plans that morning, I'd spent hours helping Neil at a small reno job we'd taken on—redoing a leaning cottage porch. My jeans were dusty, my boots caked with dirt from crawling beneath that porch all afternoon. The posts needed to be checked there for insect damage or any rotting. So I was tired and had little patience for more work. Which it seemed Neil was lining up, after hauling me here on our way home that evening."

Jason quiets as Maris glances at him, then right back at the old cottage in front of them.

"I looked at this very building—this one-story shanty," he continues, hitching his head toward the shadowed cottage. "At its two small peaks over the front porch, and the added room giving the cottage its L-shape. Honestly, I thought it seemed ready for the wrecking ball."

"And Neil didn't?"

"You got it. The old place hadn't seen a coat of paint in ages, and some of the window glass was shattered. Then there was the faded life ring," he says, pointing to it still hanging on the front wood siding. "That life ring seemed a cry for help to save the abandoned cottage."

"Abandoned? I don't understand. Wasn't this for a client?" In the near darkness, she turns to him. "Should we even be here? It's private property."

"The owner won't mind, Maris."

"What *is* this place?"

They're the same words Jason once asked, with the same disbelief. Her wonder is the same wonder *he* felt when he first laid eyes on this cottage.

The day was warm, like this one.

Jason was tired then, like he is today.

But instead of Maris standing beside him, Neil did.

Neil—with *his* arms crossed—nodding to the same run-down cottage while motioning for Jason to have a look.

He tells Maris all that now.

~

"What is this place?" I asked my brother beside me.

"Don't say anything, Jay. Just hear me out."

"This better be good because I'm beat. Need to take a shower and eat some dinner."

Neil walked across the dried-out front lawn. Work gloves hung from the back pocket of his jeans. The stubby grass snapped beneath his construction boots. Halfway to the front door, he stopped and looked at me. "This is our next project."

"What?" I walked over that crappy lawn. Taking things in, I noted the missing pavers in the walkway. Piles of dried leaves accumulated beneath shrubs. Neglected tree branches swept along the roof. There was a broken birdbath in the yard, and spiderwebs dangling from the cottage eaves. "We're booked already, Neil. Busy enough," I said, waving off the dump.

"Come on, we can fit in one more job. We'll put in time on the weekends. Some evenings."

"But it's a foreclosure. Didn't you see the sign? It's bank-owned, and the bank sure as hell won't hire us to remodel. Let's go," I said, turning back to our pickup truck. "Nothing for us to do here."

"Yes, there is." Neil was standing at a window with his hands cupped to the foggy glass. He didn't say another word until I looked over my shoulder at him. "Flip it."

"Flip it?"

"Hell, yeah."

"You're crazy."

"No, I'm not." Neil beckoned me closer. His wavy hair was a mess; his tee, soiled; and his voice, excited. "Think about it, Jay."

"We don't do flips."

"Until now."

I scrutinized the cottage again. "It's too much. This place is shot."

"Listen. I've been researching them. Flips. We'll make some quick cash so we can finally get that studio you need. How long do you really want to work out of Mom and Dad's house?"

"Point taken." I walked closer and looked through another window. The room inside was shadowy, making the details obscure. I stepped back then and eyed the outside walls. "But we don't have enough cash to buy this property."

"We'll get financing, or maybe Dad will front us some dough." Neil joined me and studied the cottage, too. "No one will want this place," he said. "So it'll be a steal."

"Because it's blight."

But still, Neil hooked me already. I wandered around to the backyard. There was a patio. And a back porch looked tacked on without a permit.

"You want Barlow Architecture to be taken seriously? To be legit? You need a studio, man," Neil said, coming up behind me. "Don't need to be talking business with clients on our side porch anymore."

I shook my head. This cottage was one of the worst I'd seen. "The land's worth more than the building."

"No. No, it isn't. Those walls hold a lot of history. There are plenty of rough-hewn oak planks inside. And look at the fish-scale

191

trim over the windows. I mean, the cottage tells a story, Jay."

"What I'm checking out is the foundation. Is it really stacks of bricks?"

"And Dad's a mason. He'll help us get a new foundation in."

We circled the cottage as the sun set. Neil tossed around ideas that might draw out the character of the place.

Save the wood siding.

Sand it, restore it.

I jumped in with my own thoughts.

Make the back porch an open-air dining space.

Everything we said as we walked across the dried lawn, and brushed aside weeds, and squinted into dirty windows, gave the cottage new life already.

"I don't know, Neil. Our schedule's jam-packed."

"Listen, Jay. We'll do the work ourselves. You and I'll swing sledgehammers and get the demo done. Some of my crew will pitch in. And we'll do it fast—flip it. Sell it. Turn a nice profit. Get that studio and make a name for ourselves. Actually have space for a big old drafting table for you, a workshop for me. The auction's in a few days," *Neil said while straightening a loose piece of siding.* *"Come on, bro."* *He turned to me then.* *"Let's do it."*

~

"And we did," Jason says over his shoulder as he shines a mega flashlight and unlocks the front door. "My brother convinced me and we bought this place." He shoulders open the sticking door and walks inside, swiping away dust and cobwebs.

192

Maris follows behind him. The cottage is as raw as can be. It's old and damp. Dust is everywhere. The windows are filthy. Plywood covers broken panes. Jason shines the flashlight because the electricity has been shut off. Everywhere that flashlight beam lands, Maris sees his and Neil's story. There are two sledgehammers leaning against a wall stripped to the studs. Wood trim remnants, broken drywall pieces—rusted pipes, even—spill from big buckets. An old leather tool belt hangs from a random hook on the wall. The clips and belt pouches are filled with well-worn wrenches and a dusty hammer and nail puller and pliers and stubby pencils and matted work gloves—all of it untouched for a decade. In the dust floating in the low slant of that flashlight beam, it's like she's seeing the spirits of that summer Jason talks about.

"You *kept* this?" she asks.

"You kept Shane's engagement ring. I kept this old cottage."

She glances at him, and at the way he says this matter-of-fact. There's no anger, no antagonism. Just the truth of it. "This place is really *yours*?"

"It is."

"But … what are you *doing* with it, Jason?"

"Nothing."

"Nothing?"

"Neil and I got as far as the demolition when the accident happened." Jason shines the beam of light across the shadowed front room. There are dark rafters above and scraps of wood on the floor. A few thick wires dangle from the ceiling. The musty air hangs so thick, you can almost taste the dust.

"But Jason, you left it … like *this*?"

"At the time, I was missing half a leg. Months of physical therapy were ahead of me. My whole life—it stopped."

"But not forever."

"It seemed it to me."

Maris squints into the shadows. In the corner, torn-down drywall pieces are stacked in a pile. A bucket is flipped upside down near rotten trim molding leaning against the wall.

"After the accident? When I was in a bad way?" Leaving the front door open for ventilation, Jason walks across what must have once been a living room. "My father brought me here in my wheelchair—before I was even fitted with a prosthesis. He tried to help me. To nudge me to keep living, I'm sure." Jason's voice is low and a little hoarse. "He wanted to motivate me to get up in the mornings. I see that now. So he offered to work with me on this. *Anything*. Anything to keep me going."

"Oh, Jason." Maris sits on that overturned bucket and looks at the destruction around her in this tiny cottage. It mirrors the destruction of his life back then.

"Dad finagled my wheelchair inside and gave me a piece of his mind, actually," Jason goes on. He walks to a window and glances outdoors, then turns to her. "Said fixing up this place would be a better form of rehab than what I was headed to. So do you know what I did? Waved him off.

Then I wheeled myself through some of these rooms. It was quiet, I remember. Dead quiet. Just the sound of my wheelchair running over the debris. When I came back to this room here," he says, shining a beam of light across the gutted living room, "Dad was standing right there. At the fireplace. Told me if I wouldn't finish the job, put the cottage on the market for someone else to handle." Jason walks to the fireplace and brushes a hand across the dusty mantel. "I told him no. *Not happening, Dad.* My exact words, I never forgot them."

When Jason walks around the small room now, his feet crunch over the debris littering the floor. There's anxiety—maybe anger—in his movements, in the way he sets the illuminated flashlight on the mantel. The way he lifts a sledgehammer. The way he hefts it in both hands. The way he paces.

And Maris sees it—sees how this place brought him back a decade in time. He's there now. With his father.

"Dad? He was fed up with me that day. Tossed up his hands and walked out. But I couldn't. Couldn't walk. Couldn't get myself out through the doorway by myself, either. I had to wait for my father to come back in. So I sat in my wheelchair, right there," Jason says, nodding to a doorway in the far wall, "and heard all Neil's plans in my head. *After this flip, we'll buy a small place. An office with a studio. A workshop out back. We'll be legit, man.* Shit, he was so pumped." Slightly swinging that sledgehammer's long handle, Jason taps the steel head against a wood stud. "And sitting there alone, it was like Neil was back. Like I had my brother back only weeks after he died. His voice echoed off the stripped walls. The bare floors. Echoed in my thoughts. With my father outside, oh, ghosts were everywhere in this space." Jason looks around the room. "I heard echoes of Neil's laugh. Of our arguments."

"Wait," Maris says. "Arguments?"

Jason sets down the sledgehammer. "We didn't just swing hammers demo-ing this hotbox. We swung words, too. I did *not* support Neil seeing Lauren. She was engaged to Kyle, for Christ's sake. And we went at it in here."

After a long pause, Jason grabs the flashlight from the mantel. He's quieted, Maris notices, and doesn't say much more. He just walks to the still-open front door and waits for her as she gives a last look inside before leaving, too.

"Ten years have gone by," Jason says while locking the door. "This place has been empty all that time." He walks with her across the front yard.

"I always thought this was an abandoned property," Maris tells him. "Long forgotten by someone. Passed down through some family, maybe."

"No. It's mine. I stop by every so often. Open a window, air it out." He shines the flashlight on the uneven walkway. "So that's my secret. This cottage. Maybe some day," he says, looking over his shoulder at the old place, "I don't know …"

Maris turns then. She looks at the dilapidated cottage that she'd never guessed belonged to her husband. "Why didn't you ever tell me?"

He just shakes his head, seeming unable to find the

words. All the while, she takes in the sad cottage. There's something heartbreaking about its apparent neglect, making it hard to look away.

"Well," Jason says beside her. "I have to get going, Maris. Early day tomorrow."

"Okay. But listen ..." She's distracted, still drawn to that little run-down shanty. "There's a bag of dog food at the house," she says while looking from the cottage to Jason. "Maddy's favorite. Come and get it?"

"All right. I'll pick it up now."

Maris walks to her car, stopping at the driver's door for one more squint through the shadows to that cottage. "Park on the street," she calls to Jason a moment later. "I left the dog food inside the front door."

～

The first thing Jason notices is the lantern light shining on his home's front porch. The black lantern's beside a pot of begonias on a round table. Lamplight shines from inside, too, casting a golden glow in the windows. He looks inside past the curtains, seeing the seascape painting on the faded wall, then looks to Maris when she comes out the front door.

"Whoa," Jason says, taking the bag of dog food from her. "You carried this out here? It's thirty pounds, Maris."

"I dragged it from the pantry. I'm pretty strong, you know."

"I do know," Jason tells her, setting down the bag. "Anyway ..." He clears his throat. "Thanks for seeing me tonight."

"Sure, Jason. It was nice."

He steps closer to her. After leaning in and leaving a hesitant kiss on her cheek, he moves back and looks long at her.

"What?" Maris asks.

"Well, I was just wondering." He puts his hands in his pockets. "Can I see you again?"

She hesitates before reaching out and touching his whiskered face. "Call me."

"Okay, good." He bends and lifts the dog food bag. "I will."

"Oh, and Jason? This stuff," she says, motioning between them. "This ... *dating*?"

He nods.

"No one else is to know, all right? It'll just be our secret."

"You got it," he says around the food bag.

He turns away then. The sun has set. The sky is dark. Crickets chirp. But before going down the porch stairs, he turns with a shred of hope when Maris calls him back.

"Before you go," she's saying while reaching in the doorway.

He watches. Maybe she'll ask him to stay. Or to come home. Or has an idea for their next date.

She doesn't.

Instead, she lifts out a bundle of clothes on hangers. "You didn't take too much to Ted's." She drops the short-sleeve button-downs, chinos and linen blazers into his one free arm.

"That's *it*? You're giving me clothes?"

198

She nods. "You'll be needing them, I'm sure. For work. You know," she says, patting that now-laden arm. She turns to go in, but turns back once more. "And give Maddy a scratch for me, okay?"

"Wait! That reminds me, Maris." Jason maneuvers the full load of clothes in his arms. "I *really* need her bed, too."

"What?"

"She's been sleeping on Ted's good couch and making a *mess* of it. All that fur, it's awful."

"You let her sleep on the sofa? Jason!"

"No. No, she sneaks there when I'm not around."

"Well, her bed is *just* as disgusting. You haven't cleaned it in ages! I can't have you bringing that nasty thing into Ted's beautiful cottage."

"But Maddy needs a bed. It'll keep her off the furniture."

"You'll have to buy her a nice new one, I guess."

Jason looks at Maris, seriously not believing she won't part with the dog's bed. But she won't; it's obvious by her now-crossed arms. She's calling the shots on this. So he nods and hoists up the mountain of clothes he holds.

"Goodnight, now," Maris tells him before stepping inside and closing the heavy wooden door behind her.

The door to *his* house, too.

Jason waits a second, then shifts the dog food bag against his hip and carefully walks to his SUV parked in the road. His feet step on twigs in the lawn—which needs a mowing. Shit, he's barely managing his life these days. And he barely manages holding onto everything, nearly dropping the dog food and clothes when he somehow gets his hand into his pocket. Pulling out his keys, he uses the remote to unlock the SUV's cargo door. Finally, he shoves in the thirty-pound bag of dog food. And when he fumbles with the half-falling closet of clothes draped over his other arm, Nick drives past in the Stony Point security cruiser. Jason can only nod to him while balancing his armload of wardrobe—feeling like his life is just as precariously balanced.

twenty-two

Tuesday Night

IN THE LOCAL DOLLAR STORE, garish ceiling lighting shines on rows of merchandise. Cliff wheels his shopping cart down one row after another. There are blue plastic plates, red polka-dot cups, purple jugs of laundry detergent, green bottles of soda. And yellow everywhere— yellow racks, yellow *Sale* signs hanging from the ceiling, yellow walls. In the pet row, he has one thought as he puts a disposable litter box and small cushioned cat bed in the cart: *This is so illegal.*

Yes, Cliff figures he'll be promptly busted if the Stony Point Board of Governors catches wind of this. Of a cat taking up residence in his illicit living quarters in the beach's business trailer. Oh, Cliff will be immediately kicked out and overthrown. And the previous commissioner, Lipkin? His son has been hankering to step into his father's old shoes—so he'll swoop right in and get that gold-stitched

COMMISSIONER cap on his own head.

No, Cliff thinks as he drops a feather jingle toy into his cart. *No, this is not how you maintain authority.*

At the checkout counter, he unloads his cat cargo.

"You got a cat?" the cashier asks around her snapping gum.

"A stray's been hanging around," Cliff says, giving the feather toy a shake. "Nobody's claimed it. I actually have a few flyers with me. Would you mind putting one up in the store window?" He lifts a folder from the cart and pulls out the printed flyers.

"Suppose I could," the cashier tells him while scanning the litter box price. After putting Cliff's items into his reusable shopping bag, she takes a *Found Cat* flyer from him. "Aw, what a cutie," she says of the white cat. "What's its name?"

"Don't know. She didn't have a collar or anything."

"Well, hopefully the kitty will find its rightful home."

Cliff leaves then, and walks through the parking lot with his cat supplies. He glances back just as the cashier hangs his flyer in the store window. You never know. Sometimes pets wander many miles. So maybe the flyer, with its photograph, will help that poor cat get back to its *rightful home*, as the cashier nicely put it.

But when Cliff gets in his car and turns on his headlights in the dark night, he has another thought. Especially when he glances back and sees that white cat picture plastered on the store's window. Problem is, with the way that darn feline's been eating him out of tuna, and napping behind the file cabinet, and batting around tiny pieces of paper, Cliff fears the cat already *did* find a rightful home. His!

⌒

Sitting on his front porch, Kyle notices the lights twinkling around the windows. He glances at Lauren painting her toenails on the little porch sofa. A lamp shines close as she leans over her bent knee and brushes on silver polish. He remembers how when they first looked at this house, before buying it, Lauren had one wish: to string tiny white lights around the porch windows at Christmastime. Minutes later, she'd amended her dream: *No, all the time,* she'd added.

And she made her own dream come true, switching on those lights practically every night since living here—no matter what.

How much of dreams coming true is just that—making it happen yourself. Lord knows, Kyle tried at his boardwalk meeting today. Tried to make his dream of peace among the friends and Shane come true. Hearing the waves lapping on the bay across the street, he takes a long breath of the misty night air. Maybe it still will.

"I emptied another moving box," he tells Lauren now. "We moved here in June, Ell, and the boxes stacked in the front room just don't end."

"I know. And I was hoping to turn that space into my art studio."

"Yeah. Me, too. One box at a time, I guess."

203

"What did you unpack?" Lauren asks while giving her nail polish bottle a shake.

"Car cleaning supplies. Wax, soap, sponges. I'd been looking for that box, and unloaded it all in the garage."

"Oh, good." She dabs the polish brush into the bottle. "But I don't know how many more waxes your truck will need. Maybe we can replace it soon?"

"We'll see. The a/c crapped out, and I'm hearing a funny clicking under the hood." Kyle clasps his hands behind his head and sits back in his wicker chair. The kids are asleep; crickets chirp; a train whistle blows as it nears on the tracks behind the house. This is the time of day when either nothing matters as you sit in your castle ... or everything matters and will keep you up all night.

In the quiet after the train blows past, a cell phone dings.

"Is that you? Or me?" Lauren asks while edging a nail with polish.

He picks up his phone from the end table. "Me. It's a text from Nick." Kyle's quiet while he reads the message. "Oh, man. I *knew* it."

"Knew what?"

"They're getting a divorce."

"Who is?"

"Jason and Maris."

"They are not!"

"From what Nick says?" Kyle flashes the phone screen in Lauren's direction. "After he took down the flag on the beach, he drove around on patrol. Saw Jason in front of his house. Says he was loaded down with *clothes*, Ell. Clothes *and* dog food."

"Really?" Lauren stretches out her arm to take the phone.

"Yep. What else can it mean except Jason's not coming back. Which means divorce, no?"

"Don't jump the gun, Kyle. It could mean *anything*."

Kyle takes his phone from her, saying under his breath, "Now I'll *never* sleep tonight. Everything matters today. *My truck. Shane. Unpacking. And now this.*"

"What are you talking about?"

"Nothing." He reads Nick's text again. Hoping for a different answer, Kyle types back, *Say it ain't so, Nicholas.*

~

Oh, life, life. Doesn't Maris' life somehow find its way onto the page? Especially if she's bothered by something.

Tonight, she is. Seeing Jason's secret cottage alarmed her. Saddened her, especially. And she doesn't know how else to process the ghosts, the shocking loneliness inside the walls of that dilapidated cottage.

So once Jason drives off after their date, she eventually goes out to her writing shack. There, she lights several dusty hurricane lanterns. They flicker beside her laptop, on the round table, and even in the propped-open doorway. Lanterns are everywhere. The golden light casts wavering shadows on the shack's white-painted wood walls, and on the shelf of duck decoys—bringing them oddly to life.

In the misty night then, she sits alone at her computer and begins typing a passage in DRIFTLINE. Grains of sand fall from the pewter hourglass' top bulb to the bottom. The creaking call of the katydids, rhythmic and repetitive, keeps pace with her clicking keyboard …

The cottage goes oddly quiet, right in the thick of the hurricane. Oh, the storm still blows outside. Crashing waves roll onto the beach. The sound of that roiling water comes right through these thin cottage walls. And the wind, it whistles. Does something else, too; he can tell. It's lifting shingles right off the house. Ripping them off so that those shingles fly against the boarded-up windows before veering out into the ether.

But there is a new quiet inside the house. The voices stopped. The talk and laughter of everyone downstairs had risen to his room—until now. Now there are no more shrieks of fear when thunder crashes. No more yells of surprise when some debris blows against the house. No more jokes; no more reminiscing as the friends reunite on this stormy weekend. They had such plans, too. There's food to be had, liquor to be drunk, music to be danced to, games to be played.

So the sudden silence is odd.

On his way downstairs to check out this new quiet—and to be sure everything is okay—he stops. Right there on the shadowed steps, he stops and warily sits himself down. What he's seeing looks a little eerie. You could think at first that they are ghosts, the people silently dancing in the living room. Candles are clustered on the hearth. A few flicker on the mantel, too, beside vases overflowing with wild beach flowers the women cut before the storm hit. So there is a fragrance wafting in the room. A subtle, sweet fragrance.

And ghosts.

Because those candles, they cast the friends in silhouette. Three couples are slow-dancing to the storm. Not to music—the power is out, after all. But that doesn't stop their storm-dance. Their bodies press close. One of the friends holds a drink in his hand that's draped around his girlfriend's back. Another couple slows their dance to the slightest sway as they deeply kiss in the dark shadows. Bare feet whisper across the hardwood floor. One of the guys must've ventured outside in the storm. His hair lies damp on his head; his sweatshirt hangs loose. Their bodies all move with a grace counter to the frightening chaos outside the cottage. A chaos almost beating it down with wind and water.

But inside? All's calm.

Sitting on the step, he watches through the staircase balusters. Six adults look like ghosts. He's sure some part of their dance will linger ever in the cottage. On stormy nights, might future residents catch a glimpse of a shadow waltzing past? The silent dancing is too powerful a sight to not leave some essence behind. The couples don't let up as they keep their feet shuffling, their faces pressed to shoulders as their bodies glide around the room.

As he watches, he takes in the space. The flickering candles at the fireplace. The hulking shadows of furniture that have been moved aside. The storm ghosts, swaying.

Which is when he sees her. She stands in the room's far doorway, watching too. And as if she senses his eyes on her, she looks at him sitting on the stairs then. But she doesn't move.

He does.

He silently goes down the stairs and circles around the room's perimeter. All the while, the wind whistles; seawater splashes on the

207

beach and washes beneath the raised cottage. The night is black, except for the candlelight. Finally, he stands near her. Stands there, tips his head and wordlessly opens his arms. She smiles, hesitating before taking her own quiet steps into those arms. When she does, he sweeps her into the candlelit room so that they become shadows as well.

And their storm-waltz begins. He holds her close, feeling wisps of her hair against his face in the darkness. Hearing softest whispers around them. They move in the silent, ethereal storm-dance, forever haunting the room with their own ghosts now, too.

Maris takes a long breath and sits back. The words, they just flowed from her fingertips. And she knows why. She gets up and stands in the shack's open doorway. The night is dark; the big maple tree in the yard an even darker silhouette. Beyond it, she can see Jason's massive framed photographs of finished renovations. The pictures hang, illuminated, in his barn studio and are visible through the wide double slider. They're grand—the cottages he's designed—breathtaking, stately … and done.

She looks out in that darkness toward the bluff. But what she *sees*—what she can't get out of her mind—is an abandoned shanty also in darkness right now. Overgrown trees and shrubs conceal it. A ruined walkway keeps life away. Windows are covered in plywood.

But the cottage still stands. God only knows what ghosts linger in its walls.

There's no denying they're there, though. Because for

Jason, *everything* from one tragic, hot summer day ten years ago is long gone.

The crash site was wiped clean soon after the accident.

The totaled motorcycle was junked.

And Neil? In a coffin six feet beneath the ground.

Everything from that day, gone.

Except for one thing.

All Jason has left of that summer is one utterly haunted shell of a beach cottage.

twenty-three

Early Wednesday Morning

Swell," MARIS SAYS TO HERSELF after sipping her orange juice the next morning. She can't tell if the juice is a little warm. So she opens the refrigerator and sets her palm on the orange juice carton. It *feels* cold, but cold enough? So is the refrigerator on the fritz now, too? Or is it just that it's been so unbearably hot out, the appliances can't keep up with the heat? Not taking any chances on spoiling her food, she bumps the fridge temp down a notch.

That's right, she thinks then. This is one of the reasons she needs Jason to stay away now—to pull off her secret kitchen reno. The one *anybody* would realize the second they walked into the tired old room. The dead giveaway? All the countertop and backsplash samples still strewn about, for one. She stands a honey-colored backsplash tile on her counter so that it leans against the wall behind it. The natural colors in the stone remind her of beach colors—

210

beige streaked with grays and creams. As she stands back for a better look, her cell phone rings.

"Hey, Cody," she says upon seeing her kitchen contractor's name on the caller ID. "I'm so glad you called."

"Good news, Maris. Your dumpster's being delivered next week. Right after that Stony Point Hammer Law lifts," he tells her. "Wanted to make you aware so you can plan."

"Excellent." And it *is*, she knows. But now a new worry nags at her. "Listen, Cody. Can you drop the dumpster way in the back? I don't want it visible from the street."

"Why not?" he asks before saying something to a worker nearby.

And Maris can just picture it. Cody must be calling from some job site, where he's getting his crew situated. He'll have on his tool belt and be holding a clipboard denoting the day's work. He's meticulous like that, and is one of Jason's top contractors. "Well, here's the thing, Cody. It's just that ... well, okay. This kitchen reno is a surprise for Jason. Yes ... a *surprise*," she lies. "He's away right now. You know, for the show," she adds, spinning out that lie even more. "He'll be gone for quite a while, actually, back and forth to CT-TV in Hartford, doing publicity stops ... and I want to surprise him when he gets back. But if any neighbors or our friends *see* that dumpster, they'll say something to him. You know how it is. Small beach community? Everybody talks."

"Okay. We'll be discreet," Cody says just as someone hammers a wall, or cabinet, or floor on the site. "Best we can, anyway."

"Um, well, if you can be *more* than discreet. It would really be best if you bring the dumpster up the driveway and around back. It's a little bit of a twisty turn, but it is possible. That way you can tuck the dumpster behind the deck."

"But I'm not sure we can maneuver that thing up there—"

"Oh, you *have* to. I mean ... it'll be better behind the house, because you can just throw the kitchen demo debris right off the deck into the dumpster below!"

"Got it." The beeping sound of a truck backing up comes through the phone then. "So we're good here?"

"Wait! There's just one more thing." Maris walks to the kitchen slider and looks out to the backyard. The lawn is getting high with Jason away.

"Name it, Maris. Your husband's pulled a few strings for me in the past, so happy to oblige."

"Well. I know you work with Jason on a lot of his jobs. But *please* don't say a word to him about this, if you see him around. Tell your guys, too?"

"He *really* doesn't know?"

"No."

"I find that hard to believe. I mean, the dude's got *everything* documented and listed in that phone planner of his."

"Not this." Maris turns back to the kitchen and imagines it remodeled in all the cool colors and calming textures she's leaning toward. "It's something special I'm doing." *If only I can keep Jason at Ted's long enough*, she thinks. "So *promise* you'll keep it under your hard hat?" she asks Cody. "It means the world to me."

"Sure thing," her contractor says. "It'll be our secret."

~

Maris can only hope. Because *something* good's got to come out of this summer. If Jason wanted to walk out? Fine. He had his reasons. But that's when the house became *her* domain. *She'll* decide the fate of these walls. And that new kitchen she's been dreaming of for two years? Oh, by hook or by crook, it's happening.

So it's time to finalize material choices. First priority goes to the tiles and countertops in stock at the design center's warehouse. It'll shave weeks of waiting off her project that way. She lays a large tile on the floor. That choice is easy. She's definitely going with this tile that looks like wood—driftwood, to be exact. It's got that nice gray-brown blend that's very beachy.

Next she turns to her island-top samples. Carrara marble versus quartz is the issue here.

"Yoo-hoo!" a distant-sounding voice comes through the slider screen.

"*Oh, shoot,*" Maris whispers while grabbing some samples. "*Eva!*" Quickly she places an armful of marble squares on the pantry floor.

"Maris?" Eva calls out from her golf cart in the driveway below. "Are you in the shack, writing?"

Maris looks from the pantry to her sample-strewn

kitchen. "In the thick of it," she calls back to Eva. "Just getting some notes. Be right there." As she says it, she realizes she'll *never* get all the tile and countertop pieces hidden. So she's *got* to keep Eva outside, lest she sweep in and completely micromanage this kitchen facelift. Maris can just imagine Eva's whirlwind orders—*This is the latest trend.* And, *Cottages are all going with white color schemes.* And, *Why not remove this wall to open things up?*

No, no, no. Maris wants this to be her kitchen vision, and hers alone. Leaving the mess behind, she instead brushes tile dust off her black ribbed tee and faded denim skirt. Then she grabs her keys from the counter, her straw cowboy hat from the wall hook and wiggles into a pair of flip-flops. After locking up the slider, she hurries down the deck stairs just as Eva is getting out of her golf cart.

"Aren't we having coffee outside? Like always?" Eva asks.

"Not today. It's too hot on the deck. There's not even a breeze." Maris puts on her straw hat while walking straight past her sister. She lifts the take-out coffee tray and pastry bag from the golf cart passenger seat and climbs right in. "Let's go to the boardwalk," she says while shifting the coffee tray on her lap. "It's cooler near the water."

"Huh?" Eva looks from Maris to the deck—fully shaded by the maple tree.

"Come on!" Maris says, motioning to Eva. Her sister is dressed all summer chic in her scalloped shorts, half-tucked blouse and white slip-on sneakers. Heck, Eva could *walk* to the boardwalk and not break a sweat. Whereas Maris feels

214

like she's sweating bullets—just from how close Eva came to discovering her kitchen reno secret. "Let's go, sis."

"Okay," Eva tells her as she gets in the golf cart and pulls out of the driveway. "The boardwalk it is."

~

This is the time of year when folks push the limits around here. After the long summer, they get antsy to knock down cottage walls and raise roofs. So sitting at his tanker desk, Cliff writes a clear reminder for all Stony Point residents. His fingers type with conviction, sternly hunting and pecking each letter. He notes that the Hammer Law lifts next Tuesday, the day after Labor Day.

Any construction prior to that day will be duly noted and appropriately fined, he types. *NO exceptions*.

"The rules …" he says while typing the letters, "are the rules."

Pushing back in his ergonomic desk chair, Cliff rereads the notice on the computer screen before sending it to his printer in the other room. Which gives him just enough time to enjoy the sugar doughnut he picked up at Scoop Shop earlier. After his doughnut and coffee, he'll post the notice on the community bulletin board and swing by Elsa's inn. She might need a hand with last-minute grand opening preparations.

Leaning over his desk, he bites into the doughnut. When he does, sprinkles of sugar drop onto the desktop blotter. Another bite, more falling sprinkles.

And a jumping cat—leaping straight onto his desk. Her eyes are riveted to the sugar sprinkles, which she immediately bats at with her white paw.

"Hey, hey," Cliff says, pulling back. "You'll get those on the floor and then I'll have ants!" When he takes another bite of the sweet doughnut, more sprinkles fall.

And more paw action ensues. But this time, the cat pats at the sugar and then licks its sweetened paw! *Well, that's one way to clean off the desk*, Cliff thinks. While the cat's sugar-dabbing, he checks his voicemail. There are no lost-cat calls. No one claiming a pretty white feline as their own. The cat's a complete stray.

"But a friendly one, at that," Cliff notes. "Just took some time to warm up."

As he says it, the cat touches more of the fallen sugar grains.

"Oh, no you don't." Cliff takes his napkin and sweeps the loose sugar into his hand. "Sugar's not good for you. Off you go now. *Shoo!*"

And darn if the cat doesn't answer back. She gives a soft mew and moves to the corner of the desk. There, she sits tall and watches him.

Which gets Cliff to thinking as he's about to head out to Elsa's. The cat's looking very regal, sitting all straight like that. Regal enough to actually give to Elsa for a grand opening gift—a lovely inn mascot.

"Now, that's not a bad idea," he muses while the cat sniffs around for any lingering sugar. Surely the beach inn would make a nice forever home. And heck, the new cat would even make little Aria smile. *Sorridi!* he thinks. Yes, it's the *best* idea he's had all morning. Oh, his gift might be late. The scrawny stray will have to be vet-checked first, and groomed, *and* fattened up some. He'll have to come up with a proper name, too.

Which gives Cliff something to ponder. He walks to the printer in a small side room. "Snowflake," he says, glancing over at the white cat. "Pearl is nice, too. Like a pretty saltwater pearl. Or Star, maybe." Retrieving his printed bulletin board notice, he turns back to the office. When he does, there's a clattering noise coming from his desk. "What the heck?"

The cat is batting around his lucky domino now! She swats it, then gingerly pats at the white dots on it. By the time Cliff gets to his tanker desk, the cat's knocked the black domino to the floor. Cliff scoops it up, running his thumb over its faded white pips.

"Can't be having any of that," he says while pocketing the domino. "Your little paws will rub off all the lucky pip dots." With that, he takes a scrap of paper, crumples it into a ball and tosses it across the room. The cat jumps off the desk in high pursuit, swatting at the tiny paper.

"Why you look like a white pip yourself," Cliff remarks. "And maybe you'll bring some domino-luck to Elsa's inn, too." He walks over to the cat and gently pets its silky head. "By golly, I think you've got a name. *Pip!*"

"Oh my God," Maris says as she bites into some delectable pastry. "What are you feeding me now?"

"Lemon-blueberry crumb bar." Eva picks one out of the bag for herself. "With fresh blueberry filling. And the crumb topping's drizzled with lemon glaze."

"You *made* these?"

"Me and Tay did, last night. Then we chilled them."

"Mmm. What a breakfast. Wish I could whip up stuff like this."

"You'd have to do something about that ancient kitchen of yours first," Eva says before taking a hefty bite.

They sit beneath the boardwalk shade pavilion. Though it's the last day of August, the beach will be crowded—especially with the way this blazing heat hasn't let up. Maris figures people just don't want to say goodbye to summer. Already, colorful umbrellas line the beach. Sand chairs are set out, reserving families' regular seaside spots. A few people wade in the cool Sound, drizzling drops of water on their shoulders. She could sit here all morning, looking out at that blue sky, hearing the seagulls cry and watching sparkling ocean stars twinkle on the sea. Oh, to have that life.

"Hey," Eva says after another bite of her crumb bar. "How about Kyle's meeting here yesterday?"

"I know. Pretty shocking."

"No kidding," Eva says around her mouthful of food. "To think that for all these years, Kyle and Shane lost so much over a misunderstanding."

"We *all* did, after the way we judged Shane back then."

218

Maris pauses, holding her half-eaten crumb bar. "I'm actually kind of ashamed of it now," she admits before finishing her pastry.

"I guess in the heat of the moment that night around the bonfire, our emotions got the best of us."

"And we're all feeling some regret today, I'm sure. I know I am." Maris shakes her head. "And the worst part, according to Jason? It was all for nothing. Just *nothing.*"

"Wait. You *talked* to Jason afterward?" Eva asks.

"I did," Maris lets on, without mentioning their secret date last night.

"How's he doing?"

"Okay."

"*Okay*," Eva repeats with a nod. "Does that mean he's coming back?"

"It means we're talking. We're … trying."

"Well, just say the word and I'll go give that husband of yours a piece of my mind."

"Thanks, Eva. But leave it to me, okay?"

"Fine, then."

"Anyway, Jason's pretty beat, running on fumes. Which explains some of his interview blunders."

"Among *other* blunders."

"Eva! Dial it down." Maris swats her sister's arm. "Listen, I talked to someone else, too," Maris says while plucking her blueberry-sweet fingertips from her mouth. "Ted Sullivan."

"You *did?* When?"

"Yesterday. After Kyle's boardwalk meeting." Maris

sips from the hot coffee Eva brought her. "I invited Ted over, thinking maybe he saw something in Jason that could help me."

"Wait. Isn't Ted supposed to be on some cruise?" Eva asks.

"No, actually." Maris tells her sister how Ted made up the cruise story—on the spot—when he saw Jason a week ago. "So that Jason would stay in his cottage, a safe place. Ted was *that* worried about him when Jason told him we were taking some time apart," Maris goes on. "So the cruise is actually a little white lie."

"How do you like that?" Eva says of the nonexistent cruise. "Ted would do anything for Jason, wouldn't he?"

"Seems it. I was really surprised when he told me *that* secret."

They're quiet for a moment, until Eva admits, "I've got one, too."

"Got what?"

"A secret. And you'll be surprised with *this* one, too." Eva peels the lid off her take-out coffee. "So hold on to your cowboy hat."

"Jeez, what now?"

"Taylor failed her driving test."

"She *did*? After Matt worked so hard practicing with her?"

"Yep. Messed up in one of those multiple-use lanes," Eva explains. "You know the kind—either side can use them as a turn lane."

"Those lanes *can* be tricky. What's Matt say?"

"Heck, he misses all the fun. He's away at state trooper training this week. Giving seminars to the new recruits."

"Well." Maris cups her coffee close and takes another sip. "She'll try again. And maybe Tay will be a little older and wiser next time."

"If I can ever fit *in* a next time." Just then, Eva's reminder-alarm goes off on her phone. "See? I've been so busy lately. Have a closing in an hour, so I've got to run." She stands, brushing crumbs off her scalloped shorts and adjusting her leopard-print belt. But suddenly she stops brushing and instead directs her eagle eyes out at the parking lot beyond the boat basin. "*Wait.*" Eva leans over the boardwalk railing and squints. "Speak of the devil, is that *Taylor*?"

Maris stands and looks, too. She can't miss Eva's daughter with her long blonde hair, short-shorts and striped tank top. "Oh, it definitely is."

Eva finishes her coffee in a long swallow. "But she's supposed to be at Parks and Rec, *working*."

"Well, she's actually getting in a car, Eva."

"*What?* With who?"

"Hmm. I think it's a boy, sis."

"No way!" Eva jams her crumpled napkin into her coffee cup.

"Oh, look." Maris points to the boy then. "He's setting out cones. Aw, he must be helping Tay practice parallel parking. That's so cute."

"Ahem, ladies?" a voice asks from behind.

They turn to see Nick approaching in full guard

221

uniform: black shorts, khaki button-down with epaulets, walkie-talkie clipped on belt—the works.

And he's pointing to their boardwalk seat. "Is that a *food* bag I'm seeing?"

"Do you *see* any food?" Eva asks.

"I see crumbs," Nick tells her, just as she reaches into the bag and tries to bribe him with a lemon-blueberry bar. "No food on the beach, Eva. You know that." He pulls out a ticket pad from his uniform cargo shorts pocket. "So Maris," he says while jotting on a ticket, "how's Mr. Barlow doing? Saw him last night, getting into his truck."

"What?" Eva whips around to Maris. "Jason was *here*?"

When Maris shrugs with a small smile, it's not enough to hold Eva's attention. Taylor's apparently got dibs on that. "Listen. Never mind *Jason*. Nick," Eva says, turning to him now. "Tell me something." She points toward the parking lot. "Who *is* that?"

"Where?" Nick asks, looking up from his food-violation ticket.

"In the parking lot," Eva answers.

"Taylor. Your daughter."

"No, no!" Eva shakes her head. "Who's *directing* her?"

"Oh, that's Gage. Nice-enough guy." Nick puts a knee on the boardwalk bench and watches the driving lesson going on behind them. "He's our new parking lot attendant. Makes sure everyone has a Stony Point parking sticker in their window. You know, that kind of thing." Nick rips the ticket off his pad, gives it to Eva and starts to walk away. "I'll go check to see if he's found any violators."

"What? Twenty dollars?" Eva glares at the ticket then calls after Nick. "Why do *I* get the ticket?"

"You tried to bribe me," Nick says, backtracking and scooping up the bribery crumb bar off the boardwalk bench.

"*Oh!*" Eva stamps her foot, then just as suddenly grabs Maris' arm and yanks her close. "Listen," she says. But her eyes? They're locked onto this Gage kid now. "*Nice-enough guy* hanging around my sixteen-year-old daughter?"

"Maybe it's nothing." Maris pats Eva's hand—the one still locked onto her arm. "And he *is* helping her."

"But Tay never told me about this … this … *Gage*. Even when we were baking last night. And now look. Look! She's giving him a *hug!*" Eva hisses.

"Oh, that's just the way kids are these days." Maris watches Taylor trotting back to the Parks and Rec area, where groups of young children are doing a summer craft project. Sand pails and paintbrushes are strewn on picnic tables. "She must've been on a break, Eva. Don't jump to conclusions. He *could* just be a friend helping her."

"Right." Eva takes a quick breath while watching Gage closely. "A friend with his own car. You know, Taylor *has* been doing her hair differently. *And* wearing more makeup. Actually, Maris?" Looking worried, Eva turns to her now. "Tay hasn't even been home that much lately, either."

"Oh boy." Maris picks up the food bag still packed with a few of those fruity crumb bars. "You know what we may have here?" she asks, nodding to Taylor.

"Yes. *Trouble!*" Eva grabs up her coffee cup and starts

down the boardwalk toward her golf cart in the parking lot.

"No. I'll tell you what this is," Maris says, hurrying along to catch up, pastry bag in hand. When she gets to her sister's side, she leans close. "It's *another* Stony Point secret … floating around in all this sweet salt air!"

twenty-four

Late Wednesday Afternoon

SHANE'S ALWAYS THOUGHT THE SALT air smells sweetest at this time of day—late afternoon. After coming ashore, he walks along Rockport's docks as the sun sinks lower in the pale blue sky. The harbor water is calm. And the sea air hovering between daytime and twilight hours is laden with that misty salt.

Across the street from the docks, the Red Boat Tavern is quiet right now. Turning in, he orders a sandwich to go, drops his duffel, takes off his cap and waits at the bar. Wine goblets hang from a rack up above. A news anchor talks on a nearby mounted TV. Behind him, a wall of windows faces the harbor across the street. Tall café-style tables line those windows for bayside dining. Folks usually sit on stools there to watch the water while they eat. But it's early still. The crowds grow here closer to sunset. So the window stools are empty, and only a few are occupied at the bar.

225

"Surprised to see you, Shane," the bartender says as he sets down a glass of beer. "Thought you were maybe out to sea on one of the big boats."

"No. I stick around Penobscot this time of year. Shorter trips with the local lobstermen. Sometimes out only a day at a time—start at three in the morning, home by dinner." He takes a long swallow of his beer. "Home and beat."

"Ayuh. Makes for a long shift," the bartender says.

"I'll be on the offshore boats soon enough, later in the season. Out for two-week trips on those. So this local work is nice. Keeps me around these parts." Shane glances over his shoulder toward the harbor outside. "Just got back a half hour ago."

"Was it a good run? Fill those lobster pots?" the bartender asks while pulling two glasses off the ceiling rack.

"Sure did. Oh, let me tell you a story, though. Had a rough start this morning when the sun came up."

"How so?" The bartender fills the two glasses with a white wine.

"Bank of fog settled in. Couldn't see your hand in front of you. An old boat, thirty-eight footer, was coming in—though we didn't know it. Not until she passed by like a sudden ghost moving through the fog and nearly sideswiped us."

"Shit, close call?"

"Pretty much. Man, that incoming boat was roughed up by the sea. Captain was, too, the old salt. An old-timer lobstering with not much more than a compass and a rope it seemed, from the looks of him. All grizzled and weather-beaten. Almost expected the dude to have an eye patch and skull-and-crossbones hat." Shane hitches his head to a pirate statue standing beside the bar's entrance door. "Like your buccaneer there," he says.

"Ha! Well, enjoy your grog, matey. Glad you made it back okay."

"Yeah. Me, too."

Just then, a waitress approaches with his take-out order. "Ahoy there, Shane." She touches his arm as she passes by. "Thought you maybe went overboard. Haven't seen you around lately."

"Good to know I've been missed here," Shane tells her while raising his glass in a toast. "Been in Connecticut, Mandy. Family matters for a couple of weeks."

"Family?" Mandy sets down his sandwich with all the trimmings, bagged and wrapped up to go. "You never mentioned family before."

"Got a brother there. Sister-in-law."

"Oh. Have a nice visit?"

"That I did."

Mandy reaches over and places the two filled wineglasses on her tray. "Well, stop by my place later." She brushes her fingers through Shane's salty hair, whispering close, "*I'll cook you up a real meal, Sailor.*"

From where he sits on the barstool, Shane looks back over his shoulder at her. Her blonde hair is in a loose braid; her smile, easy. She throws him a slight wink, too.

"Maybe another time, Mandy." And he sees it, the bit of suspicion in her long squint at him before picking up her tray of drinks.

"Door's always open," she tells him as she breezes off to her waiting customers.

Shane sits alone then, nursing the rest of his draft beer.

"Anything else, my friend?" the bartender asks when he walks past.

"Nah. Thanks, man. Been a long day." Shane stands and puts on his cap before grabbing his duffel and the bagged sandwich, too. "Going to hit the road home."

~

He walks the few harbor blocks to his house. The distant water is deep blue at twilight; wild roses climb among rocky ledges. While carrying his duffel and food, one thing Shane knows for certain is this: As much as he likes being out at sea, he also likes seeing his dockside home when he returns. He gives a long sigh when the tiny, silver-shingled house with its paned windows comes into view. Red geraniums spill from a window box. Off a ways behind it, lobster and pleasure boats both are docked at day's end. The moored vessels bob in the calm bay.

It's all a sight for sore eyes, and shit, Shane can't get home soon enough now. All he wants to do is kick off his work boots, eat his dinner and relax his weary bones. He's sweaty and needs a shower, too. Mostly, though? After having two weeks off, he's really feeling some kinks and aches. The hard work got to him this trip—from baiting and lifting empty traps, to hooking buoy lines and hauling pots up from the bottom of the sea, to banding claws and filling the lobster tanks.

But approaching his mailbox, lobstering is the furthest thing from his mind. Now? Now his thoughts turn to Celia and the note he mailed off to her. It's too soon to get a letter back, having only been a few days. Still, while thumbing through the envelopes accrued in his mailbox, he wonders if he should've sent her that note, after all. Where could it even lead?

Not that he won't find out Friday, when he goes to Connecticut again. Should be a short stay this time. Back on the boat first thing after Labor Day.

Which reminds him. He's got to call and see if that little beach bungalow is available for the weekend. Because he wouldn't dream of missing Elsa's Ocean Star Inn grand opening. Knowing Elsa, it'll be the bash of the summer. Celia will be there, too.

Hefting his duffel, take-out dinner and mail now, he's walking to his front door when he hears a familiar voice.

"Shane! Good to see you back!" a neighbor calls over from his driveway. He's soaping down his car in a quick wash. "How you doing there?" he asks.

"Not bad, Bruno." Shane sets down his duffel, resettles his cap on his head and walks across his friend's yard. "A little tired. You know."

"Sure, guy. Hey, listen," Bruno says while picking up the hose and spraying his car. "Looked after the place for you. Gave the flowers a drink."

"Appreciate that," Shane tells him with a tip of his newsboy cap.

"And someone was here looking for you. Sunday, I think. Yeah, the day you left."

"For me?" Shane asks, not mentioning that he actually saw Celia on the docks.

"Yessah. The lady ... *Celia*, I think her name was. Seemed like she was from away."

"Celia. Yeah, I know a Celia."

"Well, she was in an awful hurry to catch you," Bruno says while spraying soap off his tires. "Did you see her?"

"No." Shane steps closer. "She say anything to you? Why she was here?"

"Not much. Had a baby with her, cute little thing. Said she was a friend stopping by for a visit."

"I must've just missed her, then."

"Oh, too bad."

"Yeah." Shane turns to get back to his house. "Thanks for letting me know," he calls over his shoulder as Bruno gives a wave.

~

So she wasn't a mirage. Wasn't a figment of his imagination. Celia was really here. In Maine. But why? Why would she ever make that five-hour ride with her baby? Now, as he picks up his duffel and heads to his front door, Shane's more than a little worried about her. Actually, as he holds open the screen door with his foot and maneuvers the key in the lock, he hopes everything is all right.

Inside, like on every return trip, his closed-up house

feels musty. He sets down his duffel and the mail, tosses his cap on a chair and opens a window. Some fresh sea air will do the place good.

But before going to the kitchen to eat the sandwich from the bar, he lingers near that open window. On a table beside it, his old red sailboat is propped against a lamp. Whenever he sees that toy boat, he thinks of the times he and Kyle hunkered down on their knees in the marsh. They'd set that boat a-sailing and spin out some seafaring yarns. Hell, picking up that boat, Shane feels like he's been an old salt telling sea stories all his life. He runs his hand along the mast, then sets the boat back down.

His happiness jar is on that table, too. Right beside the boat. Right where it should be.

The house is quiet. Evening settles on the harbor town outside. Shadows grow long, so he turns on the table lamp. Standing there, he hesitates for a moment. Finally, he takes the top off that happiness jar, reaches in and lifts a few pieces of Celia's frosted sea glass from the sand. The pieces—green and white and blue—feel cool in his palm. Briny. And soft, somehow. He closes his hand in a loose fist around the sea glass, jostles the pieces, then gently sets them back on the sand in the jar.

twenty-five

Wednesday Evening

SHE WEARS ALL BLACK TONIGHT.

Elsa gives a last look in the mirror. Her fitted black tank top over black capris with the shredded hem needs a finishing touch. And she knows just the thing. Carefully, she lifts her gold etched-star necklace and clasps it behind her neck.

But no matter how warm the day, evenings by the sea bring a dampness to the air. It'll be cool sitting on the outdoor patio at the Dockside Diner—where she's meeting Mitch for their second business meeting. So she slips into a white open-weave topper, buttons the two carved wooden buttons and dashes outside. With her black straw tote slung over her shoulder, she locks up the door and, keys in hand, heads to her car.

Stops still in her tracks, too, at the sound of a particularly familiar voice calling her name.

"Elsa!"

She turns to see a vehicle pulling up to the curb. It's one of those off-road-looking SUVs. The top's been removed, leaving some sort of roll bars exposed. And the hefty tires make the gray safari-style vehicle ready to cruise the beach sand!

"I'm just headed to the diner myself," Mitch Fenwick is saying from the driver's seat, all while motioning her closer. "Hop in. We'll go together."

"But ... Well," Elsa says, glancing at her own plain sedan in the driveway. "I don't want to inconvenience you."

"Nonsense. Why go to the same place in two vehicles?" He lowers his sunglasses and looks at her over the frames. "What's the point of that?" he asks.

Elsa gives one last look at her staid car before shrugging. "Okay," she says, dropping her keys in her tote. "Okay, then." She walks around Mitch's open-air vehicle and climbs in the passenger side.

"Hope you don't mind a little wind," he tells her.

"Oh, I *welcome* it," she admits, settling into the seat. "This heat has been just stifling."

"Indeed it has. Now, buckle up," Mitch says. "And before I forget, I believe this is yours?" He lifts a sandy-gold silk scarf from the console.

"There it is!" Elsa takes the scarf as he pulls the vehicle away from the curb. "And it's just what I need in this breeze." She rolls the silk fabric and ties it around her head to keep her hair in place. While Mitch drives the beach road, she also lifts a huge pair of sunglasses out of her tote and sets them on her face.

Well, now. This is interesting, she thinks as they pass the shingled cottages and little bungalows. The view from up here is mighty fine, actually. Sitting in the roofless vehicle, she feels that light breeze, and occasionally catches the scent of someone's backyard barbecue. Yes, it's that kind of night when everyone's outdoors enjoying these fleeting summer evenings. At the stone railroad trestle, Mitch cruises right on through, tapping the horn and waving to Nick standing guard there.

Nick—who does a double take, Elsa notices. He squints and tips his head at the two of them coasting by. Elsa gives him a casual wave as under the trestle she and Mitch go. When she steals a look back before Mitch turns onto Shore Road, there's Nick. He's standing right in the street, hands on hips, as though he cannot believe he saw her roll past in these spiffy wheels.

On the way to the diner, she and Mitch share some small talk—about the day, the weather. But not much is said, not with the noise and wind that comes from the top being off the vehicle.

And the funny thing is? Elsa likes it. She *likes* feeling that salty wind and hearing the traffic noises. After spending the day still wrangling issues delivered Monday in her surprise certified letter, this is a welcome change. There's a certain freedom to driving along in Mitch's safari-style open-air vehicle. Her new worries and fears brought on by that letter simply blow away with the wind whipping her now-scarved hair. She glances over at Mitch. The wind lifts his fading blond hair, too. But his sunglasses propped on top of his head somewhat keep it all in place. He's dressed casual for their meeting—a loose linen button-down turned back at the sleeves, over brown chino pants rolled at the cuff. Two-strap leather sandals on his feet keep the look really easy.

With a long, just-as-easy breath then, Elsa discreetly—*discreetly*—extends her arm out the window and catches some of that salty breeze between her cupped fingers. This is the life, this letting all her troubles blow away with that wind as they cruise the beach roads. By the time they pull into the diner parking lot, she feels like, well, like a new woman! Or at least like the woman she was *before* those serious troubles set in with Monday's letter. So when Mitch parks and gets out of his vehicle, she takes off her returned scarf and ties it on her straw tote strap for safekeeping. Giving her hair a quick *zhuzh*, she then takes Mitch's hand as he helps her step out of the SUV.

"Shall we?" he asks, sweeping his arm toward the outdoor patio.

As if he even had to ask.

～

Elsa's not sure the diner would've looked as magical if she'd driven here in her sedan—with the windows sealed tight as the car's a/c kept her cool. No. After that windblown, freeing cruise with Mitch, the whole night takes on a new feel. They cross the parking lot toward the outdoor patio.

With the sun setting, tiki torches glimmer near the patio. Flames dance, too, from Kyle's new decorative firepit—around which several customers sit. The grill station is sizzling with food.

But most intriguing to Elsa is this: the large lattice-type fence panel draped with fishnet. Because what's in front of that fence panel is a live-music stage. A stool is set near a microphone stand, with a few small amplifiers there, too.

"Sure appreciate you meeting with me again, Elsa," Mitch is saying as he pulls out a chair for her at a table off to the side. "It's a big help."

"I'm glad to, Mitch. And anyway, who wants to cook in this heat? Being here is a nice break for me, too."

Right as Mitch grabs a seat across from Elsa, Kyle saunters over from the grill station. He's got on his white chef apron and sets down two menus. "What's up, guys?" he asks. "Surprised to see you two here."

"Good evening, Kyle. Elsa and I've got a working dinner going on," Mitch explains, hanging a small canvas messenger bag over the back of his chair. "She's giving me some pointers for being on-camera."

"That's *right*. For *Castaway Cottage*," Kyle says with a nod. "Jason and his crew will be ramping things up soon, no?"

"After Labor Day." Mitch leans back in his patio chair, lifts a sandaled foot to his knee and crosses his arms over his chest, all while taking in the illuminated tables around them.

"Is Lauren around?" Elsa asks Kyle.

"Not tonight. She covered for my head waitress all day,

and is home with the kids now," Kyle says. "She's doing some driftwood painting to restock our inventory."

"Tell her I said hello?"

"Of course."

"Well I must say, Kyle," Elsa goes on. "I am just *amazed* at how this outdoor patio *transforms* the diner vibes."

"Definitely," Mitch agrees. "The tiki torches, umbrella lights. Nice place you have here. I'm duly impressed."

"Appreciate that, Mitch. And hey, we've got entertainment, too." Kyle points to the small stage area. "It's acoustic night."

"Perfect. Music beneath the stars," Elsa remarks. "Do you do this often?"

"First time," Kyle explains. "The outdoor patio's been a big hit. But studies show that slow music gets patrons to linger even *longer*."

"From the looks of the crowd here, your diner will be doing the business tonight," Mitch says, nodding to the filled tables.

"Sure hope so." Ready to take their order, Kyle nods to their menus. "In the meantime, what can I get you two?"

⁓

As soon as Kyle returns to the grill station, Mitch pulls his notepad out of that canvas messenger bag he'd brought along. "Time for a tip or two?" he asks. "Before the food gets here."

Elsa pulls her chair in closer. "Excellent idea. Where'd we leave off the other night?"

"Let's see." Mitch flips a few notepad pages and reads some of Elsa's tips. "Hydrate, and physically relax. Particularly the arms."

"Yes, of course. Which was when I got that sliver!"

"Feeling better now?"

"Much. It's all healed, thank you," Elsa says while holding up her hand. "And I've been giving your filming some thought since then. A *really* important piece of advice is to ... bring something personal to the televised segments."

"Personal?"

"Yes. It gives that human angle viewers connect with. For instance," Elsa says, sitting back when a waitress delivers their drinks and silverware. "When I lived in Milan, I always wrote inspiring sidewalk messages outside my boutique—"

"Milan! Now I just knew there was some ... *air* about you. That you weren't from these parts," Mitch says, leaning back and squinting over at her. "So you hail from somewhere other than this salty beach town."

"Oh, I actually *am* Connecticut born and raised. But I spent much of my adult life in *il bel paese*."

"The beautiful country?"

Elsa nods, smiling. "I studied abroad in college. In Italy. Married a wonderful fellow I'd met there, too. He swept me off my feet, and it turns out I never left. And while raising our son in Italy, I opened a clothing boutique in Milan. Oh, how I loved that little shop. I owned it for many years. But once my husband died, and my son moved to the States, my life there ..." She turns up her hands.

"Quieted?"

Elsa nods again. "And all it took was one wedding invitation from my niece to change things."

"Would that be Maris?"

"It is!"

"Ah, yes. Jason's wife. She called me earlier," Mitch says as he scoots his chair around closer to Elsa. "She'll be touring my cottage before demo begins, too. For inspiration for the novel she's writing."

"*Magnifico!* Maris will so appreciate seeing up-close the details of that beautiful beach house."

"But *you*," Mitch continues. "You said Maris' wedding invitation changed things?"

"It did." Elsa slides her chair a little closer to Mitch as she explains. "I came here for her wedding, two summers ago ... and my life was uprooted again. This time back to Connecticut—as I never returned to Italy once I reconnected with my family in Stony Point."

"And here you are." Mitch tips his head, watching her beneath the umbrella's twinkle lights. "About to open a grand beach inn by the sea."

"Yes. Yes, I am." With Mitch's steady gaze on her, Elsa clears her throat then. And sips her water. "Which brings us back to your next tip."

Mitch sets his pen to paper, still watching Elsa closely.

"So when my inn's renovation was happening, I brought something personal to the filming. We did a segment on my *inn*-spiration walkway, where I write motivating, uplifting phrases with chalk on a prominent part of the inn's stone patio. Just like I did outside my Milan boutique. And we did a segment on my happiness jars—"

"Happiness jars?" Mitch glances up from his writing.

"Yes." Elsa looks at him sitting so close. She notices the chain and beaded necklaces beneath his open shirt collar. Notices how he watches her while waiting for her words. "Mason jars," she quietly says. "I put a bit of beach sand in them, then add happy mementos from any special day. You know, flower blossoms, a seashell maybe. Or a photograph would work. I got the idea from Maris, who made a happiness jar to commemorate her wedding to Jason."

"Okay," Mitch says while jotting a note in his pad. "*Personalize* a segment or two."

"Yes. With some *quirk*. Or some *personality* of the property, even."

"Like the beach binoculars you saw on my deck."

"Of course!"

"I can connect them to Kate, who always loved coming across them in our travels."

"Yes, you see? A personal story," Elsa says, just as the waitress delivers their red-plastic dinner baskets. They shuffle between them a veggie-burger basket and a triple-decker turkey club. Both baskets are lined with tissue paper, with French fries in one, onion rings in the other. Paper cups of coleslaw and potato salad are on the side.

And just as Elsa leaves a curl of ketchup on her fries, the packed patio quiets at the first strums of a guitar. The microphone is tapped next, and the singer clears her throat. "Thanks for joining me this gorgeous summer evening," the singer says as Elsa lifts a ketchup-laden fry. "I'm Celia Gray."

"*Celia!*" Elsa whispers, leaning back in her chair for a better look. Yes, it's Celia sitting on the stool with her guitar in her lap. She wears a teal fitted top over a long black lace skirt. A wide silver belt wraps around her waist; her silver thumb ring shines in the lone spotlight.

"Someone you know?" Mitch asks as Celia slowly strums while tuning a few strings.

"Yes. Yes, it's Celia! She's my assistant innkeeper and lives …" Elsa pauses as she quickly loosens the silk scarf from her straw tote handle. "Celia lives in my guest cottage behind the inn."

"I have some special songs to play for you beneath the stars," Celia is saying, her soft voice soothing as she leans close to the mic.

Just then, Elsa waves her scarf, silently getting Celia's attention. Celia squints through the shadows, and when she makes out Elsa? She waves a few fingers right back.

⁓

Like a bit of summer magic itself, the evening keeps casting its spell on Elsa. As she and Mitch enjoy their basket dinners, Celia serenades the diner crowd with easy songs. Twilight falls on the patio, too. At the harbor further down the street, Elsa can see silhouettes of anchored sailboats floating on the sunset's red-tinged water.

Magic. Yes, summer magic at its finest.

Even more so with Celia's singing. She stops by their table between songs; her long gauzy skirt flowing; her auburn hair, down.

"I was so surprised to see you here, Elsa!" Celia says, bending and giving her a hug.

"Same here," Elsa admits. "Won't you join us for a few minutes?"

Pulling up a chair then, Celia tells her, "I'd love to."

"And where's Aria tonight?" Elsa asks. "With Taylor?"

"She is. Taylor's babysitting at my place."

"Good. That's good Aria's at home." Elsa turns to Mitch. "This is Celia, Mitch. Celia Gray."

"How do you do, Celia?" he asks, extending a hand. "Mitch Fenwick."

"Pleased to meet you," Celia says, shaking that hand and nodding.

"Celia is the mother of my beautiful granddaughter, Aria."

"Is that right now?" Mitch tips his head, drawing his hand down his goatee. "Elsa mentioned that you live in her guest cottage?"

"I do." Celia squeezes Elsa's hand. "So Aria gets to see her *nonna* every day."

"Mitch," Elsa explains with a sad smile. "Celia was engaged to my son, Salvatore, when he passed away last year."

"Oh, no. Now I am so very sorry for your loss, Celia." Mitch sits back and eyes them. "For *both* of your losses. That is *very* tragic, especially for the little baby."

242

"*It is*," Celia whispers. "So I'm *really* thankful Aria's close to Elsa here."

"Me, too," Elsa says. "Mitch lives close by too, Cee. His place is the last cottage on the beach."

"Yes, of course! Jason's next castaway?" Celia asks.

"That it is." Mitch looks from Celia to Elsa. "And Jason thought that Elsa could give me some filming tips."

"So you see, well … that's why we're here," Elsa explains. "Having dinner here, I mean. It's business. What I'm trying to say is that we're talking about the show. *Castaway Cottage*," she adds with a quick smile as she looks from Mitch sitting casually beside her, to Celia—then back to Mitch.

"*And* enjoying the music," Mitch adds. "Really dig the sound of your songs, Celia."

"Thanks so much. I'm trying out a few new ones tonight." Celia stands then. "Speaking of which, I better get back to the show," she says with a wave. "Nice meeting you, Mitch."

⁓

"Now. Where were we?" Mitch asks as Celia heads to the stage.

Oh, Elsa knows just where they were. Sitting outside on this summer night, they have *not* been talking business. Instead, they've been swapping personal stories along with the swapping of French fries and coleslaw.

And Elsa's been enjoying every minute of it.

243

JOANNE DEMAIO

She knows why, too. It's because this evening is a distraction. A perfect distraction from what's been filling her days all week: upsetting news, secret phone calls, difficult conversations. All of which she's had enough of for the time being. So she scoops up a forkful of coleslaw instead.

"You were telling me about the history of your cottage, and that little Sailor boy," Elsa says, her coleslaw-covered fork hovering. "The one who went missing during a hurricane?"

"That's right." Mitch draws a hand along his goatee. "Poor kid. Folks thought he maybe got swept out into the waters. Or crossed the rocks toward Little Beach in a panic when the hurricane struck. So Gordon, my wife's father—"

"Your father-in-law?" Elsa asks.

"Would've been. If he'd survived."

"Oh, no."

Mitch nods.

And as he tells her how Gordon paddled out in the storm waters searching for little lost Sailor, and how Gordon went missing—never to be found—Elsa listens, riveted. "But what about the boy with the little sailor cap?" she asks.

"Turns out a neighbor saw him running home. Winds were a-whipping, tree branches and wires were coming down. So she grabbed him and brought him into the safety of her own cottage. But by the time Sailor's mother, and Kate's family as well, found out?"

Elsa drops her voice. "It was too late."

244

"It was. Gordon had already pushed off in his rowboat and rounded the point toward Little Beach. That's where Jason found the long-lost boat, all these decades later. Buried in the dunes there."

"And poor Sailor. Does he have a real name? Do you know what *ever* happened to him?"

"No. He's turned into the stuff of legends, this mystery boy. His family left and never returned to Stony Point. And the neighbors only knew him as Sailor, because of that blue-and-white cap he wore. Jason's actually having a blue-and-white awning installed on the cottage as a tribute."

"What a heartbreaking tale," Elsa admits, shaking her head.

"My wife, Kate? Like I said, Gordon was her father. He died so young, gone too soon."

"That's a terrible fate. I know, because it happened to me. My son? Salvatore? After contracting rheumatic fever as a child, his heart was damaged. We lost him during valve-replacement surgery a year ago now. He was only thirty-six."

"Elsa." Mitch leans over and takes her hand in his. "It pains me to hear this."

"Thank you. My Sal? He was a Wall Street wizard, ready to retire from the rat race there and settle at the beach. Help get my inn off the ground. But it wasn't to be."

"I'm sure he'd be proud that you're going forward with the plans."

Elsa pulls her wallet out of her tote and shows Mitch a glossy photograph of Sal. "He left such an impact on my loved ones here. Celia, Jason, Maris—everyone—in the short time he was with us." As she says it, though, Elsa realizes something. Talking about Sal, she's actually *smiling* now ... and it feels okay. She knows Sal would be nodding his approval at her smile.

"My daughter, Carol, she took it very hard when Kate died," Mitch reveals. "She misses her mother and struggles still with the loss."

"I can certainly understand that. But you know, Mitch." Elsa leans close. "Something my Sal said might help her."

"Really now ..."

Elsa nods. "Sal would tell me, and the others, to smile. Even when we're sad. That it helps lift you to a better place. And ultimately? It will have you live the way of an old Italian proverb."

"And what would that be?" Mitch quietly asks as Celia's guitar strumming winds through the salty air.

"To tell your life in smiles, not tears. *Sorridi*, Sal would often say."

"Smile?"

"Yes. And we would." Elsa wipes a random tear from her cheek, smiling as she does. "It works," she assures him. "I promise you."

"Now that is a tip for the books," Mitch tells her as he opens his notepad and jots a few words.

"Yes. Smile for the camera. And ... *breathe* when they're filming. Jason taught me that one. Deep breathing techniques open your mind, too." She takes a long salt-air breath then.

"*Breathe*," Mitch whispers as he continues jotting.

Elsa looks out on the patio as Celia plays one of her new songs. It's an upbeat song that's got folks foot-tapping. A few couples take to a small dance area, where they swing and sway on this summer night. Oh, memories for sure—sweet ones—are being made as they do. *That* gets Elsa smiling, too.

"Another easy tip?" She pats Mitch's arm. "Exercise. You might get tense even before the cameras show up. So take a ten-minute walk on the beach. It helps loosen up muscles."

"I like that idea, Elsa. Maybe you'll join me on some of those walks?" he asks.

"Sure. Just give a wave through my inn's secret path. If you're tense, you'll ..." She pauses as she watches the dancing couples. "Shake it off with a walk!"

Mitch looks from the dance area—roped off with swimline attached to decorative wood pilings—to Elsa. "Can shake it off with a dance, too." He sets down his pencil and reaches for her hand. "Come on," he says, hitching his head to the dance area. "Let's shake it out."

"What?" Elsa glances at the people dancing. "I ... I don't know, Mitch." She slips her hand out of his hold. "Maybe it's best if—"

Mitch stands and gives Elsa a warm smile. "Just one dance?" he asks, extending a hand again.

"Are you sure?" She places a tentative hand in Mitch's as he tugs her to her feet.

"Oh, Elsa. It's *strictly* business."

twenty-six

Moments Later

WITH ELSA HERE TONIGHT, CELIA'S secret is up—this on-the-sly singing gig.

Not that Elsa much noticed. All evening, whenever Celia looked over at Elsa and Mitch at their table, funny how there wasn't much note-taking happening. Instead, there's been laughing. And leaning close. Elsa even clasped Mitch's arm at one point. Well, for crying out loud, Celia actually has to keep an eye on Elsa—which is distracting her from her guitar strumming.

Because, *really*? Celia does a double take. Mitch is standing and holding out a *hand* to Elsa? Okay, this is one suspicious-looking *business* date. A date, definitely. But *romantic* date is more like it.

So while Mitch and Elsa *dance* now, Celia continues playing her tune. It's a song relaxed as a summer night, casual and upbeat.

Oh, the moon knew, didn't it? she sings. *Smiling down on our midnight walk.*
And the stars, they knew too ... wisely winking at our talk.

Yes, it all happened. Celia remembers while sitting on her stool and strumming her guitar. The night Shane walked her home after she'd slept with him a week ago, all of nature seemed to smile at them beneath the midnight sky.

Oh, how this song could *really* use Shane's harmonica. If only he were here, jamming with her. Standing off behind her just a little, bending and getting into a riff. When he did that at The Sand Bar, people loved it. The cheering and clapping rose right with the first lick from that harmonica.

Alone on stage, Celia keeps strumming, singing the next verse of her new song.

And when we strolled the sandy path to the beach,
Dune grasses whispered my secret ...
One they'd never breach.

Holding her guitar, she shifts and looks down the street toward the distant harbor there, but thinks of another harbor—one five hours north. Leaning toward the mic as she sees *this* harbor dotted with lights, she sings her next lines—sending out a secret salt-air message.

All around us, yes, the magical night-world knew, Celia sings, her eyes dropping closed, *that I ... yes I ... was so in love with you.*

Okay, so the crowd likes her song—that's obvious by the dancing. But Celia hears a *renewed* clapping and cheering start up. It gets her to look closely as folks gather at the edge of the dance area.

Well, I'll be, she thinks. That Mitch Fenwick has got some fancy footwork going on. The way he's slipping and sliding those sandaled feet, Celia hasn't seen anything like it. It's like he's strolling in place, his feet striding in rhythmic movements. Apparently the people gathering around aren't the only ones liking Mitch's summertime shuffling, either. Because there's *Elsa*, holding his hand and trying to match his dance steps—move for smooth-footed move.

What it does, seeing Elsa live it up a bit, is this: It gets Celia smiling, too. Smiling and inspired to go off on her own impromptu guitar jam—throwing in a few slap strums to give a drumbeat feel. And to keep Mitch's feet mighty happy as she does.

⁓

"A little bit of shagging loosens us up, too," Mitch tells Elsa. His left hand holds her right as he dances close, then backs up in his smooth-striding steps.

"*Shagging?*" Elsa asks, trying to keep her feet moving as smoothly and gracefully as Mitch's. His feet stay close to the floor, skimming along through each turn.

"The dance," Mitch explains while turning to the side. "It's the South Carolina state dance. And Celia's tune is custom-made for it."

Elsa watches Mitch's feet move without kicks, without bouncing. The dance seems to be mostly from the waist down. Why the way he's stepping his leather-sandal-clad feet? It could seem like he's got rubber knees.

"Here. I'll show you a few steps," he tells Elsa as Celia really strums her guitar now. Holding Elsa's right hand, he nods to her other arm. "Bend your left arm, with your hand at waist height."

Elsa does as Mitch keeps his feet moving.

"Take small steps," he tells her. "Mirror mine. One-and-two, three-and-four," he says, shuffling his feet. "Five, six."

Elsa does just that, slowly at first. Taking a few missteps, too. But then? As Celia romps along on her guitar, Elsa gets it together. She likes this dancing from the hips down. There's something mod about it, and she gets into the rhythm. Mitch holds her right hand, stepping close, backing away, slowly turning her alongside him.

But there's more. Elsa hears cheers and clapping coming from the tables. Other couples sidle close, listening to Mitch's instructions and ... *wait* ... why, they're *shagging* right along with them. When Mitch holds her close for his next round of steps and they move in sync, it's obvious *he's* having fun, too.

But it's his touch, and the twinkle in his eyes—eyes that *don't* leave hers—that tell her something more. Why, for heaven's sake, could it be? Yes, she's actually on a *date*. Oh, Lordy. An honest-to-goodness date with Mitch Fenwick ... at the Dockside Diner!

With all the music and lights and spinning around beneath

251

the twilight sky, it's a fine date, too. One that has sent all Elsa's troubles—all her news received in one particularly upsetting letter—fading away into the summer mist.

Yes, dancing with Mitch outside the diner, Elsa's not thinking about the shocking words in that letter she'd received.

Not thinking about the umpteen phone calls and arrangements she's secretly been making since.

Not thinking of how she'll break the news to everyone at Stony Point.

No. When she's here with Mitch, she stays right in the sliding-and-shuffling moment.

Elsa doesn't think. Doesn't fret.

She simply shags.

～

Well. The last thing Celia wants to do is stop this song. Especially with the way everyone's dancing, and laughing, and having a grand old time.

"Come along on my song," she calls into the mic, her fingers guitar-strumming. Even Kyle is tapping his feet at the grill. He gives a full twirl, too, while flipping a burger high in the air.

But still, from all her open-mic nights at The Sand Bar, Celia knows the ropes. It's really important to change up the tone, so she segues into a slow, bluesy number now. Some people, breathless from the faster dancing, scatter to their tables.

Others stay in the dance area. A few couples step into each other's arms and lean close. Heads rest on shoulders. Hands reach around waists. Words are whispered.

This is a moment meant for soft serenading. So Celia quietly sings into the mic, her voice breathy. *"Twinkle, twinkle, ocean star … How I wonder what you are."* She slows the song's pace, then, so that it's nearly unrecognizable. *"Floating on the sea so light … Like a diamond shining bright."*

Before she gets to the next line, though, she nearly forgets the words with what she's seeing.

In the shadows off to the side, Elsa slow-dances in Mitch's arms. She's dressed in a black fitted tank over black capris—with the hems shredded. Her summery sweater has long ago been shed. She and Mitch slightly sway, pressed together. Beneath the starry sky, they look at only each other as Mitch says something that gets Elsa to laugh. But then? Well, then he gently raises a hand to Elsa's face, brushes aside a strand of her honey-highlighted brown hair—and goes in for a kiss.

A kiss Elsa does *not* resist.

Celia, stunned, looks quickly to Kyle, then right back to that kiss—still going on as Mitch's hands cradle Elsa's face.

Now *this* is a turn Celia never saw coming tonight. Elsa's getting herself into a boatload of an entanglement. And what can Celia do?

Nothing, except play on.

twenty-seven

Wednesday Night

EVEN NOW WITH THE SUN setting, the heat doesn't let up. Jason thought that sitting out on Ted's deck, there'd at least be a breeze lifting off the Sound.

There isn't.

So instead of cooling off, he's perspiring. His glass of iced water is perspiring, too, with rivulets of condensation running down the glass. Even Maddy's perspiring. Panting, she walks to her water bowl on the deck and laps up a few mouthfuls. It's as though someone turned up the flame beneath these late-August days, and the hours—day or night—just simmer.

Heat or not, he's got to get this design done. Not having access to his studio, every aspect of his work takes twice as long now, at least. A few black markers are fanned out on the patio table. He picks one and doodles through a new issue at the Fenwicks'. A portion of their elevated

254

deck has to be reworked to accommodate the beach binoculars. Some sort of nook will do the trick. For inspiration, Jason brought out the beach jar Maris made for Neil on Sunday. Having the jar nearby might help channel his brother on this critical sketch. If Jason can work out the kinks on paper first, he'll transfer it to his tablet later. His recommended change also has to come in on schedule and under budget.

It helps to see the project from different angles. So he begins by sketching a distant view of the cottage, as though he were standing far down the beach. His black marker draws sweeping lines with some crosshatch denoting the sand. Feathered lines depict dune grasses on the right side of the sketch. A blue highlighter rough-fills in the Sound on the left. Round, cloud-shaped lines indicate the treetops past the rocky outcropping. Finally, the Fenwick cottage rises from the sand on stilts as Jason lets his drawing hand take over.

But three torn-out sketch pages later, still nothing. And Jason sees why. More than any *deck* design, he's actually drawing Stony Point—as though he's missing it, maybe. So he puts the sketchpad and markers into his leather portfolio, sets it aside and takes out his cell phone. Now might be a good time to call Maris. Surely she's home, sitting in their house on the bluff. Or writing in the shack out beside the barn studio. He'll ask her out on another date.

But with his phone call, too? Nothing. No answer. So he just hangs up and whistles to the dog, which gets her scrambling to her feet. "Let's walk," Jason tells the German shepherd. And she's not one to argue as they leave his work, his sketches, behind.

⁓

The beach is no different than the deck tonight. The heat hangs there like a bank of fog. Everything is stopped in its tracks by the warmth. The salt air is thick in the stillness. Even the surf, which is usually stronger here, is calm. Walking along the high tide line, Jason picks up a stick of driftwood and throws it down the beach. Maddy runs after it, then carries the stick right into the water—where she sloshes in the shallows.

Feeling frustrated that he couldn't reach Maris—that he's so out of touch with her—Jason wonders if all he's trying to do is find his way back to her. Back to Stony Point. That's why he's on the beach now. Walking the hard-packed sand usually eases his gait, his mind. But the gravelly packed sand here at Sea Spray Beach doesn't do it tonight. It's not the same as Stony Point's sand. And so the thought occurs to him that maybe he should have just stayed *there* this summer. Should never have left.

No, you couldn't have stayed, he hears right as a wave sloshes onto the beach. Jason glances over his shoulder. Whether the words are imagined, or actually Neil's spirit, the effect is the same. They get him to doubting himself.

"Not sure being away is the answer either," Jason quietly says into the still night. When he takes a breath of the salt air, it's so pungent he can almost taste it. "Maybe leaving wasn't right after all."

I told you, Neil's voice goes on when Maddy lopes out of the water and gives a good shake. *You had to stay out of the crossfire between Shane and Maris.*

"Ach," Jason says, waving off his brother, or the voice, or maybe just his own confused thoughts.

Situation would've imploded if you'd stayed and gotten involved. The hushed words come from behind him now—Neil's voice blending with the low foghorn of a faraway lighthouse.

Jason keeps walking. Implode? Oh, doesn't he know it. He thinks of the night he walked into the shack and interrupted a very private moment between Maris and Shane. There was no telling where that situation would've led without his interrupting it. Shaking his head, Jason looks out at the thinnest slice of a waning crescent moon hanging over the misty Sound. That edge of the moon casts little light, leaving the beach in darkness.

Shit, have they made a mess of things.

Don't doubt yourself, bro, comes in the hiss of a receding wave. *Remember what Dad said about fighting in 'Nam? Instinct saved him, not doubts.*

Did instinct save Jason nearly two weeks ago in the shack? His gut told him he was about to lose Maris that night, and he wasn't going to stick around to watch it happen. So he retreated. Waited in his bunker here at Ted's cottage until Maris visited her past. Until their home situation felt safe again.

And it does, now. It feels safer. Somewhat. Shane's gone, yes. But still, the damage to their marriage isn't.

Again Jason takes a long breath of the night's heavy salt air.

Cures what ails you, he hears as he deeply inhales. *Remember Dad talking about the beach in 'Nam? China Beach?*

Jason remembers. He raises a hand to his father's Vietnam War dog tags hanging on his neck. Slowly, he drags those tags back and forth on the chain. His father told him and Neil plenty of stories about China Beach. About how he could lie on the sand there, close his eyes, listen to the waves and imagine being back home in the States. Until a random chopper flew over, the loud thwacking helicopter blades nicely reminding him that he was ten thousand long, long miles from home.

A world away. A lifetime away. A nightmare away.

But one time, he told only Jason a story. It was shortly after the motorcycle wreck, and his father wheeled him across the rough terrain from their backyard, to the bluff. Everything was still raw—the accident, the amputation, the loss of Neil. His father helped Jason out of his wheelchair and sat him on the stone bench there. The old man never quit on him. Never stopped bringing him back from the brink in those days.

Jason was as down as he'd been, this one day. Not seeing much point in physical therapy, in replanning his life. A breeze lifted off the sea, the salt air brushing his face, his skin. The air was cool.

Not like in 'Nam, his father told him as he draped a

sweatshirt over Jason's shoulders. *Shit, was it hot there. But that Southeast Asia beach saved my life ... Saved my life by saving my mind.*

Jason thinks of that story now as he stands alone on a beach far from Stony Point.

Far from his life.

Far from his wife.

Hell, he might as well be ten thousand miles away in 'Nam for all the difficulties he's having getting back home.

~

In the war, there wasn't much you could ask for. Or if you did, you'd better be asking God. Because no one else in 'Nam was about to grant any of your wishes. Well, any wishes except for one, his father said that day. He sat back on his bench and looked out over the blue Sound, the blue sky. His crippled son sat beside him, silent. *You could always ask for some double-*R *at China Beach. Rest and relaxation. Rowdy and raucous. Revelry and rollick. Whichever double-*R *suited you to get by, get through, get strength. If you'd seen too much blood, killed too many VC, looked death in the eye in some godawful ambush, pined for home, even, anyone could put in a request.*

On occasion, China Beach was also the place to go when you gave up on everything—prayers included. Those were the times when someone else *put in for the furlough, for you.*

That's how I got to China Beach the first time. A few months into my tour, someone saw the state I was in. Which wasn't good. Life had gotten quickly shocking, and I needed to be reeled back just to survive.

Next thing I knew—paperwork in hand—off I went. Transportation logistics moved me through the jungle—trucked here, transferred there—and eventually got me on a two-hour helicopter ride until the bird landed at Da Nang. From there, a bus brought me to the beach.

Probably the most important ride I've ever taken.

Because when I stepped off that bus after months in the damp and dank jungle, I could've sunk to my knees and cried. That salt air, that sweet salt air was like my mama's hands cupping my face— telling me I'd be all right. Oh, I breathed it deep. Could've drowned on that air as I settled in for my three-day furlough. Coming off that bus, I walked straight to the water, dropped my bag and looked at the sea. Didn't walk in; didn't touch the water. Just ran my hands back through my hair and breathed beautiful air that wasn't dank and putrid with jungle stink. It was light, and reviving. And I stood there, breathing it. Some soldier happened along, walking the beach behind me. Clapped my shoulder and said four words to me.

Four words and kept going.

Four words that answered every damn question I'd had lately. Questions I'd ask of God. Questions that would steal my sleep. Worries that dope didn't answer. Drink didn't answer. Comrades didn't answer.

Four words. Never forgot that soldier's slap on my back, or his words as I stood there breathing the scent of the sea.

Cures what ails you.

And it did. No matter what I did those three days—swim, eat real grilled steak, drink beer, sail, throw a football, sleep real sleep— it was the salt air that did it. That cured me.

His father stopped talking then. Stopped and looked at

Jason until Jason returned his look. That was when his father delivered the words he'd brought him out there to hear, on a bluff above the sea.

That salt air on China Beach was the only thing that made me want to keep *breathing.* Keep *living. It was the beautiful air that made me want to* live. *To get home again to the beach, to the salt air here, someday.*

⁓

Jason looks out at Long Island Sound now. The sea is the sea, he thinks.

That's right, Jay, he hears when another wave reaches up on the sand. *Like Dad said. No matter where. Southeast Asia, Connecticut coast. Breathe it. Let it mend.*

Jason does. He closes his eyes and takes a long breath. All the while, he remembers something *else* from that afternoon when his father wheeled him to the stone bench on the bluff. As Jason sat there missing half a leg, missing life, missing his brother, and as his father tried to heal him—it happened. With the sun on his face, and his leg freshly bandaged, he heard it.

For the very first time, when a wave crashed into the bluff below, the sound came to him. It brought him to tears. Frightened him at first.

For the first time since the accident, while sitting there with his father, he *heard* Neil's whispered voice somehow in the splash of the sea.

Cures what ails you, Jay.

261

And when Jason looked at his father beside him, he half expected Neil to be standing beyond the bench—the voice was that real.

Expected Neil to be standing there in jeans and a tee—their father's dog tags around his neck, a rag hanging from his back pocket, his moppy hair lifting in the breeze.

Instead, his father met Jason's gaze. And his father's eyes? They were wet with emotion—whether at the pathetic condition of his only remaining son's life, or because he heard the voice in that salt air too, Jason never knew.

twenty-eight

Later That Night

NOW CELIA KNOWS WHAT A worried parent feels like.

After Eva picked up Taylor from babysitting, the coast was clear. First, Celia washed up and changed into her pajamas. She also set up the baby monitor on the front porch of her guest cottage. The whole time—as she wiped off makeup, scooped clear water on her face, turned up the volume on the monitor—she did something else, too. She kept an eye on any passing window so as not to miss Elsa returning from her business date.

"Huh," Celia says when she settles on a rocking chair on her front porch. "*Business* date, my foot." She decides to wait out here as long as necessary. Certainly Elsa will return home at a dignified hour. And so Celia sits back in her pajamas, then stands and leans to see down the street. Checks her watch. Sits again.

Until … finally. A vehicle—wait, a *party* vehicle—pulls up to the curb of Elsa's inn. Mitch's safari-style SUV is roofless! The windows are down and Elsa's sitting in the passenger seat while casually holding onto some roof-mounted grab handle. Celia stands again and leans on the porch railing this time. In the darkness, she hears muted voices, then some suspicious quiet, until Elsa gets out and walks toward the inn's door. Elsa turns, too, smiling and waving off Mitch and his … his … *wheels.*

"A-*hem*," Celia loudly manages. In the porch shadows, her arms are crossed, her foot tapping.

At the sound of her throat-clearing, Elsa looks over and veers to the guest cottage. "Oh, Celia!" she says.

Celia squints through the darkness. Windblown wisps of Elsa's thick hair escape from a gold scarf jauntily tied on her head. A scarf that she unties first, before shaking out her hair. And why … she's also *breathless*—if Celia's not mistaken.

"It's so hot still," Elsa is saying while crossing the yard. "Even at night."

For a long second, Celia does nothing except raise an eyebrow. "I have iced lemonade waiting," she tells Elsa. "Come visit on the porch. We'll sit in my wicker rocking chairs and keep cool."

Elsa hesitates. She glances back at the inn and shrugs. "Okay," she agrees, climbing the porch steps. "We haven't done this in a long time, Cee." She motions to Celia's silky polka-dot shorts with matching button-down top. "This having a pajama talk."

"No, we haven't." Celia lifts a pitcher and pours two glasses of lemonade, the ice clinking into the tall glasses. "We're so overdue to catch up on the local gossip."

Elsa sits, takes her glass and sips the lemonade. "Gossip?" she asks.

Celia simply nods. Even in the shadows, she can see that Elsa's face is flushed. Celia sets her own glass on a small table and settles in her rocker. "Is that who you've been calling this week? Mitch Fenwick?"

"What?"

"You're always on the phone lately, in the inn. Talking in a hushed voice. Ending the conversations when I come into the room."

"No! Well, yes, I'm on the phone. But not with Mitch. I mean, it's inn business as the opening nears. And ... and, don't forget. I'm still dealing with Sal's estate, too. Settling his affairs. It takes a long time." Elsa holds the cool lemonade glass to her face for a moment. "And what about *you*, if I may ask?"

"What about me?"

"A mysterious singing gig? Why the secrecy, Celia?"

"It's simple, really." Celia lifts her glass, stands and leans against the porch post while watching Elsa. "You know how music helps me process my life, my thoughts."

"I do."

"And it sometimes feels very personal to me, when I sing certain songs. So I didn't need my gig going through the grapevine. Then I'd see everyone there—Eva, Matt, Nick even. Like that night at The Sand Bar a couple of weeks ago. When Shane walked in?"

Elsa nods, listening while setting down her glass.

"With everyone there, the night wasn't even about my music."

"But they're your friends," Elsa says. "They truly enjoy listening to you sing."

"I get that. But sometimes it's more fulfilling to sing anonymously. I can be more myself that way." Celia sits again, leans close to Elsa and grips her arm. "Kyle and Lauren kept my diner gig a secret. So swear you will, too."

"Of course I will." Elsa pats Celia's hand on her arm. "But *no* one can know? Not even Maris? And Eva?"

Celia sits back and sips her lemonade. "I swear, Elsa," she insists, squinting at her. "If you tell *anyone*, I'll tell *your* secret."

"Mine? I have no—"

"Elsa," Celia interrupts. "I saw you. With Mitch."

"I know you did. And I told you I was there for the Fenwicks. I'm just giving them advice for filming."

"Giving *them* advice? There was no *them* there. There was just *Mitch* Fenwick. His daughter was glaringly absent."

"Well, yes," Elsa says, tucking a strand of that windblown hair back behind an ear. "Carol couldn't make it to *this* business meeting."

"*Business* meeting?" Celia waggles a stern finger. "You were *dancing*, and laughing." Celia leans closer and drops her voice. "And I saw you two … *kiss*."

"*Oh!* I was hoping you were maybe looking down at your guitar strings at that second." As she says it, Elsa waves off Celia's words.

266

"Elsa DeLuca!" Celia pauses until she gets Elsa's undivided attention. "You'll break Cliff's heart."

"Cee, it was nothing!" Elsa sits back and brushes her hand across her forehead. "I don't even know. People … well, people, they just act funny in the heat."

"Funny?"

Suddenly Elsa stands. Stands, twists up her silky scarf and looks out at the night first, then back to Celia. "I really have to go. It's late." She hurries down Celia's few porch steps. "And there are so many inn preparations to take care of still."

"Okay." Celia stands, too. "Goodnight, then." In her polka-dot pajama set, she lingers on the stoop and watches Elsa cross the lawn to the inn's side entrance. "I'll be over first thing in the morning," Celia calls after her. "Remember?"

Elsa briefly turns, nods and pats her heart.

"Tomorrow's the day," Celia quietly says, more to herself than to Elsa … or anyone else at all.

⁓

For such a small place, Shane's house has a really big deck in the back. The deck looks out on the distant Rockport Harbor. Now, long after sunset, he sees the dock lights shining there, and moored boats are illuminated, too. Some folks must be spending this hot summer night aboard their vessels, right on the water. Anything to escape the heat.

After sweeping his deck, Shane realizes something. His arms are sore. There's a good ache in the muscles. And

267

there's no mistaking why—he worked off a lot of anxiety on this lobstering trip. Spending all day throwing hooks to catch the buoy ropes, and pulling full, dripping pots off the hauler, well, he was a little bit manic with it all. He rubs an arm now. One of the boys onboard called him a beast this morning.

What his shipmate *didn't* know was that, hell, Shane worked so fast hoping they could finish early and return to port by dinnertime. He's got much to do before heading back down the coast for the Ocean Star Inn's grand opening in a couple of days.

Still, working fast or not aboard ship, one thing was constant. With each pot hauled dripping from the sea, the boys all waited for that lobster count. Leaning over the edge of the vessel, they watched as the hauler wound up each pot until it broke through the water's surface. Many rowdy cheers ensued then. It was a productive trip.

With the sun now down, Shane gives a last look over at the glimmering harbor before going inside. If he gets most of his packing done tonight for his trip to Connecticut Friday, it'll free up time tomorrow. Time to catch up on errands he missed—especially after being away for two weeks in Stony Point, then rolling right back into work. Tomorrow he'll do his banking, pay his bills and buy some fresh groceries, at least.

But for now? He puts away his broom, turns into his bedroom and switches on the light. He's got to pick out just the right clothes to pack for Friday's festivities at Elsa's inn. But one glance in the mirror shows his fatigue from lobstering hardcore these past few days. His hair's a mess; his eyes are shadowed; whiskers cover his jaw. There's no denying he'll have to polish up for the weekend. First of all, his brother will definitely be there. Hell, they've gone from one visit every fifteen years to one every five days.

Shane will see Elsa, too. After all the hospitality she showed him, he wouldn't miss her important day.

And he'll see Celia. Not to mention the Barlows. No doubt they'll all be there Friday.

The thing is, while tossing a folded vest into his duffel, it feels like he's on the lobster boat again and flinging that hook to the buoy line to haul up the trap.

Problem is, Shane doesn't know *what* he'll find in the Stony Point pot. Second chances? Trouble? Love, regret?

Or just a rockin' good time.

twenty-nine

Thursday at Dawn

SEPTEMBER IS HERE.

Elsa opens the inn's front door and just stands there for a moment. Dew covers the lawn. Few birds are singing this early, as though they're still waking up. Only a lone robin's call comes from the tree branches. Even the sun is just waking, the sunlight muted in the morning mist.

She's still standing in the doorway when Jason's SUV pulls up to the curb. In a moment, she steps out onto her inn's shaded front porch. Beside the stairs, ornamental beach grasses reach in a sweeping arch; hydrangea blossoms hang heavy on the shrubs. It's as though they can hardly bear the weight of this ongoing heat wave. From beneath the porch's grand overhang, Elsa watches Jason. In the day's warmth, he wears a navy polo shirt over cargo shorts—so she notices his prosthetic leg. She never knew him without it, but something's always been apparent with

Jason. Aren't we all wiser for *every* life experience—sometimes more so from the worst of them.

With Jason, that's especially true.

As he makes his way along the stone sidewalk, Elsa still watches. He's loaded down with a white bag from the convenience store and a tray of take-out coffees.

"Thanks for having breakfast with me today," he says as he nears the porch stairs.

"Jason." Elsa walks down those stairs and manages a light hug around the coffees and bag of food he holds. "I'm really glad you texted me."

He nods to her. "I wanted to see you," he says. "It's one year to the day that Sal died."

"*Oh, time ... time,*" Elsa sighs more than she says. "The way it passes." She shakes her head with that sad thought before turning to walk around the side of the inn. "Come on," she says over her shoulder. "I have our regular bistro table waiting."

⁓

The first thing Jason notices is the salt air here. He's gotten used to being at Sea Spray Beach, so much so that he's nearly forgotten how much gentler the air is at Stony Point.

Rounding the corner to the back of the inn, he also notices two plates and silverware set out on Elsa's wood-planked bistro table. There's a happiness jar there, too. Atop golden sand in the jar, there are pieces of frosted sea glass; a small driftwood stick; a white conch shell and a

271

dried hydrangea blossom—its petals pale cream and tinged with a blush of pink. A tea-light candle flickers among it all.

And then there's Elsa, wearing a knotted sleeveless blouse over her denim board shorts. Big sunglasses are propped on top of her head, holding back her thick honey-streaked brown hair. If anything, she seems accepting of the day. Her grief of a year ago has lessened. She lifts the take-out coffees from the cardboard tray and sets them on the table. Jason, meanwhile, places her wrapped egg sandwich on one of the china plates.

"Only the best today," she quietly says of her mismatched, antique china.

"Absolutely." Jason tears open a ketchup packet with his teeth, lifts the top of his croissant roll and swirls ketchup all over his steaming egg.

"Now what happened there?" Elsa asks, pointing to the dark bruise on Jason's forearm.

"Oh, that?" Jason twists his arm for a look at the nasty mark. Every time someone asks about it, or every time he sets his forearm on a table and gets it smarting, the whole visual returns of the way he fell out of bed last week. "It's nothing," he lies to Elsa. "Hit the door rushing around at Ted's place."

"As long as you're okay."

"I am." Jason pats the top of his roll onto his thoroughly ketchuped-and-salted sandwich. Which effectively changes the subject back to the food.

"I've missed our breakfasts, with you living away at Ted's," Elsa is saying as she ketchups her own sandwich.

"So it's nice to see you around again."

"Hm," Jason says, briefly squinting across the table at her. Then he hands her a small paper bag filled with toasted hash browns. "Nice to see *me*? Or the stash of goods I bring?"

"Oh, you know me well, Mr. Barlow." With that, Elsa plucks out a hash brown, dunks it in a pool of ketchup on her fine china plate and presses the whole potato delicacy into her mouth. It's seemingly beyond her control, the way her eyes close with the flavor.

In a second, Jason gets why. Lifting his hefty sandwich with both hands, he bites into the cheesy egg mixture. "Oh, man," he says around the food. "It *has* been too long."

And it has. *This* is what he wants back, this camaraderie. *This* illicit behavior—sneaking a greasy sandwich with his partner in crime—Maris' aunt. Well, at least he has today. And he'll enjoy every bite of this one breakfast.

The minutes pass easy, just like he'd hoped. They eat, and salt, and ketchup-dunk. Elsa wipes a strand of melted cheese from her chin. Jason washes down a double bite of the gooey egg sandwich with a sip of hot coffee. Elsa explains the items in Sal's happiness jar on the table: the conch shell, because he was a listener. The piece of driftwood honors his cherished wooden rowboat. Yes, easy, peaceful minutes.

But before they're done eating, Jason does something else. He reaches into his cargo shorts pocket and pulls out a deck of cards.

"What's this?" Elsa asks. "*Cards?*"

273

"You bet." Jason slips them out of their box and shuffles them. "You know how Sunday was Neil's Anniversary Mass?"

"Sure," Elsa says, dragging a hash brown through her ketchup.

"Well, the day got away from me—in a way I didn't like."

"What do you mean?"

"What I mean is this ... Last year, your son told me at the Anniversary Mass that I've been honoring my brother all wrong."

"Sal said that?"

"That's right, he did. Then he convinced me to go out in his rowboat instead of doing brunch. And Elsa? It was the best day." Jason bites into a toasted hash brown. "We loaded up the boat with some junk food," he says, raising the half hash brown he holds. "And while paddling in his boat, I told Sal memories I had of Neil. The things we did when we were kids. Riding our bikes with baseball cards clipped onto the spokes. Playing out our father's war stories in the marsh."

"That does sound like my Salvatore," Elsa says. "Remembering Neil like that with you, in an authentic way."

"Exactly. And I'm sorry I didn't do something different like that *this* year, for Neil."

"It's been a tough summer for you, Jason."

Jason waves off the thought. "Anyway," he says, "on that rowboat last year, Sal dropped anchor in the marsh and we actually had a deck of cards from the convenience store—where we'd bought the junk food."

"Okay …"

"And we sat there in the rowboat, but instead of actually *fishing*? We played a few games of *Go Fish*." Jason holds up his hand when Elsa tries to interrupt. "So I thought, well, today? You and I *could* play again. This time, for Sal."

Elsa sits back, smiles—and yes, she does it. She picks up the cards, shuffles and deals their hands.

So now their egg-sandwich breakfast is peppered with:

Do you have any threes?

Oh, you're wiping me out!

Give me your ten.

Then? Pauses as eyes drop closed with sweet *Mmms* while the gooey, cheesy sandwiches are bitten into, and while ketchup-dipped hash browns are lifted to mouths.

Got any queens?

Go fish.

Another pause or two as coffee is sipped.

All the while, they do something else, too. They share stories of Sal.

"I remember the way he'd show up at my kitchen slider on work mornings," Jason says while collecting Elsa's pair of fours. "He'd wear his yellow hard hat and have a leather tool belt slung around his waist. Shiny hammers and tape measures were stuffed into it. And man, those spiffy new work boots he wore. Always ready to get to a construction job site and pitch in."

Elsa sips her coffee, looking from Jason out to the

distant Sound. "Sal loved trying out all your livelihoods. Waiting tables at Kyle's diner," she says. "Taking security cruises with Nick. But his favorite? Without a doubt, swinging a sledgehammer at that old Maggie Woods place. He often mentioned something your brother once said."

"And what's that?"

Elsa lifts the last of her hash browns and stuffs it into her mouth. "I guess Neil said you can judge a person's happiness by the state of their home? And Sal thought that was *never* more obvious than at old Maggie's house on the hill," she tells Jason while plucking greasy fingers from her lips.

Jason nods. "She had no respect for the place."

"I heard all about the neglect ... the rodents, the fading paint, the overgrown weedy yard."

"Yep. It was the unhappiest cottage at the beach, mirroring the life inside it."

"Your brother was wise, Jason. Houses never lie. I'm so glad you and my son connected on that job and turned that house around."

Just then, Jason's cell phone dings. He checks his text messages, types something back and sets his phone aside. "Speaking of jobs? I've got to get a move on," he says, wiping his mouth with a paper napkin, then crumpling it and stuffing it into the white food bag. "Have to swing over to Ridgewood Road. A demo starts there next week at a tiny place called Beach Box. I'm the project manager on that one, so have to be sure the prep's up to snuff. Then I've got to find an hour to review a fall itinerary my producer sent me."

"Oh, Trent? I haven't seen him since filming my reno here. How is he these days?"

"Busy as hell. And making sure I am, too. Sent me a schedule for a county fair tour for *Castaway Cottage* this fall. CT-TV will have tents at them, and Trent wants me on hand for meet-and-greets."

"Really! Now *that* sounds interesting."

"Would be, if I could fit it into my jam-packed schedule." Jason drops his cell phone into his shorts pocket and scoops up the deck of playing cards. "You know what they say ... No rest—"

"For the weary," Elsa finishes. "So you better take off. I don't want you running late."

"No worries, Elsa. It was well worth it, visiting with you today."

"And I hope you'll be here tomorrow night? For my inn's ribbon-cutting and grand opening?" Elsa asks, standing too.

As he's thumbing through the deck of cards, Jason glances at her. "Wouldn't miss it."

"With Maris?"

"No." Jason shakes his head while still skimming the cards—searching for one in particular. "I'm sure she'll be there, but we'll be arriving separately." He senses Elsa watching him, but she doesn't press things. "Listen, I had a nice breakfast, Elsa." He walks around the bistro table and gives her a long hug, cards still in hand.

"*Me, too*," she whispers, patting his shoulder. "Thank you for stopping by." She reaches for her napkin on the bistro table and dabs at her eyes.

Backing away, Jason fiddles with that deck of cards again. Finally, he finds what he was looking for—and plucks the ace of hearts out of the deck. "For Sal," he says, dropping the card into Sal's happiness jar. "He had the biggest heart, and boy do I miss him today."

thirty

CELIA DOESN'T DO THIS OFTEN. There were a few times during these summer months, maybe. For Aria's christening in July. Then again for Kyle and Lauren's vow renewal. Other than that, she's kept the necklace tucked away in a flowered trinket box on a closet shelf. Out of sight, yes. But oh, often on her mind.

She lifts the necklace out of that box now. Sal's diamond-encrusted sea-glass engagement ring hangs from the chain. Before putting on the necklace, she touches the platinum ring's blue stone. The sea glass is frosted from the ocean itself—the salt water washing over the glass for years, tumbling it in the sand and rocks, smoothing it, shaping it. Celia's always sworn that when she touches the blue sea-glass stone, she can feel the very salt of the sea on her skin.

Today, for Sal, she clasps the chain behind her neck. In

the mirror, she sees its reflection. Sees the engagement ring that didn't lead to a wedding band. Their marriage was never meant to be.

⁓

A half hour later, Celia's standing on Elsa's *inn*-spiration walkway. While Aria's snuggled in Celia's strap-on sling, Elsa gently puts a ruffled white sunbonnet on the baby's head.

"Wait." Celia sidesteps and looks at a chalked message on the stone walkway. "What is this?"

Elsa ignores the words boldly written there and says nothing. Instead she adjusts the baby's sunbonnet, whispering, "*So you don't get a sunburn.*"

"No, no, no," Celia persists, her attention riveted to the inn-spiration walkway. She tips up her straw fedora and reads the words. "Somebody wrote ... *Dinner tonight. Will pick you up at six.*" Celia suspiciously squints at Elsa.

"Why are you looking at me like that?" Elsa asks.

"Because the question is, *who* wrote that message? Was it Cliff? Or ... Mitch."

Elsa bends and scoops up several freshly cut hydrangea blossoms off a bench before turning toward the hidden beach path. "Never you mind, Celia," she calls over her shoulder, her eyes clearly twinkling.

"I guess the real question is ... Who do you *want* to pick you up? Hmm?"

"Oh, *basta!*" Elsa lowers her sunglasses from the top of

her head. "Enough!" she adds, unable to conceal a small smile.

Shifting Aria in her sling, Celia follows Elsa through that path to the beach. Tall grasses sweep against their legs; the scent of the sea grows stronger. "Now don't you go breaking people's hearts," she tells Elsa in front of her. "Next thing you know, *you'll* be driving beneath the train trestle with one of two things."

"Two things?" Elsa asks around the bouquet of hydrangea blossoms in her arms. "I thought folks left with one of *three* things."

"They do," Celia says as they step out of the path and onto the sandy beach. "A ring, a baby, or a broken heart. But for you, well …"

"Yes, I know. My baby days are behind me."

"Right." Celia kicks off her flip-flops alongside Elsa's slipped-off sandals. "So be careful, or someday you'll be driving beneath the trestle with one of *two* things—either a ring, or ultimately with a broken heart."

Again, Elsa brushes her off as they approach the water's edge. The sun is coming up and the sand is warm on Celia's feet already. Umbrellas looking like swirled lollipops line the beach. As she and Elsa walk along, the waves slosh in, easy and gentle. A few teens are swimming to the raft; a woman paddles past in an inflated tube.

"I wanted to set these blossoms on the water for Sal today," Elsa explains to Celia as she nods to her armload of hydrangea flowers. "Like we did last year."

"That's what I thought, when I saw you'd cut them. And

I'm so glad. When the flowers drift away on the sea, it'll be like they're carrying our love to Sal."

"Our love. Our peace. Especially on this anniversary of his leaving us."

When Elsa tries to hand Celia a blossom, Celia shakes her head. "No. You go first, Elsa." Celia motions toward the water.

Elsa looks long at her, then steps into the sea. She wears a knotted sleeveless blouse over her denim board shorts. Slowly, she walks out until the water is up to her knees. In a moment, she turns and waves for Celia to join her.

Celia does. Wearing a white skort with a navy tank top, she wades in, holding Aria close. The water's not too cold, so Celia dips in her fingers and touches a few drops to the baby's arms, her neck.

"When I stand here like this," Elsa is saying while lifting a hydrangea flower from her bouquet, "sometimes I think of Sal's last words to me." She looks out at the expanse of water reaching all the way to the blue horizon. "He said them right before going into surgery. *I'll be seeing you, Ma.*" With a slight shake of her head, she drops the blossom onto the water and the current slowly pulls it away.

"Oh, Elsa." Celia wraps an arm around her in a side hug. "Don't you think, looking out at this beautiful summer day, that he *does* see you this morning? Somehow?"

Elsa only nods—that's it. Just a teary nod, with no words.

And Celia gets it. No words necessary. So she takes a hydrangea blossom from Elsa and touches the velvety flower petals to Aria's cheek. The baby smiles at the soft sensation on her face. "Do you know what your daddy's favorite color was?" Celia asks the infant. "*Blue*," she whispers, still touching the soft petals to Aria's skin.

"Like the sea." Elsa steps closer, watching Aria now, too.

"Yes. Like the sea. *And* the sky," Celia tells her daughter. "And blue like my sea-glass engagement ring," she adds, lifting the chain around her neck. "And like the wild beach hydrangeas. *Beach blues*, he called them all. Come on, sweetie," she says then to Aria. "Let's you and me both drop this into the sea for Daddy."

A moment passes when Celia *could* think Aria understands. The baby tips her head; she kicks her feet in the sling as though she wants to be dipped into the water. Celia walks a little deeper and pauses. She holds the flower close to Aria so that the baby's tiny fingers clasp around the stem. It's just as Celia had hoped—they both hold the flower together. Bending then, Celia releases the blue hydrangea blossom to the sea, letting the flower drift away.

~

Together they walk the length of the beach, making certain to wade in the Sound the entire time. The seawater laps at their ankles. They maneuver around children digging in the sand, or splashing in the shallows. At one point, Celia lifts Aria out of her sling and gently dips *her* toes in the sea, too. The baby loves it, cooing and smiling with each cool dip.

"So," Celia begins. "I noticed you and Jason having breakfast outside earlier."

"We did," Elsa says. "He surprised me with a little visit."

"How'd he seem?"

"Oh, you know."

"Yeah." Celia straightens Aria's bonnet. "Did he say anything about Maris? Or about coming back to Stony Point?"

"No. We really only talked about Sal."

"But Jason will be here tomorrow, right?"

"Said he wouldn't miss it."

"Good, good," Celia says. "Oh, Elsa. The inn's opening is coming up so fast!"

"It's just days away now."

"I know. But somehow, today? I just don't feel ready." Celia tips up her fedora and looks at Elsa beside her. "Do you?"

"Some things we're never really ready for in life, Cee. I mean, we can keep prepping for the Ocean Star Inn. Keep polishing, keep cooking, keep taking reservations." Elsa sets another hydrangea blossom sailing on the water. "But eventually, the *Open* sign has to be hung."

They turn and head back in the direction of the inn's hidden path further down the beach. "Still. How can the grand opening be *tomorrow* already? I mean, are we all set? Is everybody coming?" Celia asks. "I've seen you on the phone a lot this week. Did they all RSVP?"

"Oh, Celia. There *are* a few more things to iron out for the opening. Things we *do* have to discuss. But let's not talk business today?" Elsa dips her fingers into Long Island Sound and vaguely blesses herself. "Today's for remembering Sal."

"Are you sure?"

"Yes. You come over for breakfast tomorrow morning. We'll talk business then, okay?"

"But Elsa. How about later on, even? After dinner, maybe? To get a start—"

Elsa cuts her off simply by shaking her head.

"*Okay*," Celia whispers again, dipping Aria's toes into a gentle wave. "If you insist."

"I do," Elsa says. "And anyway, I'll be out for a few hours now. I have to stop at Kyle's diner pretty soon."

"The diner? Why?"

"His cook, Rob, wants to sample my relish for the grand opening's hot dog roast. I've got two options, and he wants to do a taste test to see which he should make in bulk." Elsa drops the last of her hydrangea blossoms into the water, then turns to Celia again. "I actually just got off the phone with Kyle before we came here. So I'm going to The Dockside for an early lunch." She hesitates, all while taking Aria from Celia's arms. "It'll be a … a *working* lunch."

"Oh, brother. Not another one!"

With her free hand, Elsa lightly swats Celia's arm. "Your mom's being so fresh, Aria, suggesting I'm *gallivanting* around," she tells the baby then. "Naughty, naughty."

After raising an eyebrow at Elsa, Celia drizzles some cool water on her neck, her shoulders. "Well, when we get back now," she says, "all the Mason jars need to be arranged for the ribbon-cutting. The tea-light candles are in them, but I'll set them out on the terrace."

"Okay, good. That's good. But what about Aria?"

"She'll keep me company from her playpen. Then I'm bringing her to my father's after lunch. He's babysitting her for a few days, since we'll be so busy with the inn opening up." They wade out of the shallows while nearing the hidden path to the inn. "Elsa. I was thinking. Remember when you said in June ... Let's take the summer? To just live each day fully?"

"I do. Sal tried to savor time, and we did, too." Elsa steps closer and puts Aria back in Celia's arms. "Especially you, with your precious new baby."

"Oh, and I *did* savor the summer. Every week of it, every day. Immersed myself in Aria's life, for sure," she says, kissing the baby's cheek. "Hanging out with my little beach bum."

"And a beautiful summer it's been with Aria here," Elsa agrees as she scoops up their sandals at the path's opening.

"I just can't believe it's really behind us now. Done. How can it already be September?" Celia glances over her shoulder at the beach. Ocean stars sparkle on the midmorning sea. A light breeze whispers through the dune grasses. "We'll be so busy now," Celia goes on. "Those easy days, they just floated away ..."

As she says it, Elsa squeezes her hand. So Elsa feels it, too. Feels the fleeting days, and hours. Notices how each day is getting shorter now, a countdown to summer's farewell.

thirty-one

Early Thursday Afternoon

WHEN SOMEONE LEAVES YOU, THE silence that follows is startling.

Maris stops still inside Jason's barn studio. Rays of sun drop through the skylights onto his drafting table. Two sketches are on it—as though Jason just stepped away for a moment. Maris breathes in the faint scent of barnwood that lingers in this quiet space. After setting down a box top and tin can she holds, she walks to that drafting table. The drawings there might be for the shotgun cottage reno he's taken on. Straight black lines delineate rooms; small arcs indicate doorways; dimensions are noted in tiny numbers. Maris picks up a marker and replaces the cap left off it. She sets the marker beside Jason's architectural scale, adjusts his swing-arm lamp and turns away. The clock is ticking, and there's much to be done this afternoon.

So after crossing his studio, Maris carefully balances that

flipped-over box top—filled with clipped mini sunflowers. She bought the flowers at a local farm stand on her way back from the grocery store. Halfway up the stairs to her own loft studio, she stops. Shifting the box top of flowers into her other arm, she manages to pat the mounted moose head's nose there. It's become such habit, that lucky gesture. Lord knows, a dash of luck sprinkled on any of their lives couldn't hurt.

After another trip downstairs for the tin can, she finally sits at her planked worktable in the loft. Being here in her barn studio instead of the shack, it's as though she's still a denim designer. Nothing's changed. The long table Jason made with wood from this very barn is gouged with her sewing nicks. Old fabric bins are still filled with bolts of denim—stonewashed, dark-washed, patchworked, distressed. There are more bins, too, filled with pairs of sample blue jeans. One of those will nicely do. She needs fabric glue, too, and grabs a tube off a wall shelf. Lastly, Maris lifts that old tin can she'd brought in from the deck. The can holds a large candle, one she now tips out before picking off hardened dribbles of wax inside the can. That done, she chooses a sample pair of stonewashed jeans— the denim soft and slightly faded. This project shouldn't take long.

So she picks up her fabric shears, lines them up to the jeans ... and sets it all down.

Because it's not right—*not right*—the silence in this vast barn. Jason's voice should be carrying up to her ... occasional phrases and thoughts as he prepares blueprints

288

at his drafting table. Maddy's collar should be jangling as she lopes up the stairs. Maris turns and looks to where the dog usually lies down and pokes her muzzle beneath the loft railing to keep an eye on her master below.

Maris walks to that railing now. How many times has she stood there, leaned her arms on the railing and silently watched Jason at work. Watched him calculate, draw lines and angles, print block-letter explanations, answer his cell phone. Or there were the times he'd sit at his massive L-shaped desk and engage his software to fine-tune clients' prints on the big computer screen. Framed certifications and commendations, as well as Jason's college degree, hang on the wall beside his desk.

Jason should be here, too. Here and working in this space that is all his, really.

From his architecture studio with its massive framed photographs of his redesigned beach homes, to his drawers of scales and T-squares and drafting brushes and utility knives.

From his trays of graph and tracing paper, to his supply of liner pens and calculators and rulers.

From the bookshelves holding Neil's journals, to an old workbench vice clamped onto a piece of wood.

Even the dock cleats mounted on the wall belong to him. His father made him and Neil learn how to tie a cleat hitch there.

Yes, the space is all Jason.

But he graciously gave her part of it.

So in her dedicated loft studio, Maris picks up her shears

again for this new project. She begins cutting the pair of jeans. The sound—that slicing of the razor-edge shears through the tough denim—almost echoes in the vast barn. With the razor knife then, she cuts the small coin pocket off the jeans and sets it next to the pitted can and sunflower stems.

While trimming and gluing denim pieces, Maris glances behind her at the half-round stained-glass window of a cresting wave. Jason installed it there as a wedding gift, two years ago now. Every shade of ocean blue that she loves is in the window's glass pieces.

Yet her heart is a little blue, too.

Still, with the muted sunlight coming through that wave window, she knows. The tide's ever so slightly turning in her marriage. They're dating now, she and Jason. It's a start.

Elsa tucks a loose strand of hair beneath the rolled paisley bandana on her head. She's sitting at her marble-top kitchen island, and her leather reservation ledger is open in front of her.

"Aunt Elsa?"

She looks up from jotting a note on tomorrow's grand opening date in the ledger. The voice calling her name quiets, but a loud knocking follows.

"Elsa? Are you home?" Maris' voice calls out again.

Quickly, Elsa flips the ledger closed and sets it in the dining room. "Yes, Maris. In the kitchen," she calls back.

"Come on in." As she says it, she scoops several papers off the island, too. Some of the papers are her own notes; others are the certified letter and notification that arrived in Monday's mail. Hearing Maris walk down the hallway, Elsa looks first this way, then that, before opening a kitchen cutlery drawer and shoving the papers in it.

"I'm so glad I caught you," Maris says as she nears the kitchen. "I brought something for you."

Elsa—leaning on the closed kitchen drawer behind her—feels her heart beating. She *just* made it. Everything's cleared away and out of Maris' view. There's no hint of the awful news delivered to Elsa's doorstep in this week's mail.

Oh, *shoot!* Except for the certified *envelope* that just slipped onto the floor. She grabs it up and folds it in half right as Maris turns into the kitchen.

"I made this special," Maris is saying, "to remember Sal today."

"Maris." Elsa discreetly opens that cutlery drawer again and slips the folded envelope inside. When she turns, Maris stands there wearing a short beige-and-white striped blazer over a fitted white tee and denim shorts. The shorts are shredded in spots, with a frayed hem. White leather slip-on mules are on her feet; frameless aviator sunglasses are on her face; a canvas tote hangs from her shoulder.

But what gets Elsa smiling is this: Maris holds a denim-wrapped vase of mini sunflowers. The denim is a soft shade of blue, with an added coin pocket giving a finishing touch. The bouquet of cut yellow flowers is packed into the wide vase.

"Do you like them?" Maris quietly asks, stepping closer.

Elsa nods, her eyes tearing up as she takes the flowers from Maris.

"I wrapped an old can in denim," Maris explains, "thinking of how Sal loved to cuff his blue jeans and walk the water's edge."

"Oh, he did." Elsa sets the denim vase on her kitchen island and sits on a stool there. She touches a flower, then looks to her niece.

"And the flowers?" Maris says, raising her sunglasses to the top of her head. She drops her tote on the counter and sits beside Elsa. "Well. Sunflowers follow the sun. In the morning the blossoms face east, and throughout the day, they turn to the west. And I think that's what Sal did. Coming here to the beach, he was following the sun." She reaches over and hugs Elsa. "*Trying to rest and get strong,*" she whispers in her ear.

"That is just beautiful." Elsa sits back and fusses with some of the blossoms. But she stands then, and hurries to that cutlery drawer—where a piece of her certified letter sticks out. "Salvatore would've loved that sentiment," Elsa says as she opens the drawer and tucks in the paper.

"And how are *you* feeling today?"

"Me?" Elsa turns and pushes the drawer closed behind her. "I'm good. Thinking of Sal, of course, but here's the thing. I knew he wasn't always well, Maris." Leaning against the countertop, Elsa presses her fingertips on her cheek, her neck. "After his bout with rheumatic fever as a boy, he sometimes struggled with his health. All his life, symptoms would come and go. So I believe my son's in a better place now, where he's not suffering. And I'm truly glad for that much."

Maris is quiet a moment, touching a sunflower blossom at the island. "Elsa?" she finally asks.

"Yes, hon." Elsa tucks a nagging strand of hair back behind her rolled bandana.

"I'm just wondering … well, is everything okay? You seem distracted. Or tired?" Maris turns on her stool and eyes Elsa standing at the counter. "And you're flushed!" she says, walking over and reaching out her hand to touch Elsa's forehead. "You're not running a temp, are you?"

"What?" Elsa spots her plant mister near her garden window. Lifting the mister, she gives her neck and face a cool spritz. "No, no. It's just … well, it's been *so* hot out."

"I'll say. But it's nice in here, with the air-conditioning on."

"It is." Elsa sets down the mister.

"Are you *sure* you're feeling all right?" Maris gives her a concerned smile. "Can I get you anything?" she asks.

"No, it's just that I've been rushing around outside." Elsa walks to the fridge, saying over her shoulder, "I just got back from Kyle's diner."

"The Dockside?"

"Yes. His cook, Rob, sampled two versions of my hot dog relish. You know, for the inn's grand opening tomorrow. He had to decide which would be easier to make in bulk." She pulls a carton of black-raspberry ice cream from the freezer. "Stay for a scoop?"

"Oh, not for me. I can't."

"You can't?" Elsa reaches for a bowl from the cabinet.

"No. I just swung by on my way to an appointment."

"I *noticed* you're dressed for something, with that pretty blazer. And your lovely shoes."

"Thank you, Elsa. I'm actually headed to the Fenwicks'."

"Mitch's place?" Elsa asks, looking up from scooping the ice cream.

"Yes. He wants me to tour his cottage before demo begins. As research, for Neil's novel. And I've got something up my sleeve for Jason, too."

"Ooh, do tell!" Elsa sits at the island, then immediately stands again and puts the ice-cream carton back in the freezer before returning to her stool.

"I can't say anything yet. It's a secret." Maris glances at her watch. "And I'm late, anyway. Really have to run." She grabs up her tote. "Is Celia in the guest cottage? I'd love to say hello to her."

"No," Elsa says around a mouthful of cold ice cream. "She brought Aria to her father's in Addison. He'll be babysitting during the inn's grand opening."

"Will you tell her I was thinking about her today?"

"Of course." Elsa digs out another spoonful of ice cream, hoping beyond hope it will cool her nerves, too. "By the way," she says as Maris stands to leave. "Jason stopped by earlier. With egg sandwiches."

"He *did*?"

"Mm-hmm."

"I guess I'm not really surprised. Jason loved Sal like his own brother. It was almost like he had Neil back last summer."

"Don't give up on Jason, Maris."

"I'm not." She pushes her stool close to the marble-top island. "But right now, I'm only concerned about you. Is everything *really* okay here? I know it's a hard day, but—"

"I'm *fine*, dear." Elsa nudges away her ice-cream bowl, stands and walks Maris to the side door off the kitchen. "You can cut through the path to the beach there," she says. "It's quicker."

Maris stops at the door, adjusts her tote strap and turns back. "You would tell me if something's wrong, wouldn't you?"

Elsa nods. "*Go!*" she whispers, motioning to the door. "Don't keep the Fenwicks waiting."

Maris squints at her for a long second, then drops on her aviator sunglasses and hugs Elsa before breezing out the side door. Elsa stands in the doorway and watches her niece cross the green lawn toward the beach path. Without turning, Maris gives a small wave to Elsa behind her. Before disappearing into the dune grasses of the winding path, she also slips off her leather shoes to walk barefoot on the sand.

And Elsa just stands there in the doorway.

Eventually, after taking a moment to still her heart, she shuts the door, rests her head against it and closes her eyes—her secret still safe.

thirty-two

An Hour Later

I't's ONE OF THOSE DAYS when the beach is warmer than anyplace else. The sun pulses off the sand; the seawater reflects the light and heat right back into the air; there's not a salty breeze blowing, nor a pocket of shade to be found—except beneath the colorful umbrellas lining the water's edge. The setting is as summer as summer can be.

And it's perfect.

Perfect for Maris' secret plan at the Fenwick cottage.

Perfect for the *Castaway Cottage* film crew set up on the deck, with Jason's producer, Trent, watching from the sidelines.

"Every cottage tells a story," Maris says to the camera as she lifts her sunglasses to the top of her head. "And for Jason's brother, Neil Barlow? This cottage alone holds the story *he* wanted to tell."

Nodding to Mitch and Carol then, they begin. The

camera crew follows along as Maris is given the same tour Mitch actually gave Neil years ago. Filming this is Maris' way of bringing Neil's penned words to life—by connecting his manuscript DRIFTLINE to the real-life castaway cottage that inspired it. On camera, Maris points out scenes from the book set in this very cottage.

From the sandy beach below the deck: "Where the characters have an impromptu clambake, using up all the perishable food before the power goes out."

To the kitchen: "Where the women in the story gather together every empty vase, bottle and can. One by one, they fill them with all the hydrangeas and wild beach roses they cut before a hurricane blows in and destroys the shrubs and vines."

To the living room: "Where a mysterious, silent storm-dance goes down in darkness. The characters seeming like spirits waltzing across the candlelit floor."

To the staircase: "Where the haunting scent of those cut wildflowers rises."

To the front door: "Which a character struggles with all his might to stop from blowing off the hinges when he returns to the cottage in the wind-driven rain."

Back outside to the deck railing: "Where a man stands and takes the brunt of the storm as though on the deck of a boat—the howling wind and sea spray washing over him. He stands there, taking it, until feeling a gentle touch on his shoulder."

As Maris walks viewers through the cottage and the story, and as Trent calls "Cut!" she *feels* something, too.

Feels Neil's presence right in the Fenwick cottage, right in all their lives now. It's like that sea mist that touches everything here.

Everyone else feels it, too—the boom operator; the gaffer; the cameraman. Maris knows it as they conclude the tour and the filming. Knows it from the hushed tones of Trent and the crew *promising* her they'll keep this segment secret from Jason.

"Thanks so much for agreeing to this. I know I sprung this filming on you last minute," she tells Mitch and Carol, too. "But it'll be such a surprise for Jason. Please don't let on if you see him?" she asks, taking Mitch's hands in her own.

Seeing Mitch's eyes tear up—with the mysterious way his cottage connects two brothers—yes, Maris knows.

For Jason, they are all good for their word.

～

Cliff lifts the ingredients out of his shopping bag. He sets cheese crackers, breadcrumbs and barbecue sauce on the kitchenette counter in his trailer. As he does, his cell phone dings with a text message. He turns to the small bistro table, where he'd set down his phone. The message is from Elsa.

Change of plans. Don't pick me up for dinner. I'll walk. Want to hear the gulls + breathe that sea air. To just … be.

"Okay," Cliff says as he types back. "*See you at 6,*" he whispers while plucking out the letters. He does one more thing, too. He sends along a heart emoji.

Oh yes, Elsa DeLuca has his heart indeed. And even though she's been so busy about to open her beach inn, Cliff will take any time with her he can get. Sure, lately he has to *pencil in* his wooing with sunrise coffee dates and evening ice-cream runs. But he's happiest enough simply having Elsa in his life, sharing trailer dinners, doing ordinary things together. He walks over to a framed photograph beside his futon. The picture shows Elsa flying a bat kite on the beach last fall. She wore a long belted sweater over leggings. A scarf hung loosely around her neck and windblown hair; a wide smile filled her face.

Really, Cliff thinks as he lifts the picture he took of her, *I couldn't ask for anything more.*

So he's got to make this dinner special for Elsa. Back in the kitchen, he stops at his record player and drops the needle on a Dean Martin album. Sweeping violin fills the room before Dino's voice floats in. The lyrics, words about things the singer and his love did last summer, well, they make Cliff nostalgic as he sets his bistro table.

And as he steps over a white cat in the way. Looking totally at home, it's lying in a nearby spot of sunlight hitting the floor. "Don't get too comfortable there, Pip," he says. "You'll be moving soon."

In the meantime, though, there are crunchy baked chicken tenders to prepare. And Cliff gets right to it, first putting on an apron, then dropping a scoop of butter into a pan on his hot plate. The butter slowly melts while he crushes his cheese crackers into crumbs, shuts off the hot plate heat, mixes breadcrumbs with the cracker crumbs, whisks eggs, salts and peppers, dips and dredges chicken pieces.

Or at least he dips and dredges until he's loudly interrupted. Insistently interrupted. *Vocally* interrupted by plaintive mews as Pip rubs against his legs. When he looks down at her, she actually puts her two front paws on the cabinet and stretches upward to get closer to his ... chicken?

"You want some?" Cliff asks the cat. "Raw *chicken?*"

Well, apparently so. Because it didn't seem like *anything* would get that lounging feline out of her sunlight patch. But with her intensifying mewing, Cliff believes the scent of chicken did it. So he tests his theory and cuts one chicken tender into tiny pieces. That done, he spreads the pieces on a paper plate and sets the plate on the floor.

And for the rest of his chicken-dipping-and-dredging, it's to the sound of cat-dining and simultaneous purring.

Finally, Cliff puts a covered tray of the ready-to-cook chicken in his small fridge. Once Elsa's here, he'll simply pop it into his toaster oven. For now, he cleans up the hot plate and counter and tends to one *very* serious matter— keeping Pip secret. She's got to be a surprise mascot for Elsa's inn. But *not* until the cat's plumped up and professionally groomed.

So after checking any Stony Point Beach Association emails at his metal tanker desk, he puts *Operation Hide the Cat* into full swing. The pet bed he bought at the dollar store goes into his own personal trailer-closet—the large one housing his work shirts with the COMMISSIONER patch on the pocket. His uniform caps hang in there, too. They nicely conceal the old sailor hat he wore as a boy. His Matchbox car collection is in there as well, on a lower back shelf. The closet's right behind the accordion-style door separating his temporary apartment from the office workspace. The closet's also surprisingly deep, what with the hidden hydraulics extending the trailer's rear wall. So there's plenty of room for the cat's bed, and a bowl of water, too.

By the time Cliff backs out of the space, well he figures this feline's got her own luxury apartment there. Sleeping quarters, eating area. Hoping to keep her entertained, too, he crumples a few paper balls she can silently bat around while confined. A bowl toppling with fresh food will help keep her quiet, filling her stomach and making her drowsy. If the cat sleeps through Cliff's dinner date, his secret will be safe.

There's another way to ensure that, too. Some pure good luck couldn't hurt. Stopping at his tanker desk again, he picks up his faded black domino and gives it a spinning flip—catching it midair.

"Done!" he says, pocketing the domino and tidying his desk.

⌒⌒

"Hey there, I'm Ryder. Welcome to PetPlace. Can I help you find something?"

Jason stands in front of an open-shelf display at the

warehouse-style pet store. "A dog bed," he tells the sales associate. All the while, he thinks of Ted's dog-fur-covered couch that's turned into Maddy's secret lair.

"Now are you looking for a crate mat? Or for an actual bed?"

"A bed, definitely."

"That your dog?" Ryder nods to Maddy standing there.

"Yeah. It's for her."

"What's she weigh?"

Jason looks at Maddy and pulls her close on the leash. "Madison! Put that down," he says of the squeaky cheeseburger chew toy she swiped from a display. "*Argh*," he adds, taking that cheeseburger and dropping it into his shopping cart. "So anyway, when she's behaving, she's maybe sixty pounds?"

"All right. So you need a large." The associate walks toward that section of beds. "We've got bolster, covered, elevated, luxury."

"Wait. *Luxury?* Are you kidding me?"

"No joke." Ryder pulls a luxury bed off the shelf and sets it on the floor. "It's fully upholstered with ultra-plush fabric. Two-inch legs keep it off the floor for ventilation, and it has side pockets for dog toys."

"But," Jason says as Maddy steps up onto the velvety bed, "it's shaped like a *sofa*."

"It is."

"That's the last thing I need—my dog thinking it's okay to sleep on *any* sofa," he says as Maddy circles around before lying down on the cushioned canine-couch. "Off you go," Jason tells the dog, giving a tug on her leash.

"Hey ... You look familiar," Ryder says now, squinting at Jason.

Which only makes Jason very aware of how shot he must look on this warm day that began too many hours ago. He's unshaven, fatigued and hot, and it's not even three o'clock yet.

"You're on that show ..." Ryder continues, still squinting. "*Castaway Cottage*?"

"That's me. Jason Barlow," Jason says, shaking the guy's hand. He must be all of eighteen, maybe working a summer job here. "Nice to meet you, Ryder."

"Same here. And is this the dog that carried out pieces of wood when you renovated that lady's beach inn?" Ryder bends and rubs the scruff of Maddy's neck. "Demo Dog?"

"She sure is. Maddy was my on-site assistant," Jason says. When that episode aired, Trent told him the response to Demo Dog was over-the-top thrilled. Just like Ryder's reaction here.

"Wow, a *celebrity* dog. You should get her a bandana, too," Ryder suggests. "Maybe a tartan plaid? Would look rad on her."

Well. By the time Jason's leaving the mega pet store— wheeling his cart with one hand and holding Maddy's leash with the other—it's the most *expensive* dog-shopping run he's ever made. Between the plush pillow-top lounger-bed with an ultra-firm foam cushion; the cheeseburger chew toy as well as a plush shark toy Maddy *also* swiped; not to mention three color-coordinated dog bandanas, and an appointment booked for PetPlace's grooming service, he's got one very happy German shepherd.

A happy dog—*and* an empty wallet. Add in the braided-rope leash and a rubber fetch stick with built-in squeaker? His bill toppled. Just like his shopping cart is as he maneuvers it and Maddy through the steaming hot parking lot, right as his cell phone dings with a text message. So he stops there on the pavement and reads the text. It's from Trent.

Man, your wife loves the heck outta you, dude.

"What?" Jason says to himself, then shrugs and keeps walking.

The phone dings two more times, but he doesn't check it right away. Not until he's stacked the dog goods in his SUV's cargo area, walked the shopping cart over to the cart corral, then settled Maddy in the SUV's backseat. Finally, after turning on the vehicle and blasting the a/c, he reads the two new text messages.

Wait till you see what she pulled off, Trent writes. *Epic.*

Jason doesn't text Trent back. Calling is faster. "What gives, Trent? You've been talking to my wife?"

"You bet, guy."

"*Okay.* What's she up to, besides ... loving the heck out of me?"

"Shit. Can't say."

"Come again?"

"Never mind. I'm sworn to secrecy. But you did *something* right in your life when you married Maris."

So, Jason thinks. *Trent doesn't know.* No matter what

304

conversation Trent had with Maris, he's clueless that Jason walked out of his marriage a week and a half ago. Clueless he left Maris. Clueless that other than their one date night, they've barely talked in all these days.

"And this is why you texted me?" Jason asks, turning the a/c down a notch.

"No. Actually just confirming tomorrow."

"Tomorrow?"

"Filming at your barn studio in the morning for the Fenwick project. Don't forget. Time is money, and the budget's tight. And maybe we can grab some promo footage afterward. You know, for your autumn meet-and-greets at the county fairs. You want to grab dinner later? Review that fair itinerary I sent you?"

"No can do." Jason checks his watch. "I'm out right now. Dropping off the dog next, and headed over to my shotgun cottage at White Sands. Got an appointment with the homeowners, so I'm booked solid."

"Okay, then. See you at your place in the morning. First thing, nice and early."

"Got it."

"Oh, and Barlow? You do right by that wife of yours."

"What in God's name are you talking about, Trent?"

"Like I said, can't say. It's a secret. But seriously? She's a keeper," Trent adds before disconnecting.

Which leaves Jason looking at his cell phone while wondering what the *hell* went down today—all as Maddy chomps on her new cheeseburger squeak toy in the backseat.

thirty-three

Thursday Afternoon

AFTER DRIVING FOR HOURS, AFTER passing rolling green mountains and cow pastures and white-steepled New England towns, Shane's in Connecticut.

Finally, he's pulling off the highway and onto Shore Road. Any other time, memories would be triggered by the sights: the take-out seafood shack he and Kyle frequented with their father decades ago; Hallmark Drive-In, where Shane spent long hours scooping ice cream in his teens; seaside inlets he and Kyle fished with the Barlows in their old Whaler; local dive bars right on the beach, good for a little summertime carousing back in the day.

But today? Shane sees none of it.

As a matter of fact, he pays the passing visuals no mind at all. Cruising the winding beach road in his pickup, his tunnel vision is locked only onto the pavement ahead. Any landmarks are nothing more than a blur as he continues on.

Because there's only one sight he's on the lookout for. It's the *only* landmark that matters today. The only one that will get him to breathe easier. To nod, even, with his decision to drive to Stony Point a day early.

That one. There, up ahead.

You could almost miss it, the way it's on a curving lane forking off the main drag. Overgrown roadside brush clings to it. Weedy green vines cascade over the sides. And its dark stone foundation blends right in with shadows cast by nearby trees.

Taking that turn onto the narrow lane, the much-anticipated landmark rises before him—stealing the show.

"*Oh, yes,*" Shane quietly says then. "*The trestle giveth, and the trestle taketh away.*"

He slows his pickup to nearly a crawl and does something else. He tips his newsboy cap at the railroad trestle before him. Its brown stone walls rise on either side of the street—the walls supporting the train tracks above it. And beneath those tracks? A shadowed, cool tunnel runs the length of those imposing stone walls.

A tunnel that's a gateway to a world unto itself. You arrive here, it seems, with a glad heart, or a pained one.

And sometimes? Sometimes you arrive with a little of both.

⌒〜

When Shane stops on the other side of the trestle, a security guard approaches. He wears that Stony Point uniform of

JOANNE DEMAIO

khaki button-down shirt with black epaulets, all over black shorts. Requisite clipboard is in hand, too.

"Can I help you?" the unfamiliar guard asks at Shane's open window.

"Hey, how you doing? Is Nick around?"

"No. He's got beach patrol today. On the boardwalk. Where you headed?" the guard asks while jotting down Shane's license plate number.

"Sea View Road. Rented a bungalow there."

"That right? You got a name?" The guard waits, holding pen to clipboard.

"Bradford. Shane Bradford. But hey, guy. Can you keep it under your hat for a while? I'm here for the inn's grand opening tomorrow, but arriving a little early to surprise someone." When the guard warily looks up from his clipboard-jotting, Shane adds, "Nicholas will vouch for me."

"Okay, then." The guard steps back and waves Shane in. "Friend of Nick's, you say? You're good."

And just like that, Shane leaves the trestle behind as he drives the sandy roads. It's a hot afternoon, and he leans an arm on the open window. Folks are walking from their shingled cottages and shanties, headed to the beach. Swim tubes hang from teens' shoulders. A few guys pull beach carts spilling over with sand chairs and umbrellas. A mother tows her youngster in a little red wagon. In the midday heat, flip-flops flip. Flowers wilt. Straw hats and big sunglasses offer little relief from the sun's rays.

Once he veers off onto Sea View Road, Shane finally

pulls into the driveway of his rented bungalow. Getting out of the truck, he grabs his packed duffel from the truck's bed and hoists that duffel onto the shaded front porch. Beside the door, something catches his eye. It's the painted driftwood sign with the cottage name: *This Will Do*.

"Sure will," Shane says to himself.

Wasting no time now, he finds the cottage keys right where he left them last Saturday: tucked inside an old fishing buoy hung from the porch railing.

Everything else is the same, too. The same from a week ago; the same from a decade ago, he's sure. That's the kind of place Stony Point is. It doesn't change much, week to week, year to year. He shoulders open the bungalow's front door and steps into the musty living room. Doesn't stop moving, either, passing the carved sandpipers and lantern on the fireplace mantel, walking alongside the gray rattan sofa, heading straight to his bedroom.

Funny how it feels like he never left. Like the past few days out at sea were just a dream. If he looks a certain way into the bedroom's shadows, can't he see Celia there, slipping into his denim shirt after they'd slept together last week? He drops his duffel on the bed, unzips it and takes out an envelope, then heads through the kitchen, straight to the back porch this time. The porch where he and Lauren sat and caught up two weeks ago. The porch where he and his brother talked long into a summer night, trying like hell to be brothers again.

But right now, all that doesn't matter.

The only thing that matters is Celia's letter that arrived

in his Maine mailbox this morning. Her letter alone prompted him to hightail it to Connecticut a day early.

Shane hoists himself up on the half-wall and sits there. At first, he only looks out at Long Island Sound. Thousands of ocean stars sparkle on its rippling blue waters. He takes a long breath of the salt air, too. It's different from Maine's. Here, the salt air is softer, like Celia's sea glass with its soft edges.

Celia.

He slips her letter from the envelope and reads her words again.

Dear Shane,

I got your letter. Oh, what you must've thought, seeing me there on the docks in Rockport. And I can explain. It's just that Sunday, for me, was a … dirty day. There was a Memorial Mass here for Neil, and everyone was going. But if I went, I would've envisioned my own memories in that church. About a year ago, it was actually Sal's funeral that happened there.

So I thought of that escape to Maine you mentioned. It really appealed to me, if only for that day. Oh, to sit on your deck overlooking the harbor, instead of in a church pew. To talk and while away the hours together. To let Aria get some of that sunshine beside the Atlantic Ocean. I thought, well, maybe I'd strum my guitar and you'd play the harmonica. Silly me, hopeful like that.

Anyway, don't think much of things, Shane, in seeing

me on the docks. I was only there on a foolish whim. We have a lot of salt air between us—miles and hours of it.

Fondly,
Celia

Shane shakes his head, then runs a finger over Celia's cursive. He tries to picture her alone, penning her thoughts—maybe while sitting at her kitchen table, birdsong coming in the open window. Was it a hard letter to write? Was she embarrassed to have been seen on the docks that day?

After folding her letter back into its envelope, he walks down to the private beach area behind his rented cottage. The Sound is calm; the sun, warm. He scoops a few smooth stones from the sand and skims them out over the water, one at a time. The stones skip and tumble and leave small plumes of the sea spraying behind them.

Problem is, they don't do what they've done in the past. Usually his worries are cast away with each skim. Each skipping stone takes some doubt or care with it, straight out to sea, leaving him feeling lighter.

But not today.

So Shane turns away from the Sound, crosses the small scrubby backyard, climbs the seven olive-painted steps to the cottage porch, opens the squeaking screen door and goes inside. After getting a blank piece of paper and envelope from his duffel, he returns to the back porch.

This time, though, he doesn't sit on the half-wall. This

time he sits on one of the mismatched wooden chairs at the faded white table. Sits there and reads Celia's letter once more.

"*That is such bullshit*," he whispers of her message.

Pressing his own blank paper smooth, he thinks for a moment, then lifts his pen and writes back to Celia.

～

Celia feels the day. Between the heat, and driving Aria to Addison to stay with her grandpop, then driving alone back to Stony Point on the hot highway, she's beat. The first thing she does when she walks into the guest cottage is change out of her tired skort and tank top and into something even cooler: frayed denim shorts and a scant lace-trimmed camisole. She also switches the necklace chain holding her sea-glass engagement ring for a very light silver choker. Lastly, she brushes out her hair, then loosely puts it in a side braid.

Maybe a cup of tea will help her relax, too. Plenty of busy days are ahead of her now, so this is a good time to just kick back and relax, to slip off her sandals, drag another chair closer, put her feet up and unwind. By tomorrow, grand opening festivities at the inn will roll into high gear.

Yes, this feels just fine, sitting at her kitchen table while the tea steeps. Maybe she'll toss in a load of laundry later. But for now? It's too hot to do anything much at all. The guest cottage windows are open to the warm day; barely a salty breeze wafts in. A ceiling fan moves the air around.

And it's quiet outside. No lawns are being mowed. No cars drive past. Even the birds are hushed, waiting out the heat without a song.

So when two knocks sound at her front door, she hears them loud and clear. Just two sharp raps—which get her to lower her feet from the wooden chair and hurry out of the kitchen, into the living room.

But she slows her bare feet right down upon turning the corner. Because there's an envelope, a white envelope, on the floor in the middle of the room. Okay, so someone must've slid it flying *beneath* the front door.

When she walks closer, she sees more.

Sees *her* name written across the envelope.

Which is the exact moment she also recognizes the handwriting spelling out her name. So she bends, picks up the envelope and briefly just stands there. Well, she's doing something else, too. She's calming her beating heart.

Because she knows.

Shane's here. Shane Bradford is standing on the other side of that closed front door—oh, she knows it but good.

He's standing there, waiting for her.

Quickly then, she opens the envelope and pulls out the letter—which she can't get open fast enough. The way her hands tremble a bit, the paper shakes while she unfolds it. But she takes a deep breath, straightens the note and reads the words written there.

Celia,

Don't think much of things? You're all I've been thinking of.

—Shane

Not taking a step, she looks from the letter to the closed door.

And drops Shane's letter.

Drops it right before running to the door.

Yes, she runs—*runs*—and flings that door open to see him waiting there.

Which is when she stops again.

Shane's standing on her porch. With arms crossed, he's leaning against the railing. It takes only a silent split second for her to take in the sight of him—from his dark tee with the ripped-off sleeves showing his tattooed arms, to his jeans and leather boat shoes, to his unshaven face. To his serious eyes looking straight at her through the screen door.

"Celia," he says as he tips his newsboy cap.

Celia, well, she still says nothing.

Instead she opens that screen door and catapults herself onto him—laughing and crying at once.

⁓

If ever any rogue wave has hit him at sea, Shane thinks it feels something like this.

Like Celia rushing to him. She's just like a rogue wave—rushing suddenly, out of nowhere, directly at you. Leaving you no time to even prepare.

So Shane does it. He takes the wave that is Celia full force—opening his arms to her, embracing her and lifting her right off the porch floor as he nearly loses his own balance. Her presence, her happiness, does nothing but have him smile.

And kiss her.

Then, again.

"What are you *doing* here?" Celia finally manages after one more kiss. As she says it, she touches his arm, his face.

"I came for the grand opening of the Ocean Star Inn. Elsa invited me."

"She did?"

Shane nods, then tucks his cap into his back pocket. "Before I left. Elsa said that if I could make it, somehow, to please come."

"But you're supposed to be on the water! Working."

"And I was. But the summer season's different. It's more day trips on the bay, not so much out on the Atlantic." Shane touches a wisp of Celia's auburn hair, letting his fingers slide to her neck, too. When he does, she takes those fingers in her hand and presses them to her lips. "I'm due back on the boat Tuesday," he tells her. "After Labor Day."

"Still, the inn's grand opening isn't until tomorrow," Celia says, tipping her head and stepping closer.

Shane hesitates. He looks at Celia in front of him. Her hair is in a loose side braid. She's barefoot, wearing a lace-trimmed black camisole with faded denim cutoffs. The thinnest silver chain is around her neck.

And she is utterly breathtaking.

He takes her hand in his and tugs her to the porch rocking chairs, where they sit side by side.

"Shane?" Celia asks. "Is everything okay?"

"It is." He leans over and kisses the side of her head. "Now, it is, anyway. Seeing you. I'd *planned* to arrive tomorrow. But after I got your letter this morning, I got here as fast as I could."

"But why?" she asks.

"My letter said it all, Celia."

From her rocker, she only looks at him.

"Did you read it?" he asks.

"I did."

"It's true. Every word of it. And I wanted to deliver that message to you in person."

"*I'm all you've been thinking of?*" Celia whispers.

Shane nods, just nods.

Sitting beside him, Celia leans closer and touches one of the tattoos on his forearm. She drags her finger along the inked swirls, then leans past him and looks out to the street. "Where's your truck?"

"At that little beach bungalow. I rented it a few more days. For the weekend, you know. I left the truck there and walked over to stretch my legs after that drive."

Celia stands then. Stands and takes his hand. "Well, come inside! I just made some tea. Or maybe you want something cool to drink, it's so darn hot out."

"After you," he says, motioning to the door.

Standing there, Celia looks long at him—seeming not to trust her own eyes. But finally she opens the door and leads him inside her shingled cottage. But again she pauses and turns back to him behind her. "I can *not* believe you're really here."

"I am." His hands cup her face as he leans in and lightly kisses her again. "But don't tell anyone," he says, pressing a finger over her lips. "I'm here early to see only you." He pauses, watching her watch only him. "It's our secret, okay?"

thirty-four

Late Thursday Afternoon

THERE'S SOMETHING TO BE SAID for taking the long way. For letting it slow you down some. Elsa believes that taking the long way makes your arrival somewhere even sweeter. Because before arriving, you've breathed deeper. Seen the sights. Let your mind meander as much as the road might.

And today, that's just what she needs—the long way.

It's why she texted Cliff earlier and said she'd walk to his trailer-apartment, rather than have him pick her up for dinner. Her feet need to mosey along the sandy beach streets while her thoughts work out her troubles. Even better, yes, she'll take the long way down Sea View Road. It'll bring her closer to the sea. Closer to that salt-soaked air.

After changing into black capri leggings and a sleeveless chambray tunic, she grabs her straw tote and heads out. Her

318

sandaled feet step on the sandy grit of the road. Folks leaving the beach at day's end pull tired wagons and carts behind them. Towels are draped over damp shoulders; faces are sunburnt. Elsa nods at some; gives a friendly wave to familiar neighbors she passes.

As she veers onto Sea View Road, she thinks it's been a long *day*, too. Actually, since receiving that surprise piece of mail on Monday, it's been a long *week*. And a tiring one, with the way that one certified letter prompted unexpected matters for her to privately handle. Oh, the phone calls. The difficult conversations she conducted—and cut short whenever Celia walked in.

But it's done now. All of it.

So she breathes, and takes in the sight of seaside cottages lining the street. Geraniums spill from front-yard planters; garden flags flutter in the slightest breeze; voices and the sound of clinking dishes and silverware come from screened porches.

Walking along, Elsa notices the Barlow cottage up ahead. Thick green shrubs line the side yard. There are vines of wild red roses running through the bushes, giving them a spattering of color.

But that beach house behind them? It looks more like a beach fortress. From where she stands, Jason and Maris' gabled cottage is partially concealed, with only a tall peak visible. The salt air has weathered its shingles to a dark silvery-gray. A bit of a window frame shows, too, with sunlight glinting off the white trim. And all of it grandly faces out toward the bluff and Long Island Sound. *Yes*, Elsa thinks, *a beach fortress facing the sea, facing life.* The rippling blue seawater beyond the cottage spreads to the horizon, and a bank of white clouds fills the sky.

Elsa slows and turns off the street then. She crosses the Barlows' front lawn, where twigs snap beneath her feet. But at the bottom of the front porch steps, she stops. Two cushioned chairs are on the open porch. A pot of begonias sits on a small table between the chairs. Behind the flowers, a tall paned window looks into the shadowy house. After a few seconds of silently standing there, Elsa quickly turns to leave—but stops again.

Stops, turns, walks *up* those porch steps this time and knocks on the front door before she can change her mind.

Moments later, Maris opens the wooden door. "Elsa?" she asks.

"Maris." Elsa gives her a sad smile. Maris wears the same fitted white tee and frayed denim shorts she had on earlier. Her hair is pulled back in a low twist, too, but she looks tired now. "Maybe you're busy," Elsa says, "and I caught you at a bad time …"

"What? It's never a bad time to see you."

"Okay, then." Elsa turns up her hands. And gives another quick smile. "I have to tell you something. Do you have a minute?" she finally asks her niece. "To sit on the porch with me for a bit?"

Maris hurries out the door, looks to the street, then back at her. "Oh, Aunt Elsa. I knew it. Something *is* wrong, isn't it?"

Maris can tell one thing, right away. Whatever brought Elsa to her door this afternoon isn't good. Though her aunt's dressed casual in her lacy black capri leggings and long chambray top, her face is anything *but* casual. No, it's drawn with emotion—visible even behind her big sunglasses. So Maris is concerned enough to stop Elsa when she goes to sit on one of the porch chairs.

"Come over here, close to me," Maris says as she sits on the stoop and pats the step beside her.

Elsa does. She sits right next to her. After a long breath, Elsa also lifts her sunglasses to the top of her head. When she looks at her, Maris sees it now. Sees the tears in her eyes.

"Oh my gosh. I knew it before, when I brought you the flowers," Maris says. "What's the matter?"

"I really only have ten minutes. I'm on my way to Cliff's." Elsa vaguely motions to the road. "He's making me dinner this evening. But you're right. You asked me earlier if something was wrong, and I cannot lie to you."

"Lie? Elsa, you can tell me *anything*. Anytime."

"But I didn't want to burden you," Elsa insists. "You and Jason have your own troubles."

"And I need to know yours, too. You are never, nor will you *ever* be a burden. I am *always* here for you."

Elsa does it then. Maris sees her take another long, slow breath of the sea air that cures what ails you. So it's obvious—*something* needs healing. Her aunt's eyes drop closed for a moment, too. And Maris can only think Elsa's *praying, praying, praying* for that salty air to work some magic into her life.

321

Finally, Elsa looks at her while twisting a gold bangle on her wrist. "I received bad news this week," she quietly reveals while fidgeting with that bracelet, slowly spinning it around and around. "And it's pretty much derailed me."

Maris is shocked by her serious tone. It takes her a second to even speak as she imagines the absolute worst. "*Elsa*," she whispers, gripping her aunt's arm. "Is everyone okay? Cliff? Aria and Celia?"

Elsa nods. "Yes, they're fine. This has nothing to do with anyone here. It's more ... personal."

"Personal?"

Elsa stands. Stands and walks to the porch railing, which she leans on while looking across the front yard to Sea View Road. From the railing, she turns and looks to Maris still sitting on the stoop. "Will you promise me something before I tell you?" Elsa asks.

"Of course. Anything."

"That you'll keep this between you and me? Nobody else is to know," Elsa says, still standing at the porch railing. "Nobody."

"Yes. Yes, I promise." Maris again pats the stoop beside her. "It's our secret."

"*Okay*," Elsa whispers, returning to the stoop. She sits and loops her arms around her bent knees. "Here's how it all started." Again she stops, as though uncertain what to say next.

Maris waits. In the warm afternoon air, a lone robin chirrups from the maple tree beside the porch. The late-day sun shines golden, and the colors around her—the green lawn, the wild red roses snaking through the shrubs—are all lush. They're the shades of color you remember in fond memories, or see on the pages in an old photo album.

And Maris knows, sitting close beside her aunt. *This* is one of those moments. A talk she'll think of often. It too will be a powerful memory, but maybe not as fond as others. So she drinks in those late-afternoon colors, and the sound of birdsong. *Anything* to soften the frightening words she's about to hear.

"Earlier this week," Elsa finally continues, "I received an unexpected notice in the mail."

Maris only watches Elsa now. Her dear aunt's face is sad; there's no hiding that. Regretful, even.

"At first, I thought it was good news," Elsa explains. "Everything felt so right lately. The inn about to open. Having a beautiful granddaughter. Finally getting settled in my new life here. I'd been ... happy. So holding that certified letter? I thought maybe I won a contest. Or, I don't know, a long-lost friend was getting in touch. Surely, *some* good news would be in that envelope."

"And it wasn't?"

Elsa shakes her head. "That letter, it stopped me in my tracks," she goes on. "It's like my life hit a brick wall, because suddenly everything changed. *Everything.*"

What worries Maris most about Elsa's words? They're so quiet.

Which scares Maris even more, such that she doesn't move, not one bit.

But she does one thing. Squeezing Elsa's hand, Maris

says, "I have to know, Aunt Elsa. What was in that letter?"

Sitting on the porch stoop in the shade of the maple tree, Elsa hesitates.

Only for a moment, though.

Leaning close to Maris then, Elsa tells her hushed secret—right as a summer breeze stirs the salt air.

The beach friends' journey continues in

STONY POINT SUMMER

The next novel in The Seaside Saga from

New York Times Bestselling Author

JOANNE DEMAIO

Also by Joanne DeMaio

The Seaside Saga
(In order)
1) Blue Jeans and Coffee Beans
2) The Denim Blue Sea
3) Beach Blues
4) Beach Breeze
5) The Beach Inn
6) Beach Bliss
7) Castaway Cottage
8) Night Beach
9) Little Beach Bungalow
10) Every Summer
11) Salt Air Secrets
12) Stony Point Summer
—And More Seaside Saga Books—

Summer Standalone Novels
True Blend
Whole Latte Life

Winter Novels
Eighteen Winters
First Flurries
Cardinal Cabin
Snow Deer and Cocoa Cheer
Snowflakes and Coffee Cakes

For a complete list of books by *New York Times*
bestselling author Joanne DeMaio, visit:

Joannedemaio.com

About the Author

JOANNE DEMAIO is a *New York Times* and *USA Today* bestselling author of contemporary fiction. The novels of her ongoing and groundbreaking Seaside Saga journey with a group of beach friends, much the way a TV series does, continuing with the same cast of characters from book-to-book. In addition, she writes winter novels set in a quaint New England town. Joanne lives with her family in Connecticut.

For a complete list of books and for news on upcoming releases, visit Joanne's website. She also enjoys hearing from readers on Facebook.

Author Website:
Joannedemaio.com

Facebook:
Facebook.com/JoanneDeMaioAuthor